A SISTERLY REGARD

A Regency Romance

By

Judith B. Glad

GCT, Inc.

Aloha, Oregon

2015

ISBN 978-1-60174-905-5
1-60174-905-8

A Sisterly Regard

Cover art and design by Judith B. Glad
Wisteria photo © Ina Van Hateren

Published by GCT, Inc.
Aloha, Oregon

Originally published electronically by
Uncial Press,
eBook ISBN: 978-1-60174-016-8
www.uncialpress.com

For my sisters of the heart:
Sandy, Marya, Genny, Elinor.
And in memory: Jean and Joyce...
and Neil.

For there is no friend like a sister
In calm or stormy weather;
To cheer one on the tedious way,
To fetch one if one goes astray,
To lift one if one totters down,
To strengthen whilst one stands.

~Christina Rossetti

PROLOGUE

"I wish it were not too late to change our minds about going to London for the Season."

Lord Gifford, dozing in a chair in the corner of his wife's comfortable dressing room, snorted, and then sat straighter and gaped at her. "What! What?"

"I am afraid we have made a terrible mistake, George. I have an unshakable premonition of disaster every time I contemplate the girls' London Season." Lady Gifford watched his reflection in the ornate mirror over her dressing table as she drew a brush through her prematurely grey hair.

"Nonsense! The girls'll go on marvelously. They've charm, beauty, and manners."

"My love, Chloe expects to take the *ton* by storm and will settle for nothing less than a rich and handsome husband. Phaedra dreads the whole experience and claims to be uninterested in finding a husband of any sort." She set down the silver-backed brush and turned to face him. "Chloe is certain she will be declared an Incomparable, surrounded by young, wealthy beaux, the toast of the *ton*."

"Well, and why should she not?" her husband replied, pride in his voice. "Is she not the most popular young lady in the neighborhood? I swear, I have to plow my way through the callow sprigs hanging about the house, bringing her posies and poetry. Tiresome, that's what it is."

"Oh, George, please do try to understand my concern. Chloe may be the most sought after girl in the neighborhood, but she is merely one of a few, not one of many. Her present popularity... I believe she has come to have too great a sense of her own attractiveness."

"First time I ever heard of a mother fretting about her daughter's social success. You're off the mark this time, I tell you, Isabella," he said. His impatience with the subject of conversation showed clearly in his tone.

"I greatly fear that she will disregard those rules of Society she finds too confining." She put her hands to her cheeks. "Oh, George, what if she should gain the reputation of being a hoyden? Or even fast? Just think how her Season would be spoiled. She would never receive an offer from anyone respectable. Even with your aunt's support, think of what might happen should one of those malicious old cats take her in dislike."

"Enough, wife." He came to stand before her, a stocky man of middle years with laugh lines about his mouth and strong, capable hands, which he held out to her. "Our girls will do handsomely, you'll see. With you to guide them, they'll neither put a foot wrong. Come to bed, now, love, do."

Stifling a series of yawns, Lord Gifford drew her to her feet and led her to the adjoining bedchamber with its huge bed canopied in blue.

In spite of his reassurances, Lady Gifford continued to worry to herself after the candles were extinguished. When one was the mother of daughters about to make their debut in London, one had a right to be concerned.

CHAPTER ONE

How can you be so calm, Phaedra? Our whole lives are in the balance, and you sit there with your usual blasé air. Are you not excited that tomorrow we leave for London?"

"You know I am more than a little reluctant to partake of the Season." Phaedra replied, setting aside the book she had been attempting to read. "My whole being is revolted by the concept of the Marriage Mart. One might as well be stood upon a platform in the green and auctioned off like a black slave. Mama and Papa would save a small fortune if they were to advertise us in the newspapers."

Chloe evidenced shock. "Advertise us. What do you mean?"

"Why sister, cannot you see the advertisement? 'For sale, two daughters, middling attractive, having moderate dowries, and complaisant personalities. Only handsome, wealthy men need apply.' I vow, it would cost much less than a Season and would, in my case at least, have as much chance of results."

A sidewise glance caught her sister's wide-eyed face. "If a likeness were to accompany the advertisement, the response might be better. We are not uncomely. 'Twould be even better if the prospective buyers could meet you. Your vivacity and spirit would immediately show them what a good buy they were getting. If we only let them see you; I might be sold as well. But no, that would be dishonest. Only think, the poor gentleman would think he was getting a pearl beyond price, then he would discover he had got only me."

"Phaedra, you are incorrigible. You must know I do not believe for a second that you are serious."

"Of course not, silly. I realize that you always know when I am funning," Phaedra lied, being aware that her sister did not share her peculiar turn of mind. "However, sister dear, you must know I am not nearly so sanguine about our Season as you. I do not expect us to be immediate successes, bursting upon the *ton* like the legendary Gunning sisters. I wish you would view the experience with a little more realism."

"Well, perhaps you are not hopeful of being a success," Chloe replied with some smugness, "but I intend to take London by storm. Why, with Mama's excellent taste, our wardrobes will be beyond anything beautiful. We are not unattractive. Just yesterday Edgar, the Squire's son, said I was an incomparable beauty, and everyone says we are alike enough to be twins." She rose from the window seat and crossed the room to peer at her dim reflection in the pier glass. A pleased smile showed that she liked what she saw.

Without turning away, she said, "We are well mannered and accomplished in all the feminine arts. We will, I promise you, be mobbed with admirers, as I have always been."

She set her mouth in a pretty pout, one Phaedra knew had been carefully rehearsed. "If only you will be a little less serious, and cultivate light conversation. I vow, Phaedra, if you insist upon prosing on about your flowers, no eligible man will have a second look for you. Please, dear sister, try to behave more like a young lady and less like some fusty old don at University, just for the Season."

"Will it satisfy you that I am determined to behave less seriously, for your sake, while we are in London?"

"Oh, yes, I know you will try," Chloe said, but her brief, responsive smile quickly returned to the pout. "I know you, though. You will forget yourself and begin to query someone about the wild plants to be found at his home, or some other subject equally tiresome. Before you know it, you will have the reputation of being a bluestocking."

She began to whirl about the room, her feet moving in time to the waltz tune she was humming. Stopping to gaze once more at her reflection, she said, "I wish my eyes were green and my hair golden, like Marianna Knight's. Brown hair and blue eyes are so...so common! Oh, well, I shall think instead about our lovely gowns. I vow, my pale lavender lawn, which Mama embroidered with silver oak leaves, is positively dashing."

She sketched another curtsy, gave one more whirl, and gracefully sank onto the window seat. "Or at least it would be, if it were not so demure. It is outside of enough that girls in their first Season have to look so...so maidenly!"

"And how would you prefer to appear, sister? Worldly? Brazen? Loose, even?" Phaedra said with a smile.

"Well, I would not mind being just a little dashing. After all, I wish to be noticed and not to be merely another shy young thing amongst so many. It would not harm my reputation to be noticeable, I think."

"You will be noticed," Phaedra said. "In spite of your merely passable looks, you have a sparkle about you that will bring you to the notice of all the Season's most eligible bachelors."

"Passable! I am not merely passable! Oh! You are funning again."

Chloe clasped her hands under her chin and opened her eyes very wide. This expression, Phaedra knew, was calculated to evoke feelings of protectiveness in the masculine breast.

"Seriously, Phaedra, I do want to make a splash in London. I cannot abide the thought that I will not be married before the end of the Season. I will not come home after our Season and languish here in the country. I was made for London, or perhaps even Paris."

"You would certainly make a splash in Paris, Chloe. Why, you might even last a full five minutes before you were clapped into gaol as a spy. Or had you forgotten that Boney is still in control in France?"

"Well, this horrid war cannot last forever, you know. Someday I intend to go to Paris, and I must have a husband who can take me there, in style."

A yawn interrupted her. "We should go to bed. If we do not, we will have circles under our eyes when we arrive in London and I do want to look my best."

"For that eligible bachelor who will be awaiting you upon our doorstep when you arrive, I suppose. But you are right and I am sleepy. Tomorrow will be tiring." Phaedra ignited a spill in the fire and used it to light her candle. As she pulled the door closed behind her she said, "Good night, Chloe. Dream of your handsome prince."

"And you will, I suppose, dream of flowers," came the tart rejoinder.

The February morning was cold and crisp, a perfect day for traveling. It was not yet sunrise when the family broke their fast together, and then departed to their various rooms. Shortly a wail from Chloe's room broke the silence.

"It's gone, it's gone. Oh, where is it? I can't find it," she cried. "Oh! My Season is spoiled. I cannot go!"

Her mother came running into the room. "What in the world?" she exclaimed. "Chloe, what is the matter? What can you not find?"

"My pink reticule. The one with the gold embroidery, to match my favorite gown. I cannot leave without it. Mama, we will have to unpack all my trunks, because I must be sure that I have it. No, we must search the house, for I am certain that dreadful boy has stolen it and hidden it away."

"What dreadful boy?" Lady Gifford said, while swiftly opening and closing drawers in a golden oak tallboy.

"Tom, the wretch. He has been taking my things and hiding them all week, just to plague me. He does not wish me to have a Season. He wants me to be an old maid and never have any happiness."

"Nonsense," Lady Gifford replied. "Your brother may be a rascal, but he is not unkind. Where is Peggy? Did she not help you pack your things? She will know—" She broke off as a young maid entered the room. "Oh, there you are, Peggy. Where have you put Miss Chloe's pink reticule with the gold embroidery? Did you pack it?"

"No'm, I didn't. Miss said as how she wanted to be sure she had it and would put it in her bandbox," the maid replied.

"Well, Chloe?" said Lady Gifford.

"Oh, I forgot. Let me look." The girl upended a bandbox and its contents fell upon the bed. She pawed through them. "Yes, here it is. I am sorry Mama," Chloe said. "I just wanted to be sure that I had it. It is so beautiful, with all your embroidery upon it."

Lady Gifford, not responding to the flattery, gave her daughter a long look. "Chloe, if you will continue to fly into such a passion, perhaps you will not go on well in London. No one likes to see a young lady lose her composure. Try for a bit more civility, my dear, if you please."

"I will, Mama, I promise."

"Now, you may repack your bandbox, since you were the one to disorder its contents. Come, Peggy." Taking the maid with her, she left her pouting daughter alone.

THE SISTERS REACHED THE FRONT DOOR BARELY IN TIME TO WAVE FAREWELL TO the carriage carrying Lady Gifford's maid and all the luggage. Their papa was standing just outside the door, but there was no sign of Lady Gifford. Phaedra cocked an inquiring eyebrow at him.

"Your mother had 'just one more thing' to tell Nurse. I swear, that woman was never so empty headed when we went to London before. What ails her?"

"I believe, Papa, she is apprehensive about having two daughters to pop off this year."

"Slang! Young lady, you've been around your brothers too much. It don't befit a proper young lady to use slang. Besides, we're not going to London to 'pop off' our daughters, but to give them experience of Society."

"Pooh, Papa, you know that the whole purpose of a Season is to find a husband."

"Yes, but it ain't something you speak aloud of, m'dear. You've got to watch that tongue of yours. It'll get you into trouble yet, mark my words."

Lady Gifford bustled through the front entrance, distracting them. "Here I am, at last," she said brightly. "Come girls, get into the carriage. No, Chloe, you cannot sit there now. You know you become dreadfully unwell if you ride too long facing backwards. Let your sister have a chance to sit beside me for the short while we will be on our excellent local roads. Those nearer to London are quite abominably rough. And the frozen ground will not improve them, though it will make our journey easier than the mud we had last week."

She turned to her husband. "Oh, my dear, I will miss you terribly. I wish you did not have to remain here for another fortnight." Her eyes filled and she sniffed. Phaedra, watching, bit her lower lip and swallowed the small lump in her throat. She was always deeply touched to see evidence of her parents' love for one another.

Lord Gifford, oblivious as always to watching children and servants, took his wife in his arms and kissed her thoroughly. "There, there, my love. You'll go on famously without me. Why, I'd only be in the way while the three of you are sporting the blunt for frills and furbelows. You'll not even miss me, what with fitting the girls out in the first style of elegance. I'll be in London in time for Aunt Margaret's ball, never fear." He loosened his arms and handed her into the carriage. "God be with you, love. I'll see you soon enough."

He turned away and hurried toward the house, but Phaedra knew he'd lurk behind the library curtains, watching the carriage carrying his wife until it was out of sight.

Phaedra woke from a light doze when her mother spoke. "My dear, I am afraid you must trade places with your sister now. She is looking decidedly unwell."

Indeed Chloe's face was distinctively of a greenish cast.

Once on the rear-facing seat, Phaedra fell again into sleep, disturbed only by the noise of the inn yard at their first change of horses. Her slumber was troubled, filled with scenes where she found herself in embarrassing situations and unable to find words. In one instance, she was entering a grand ballroom without her shoes; everyone stared at her naked toes and gasped with shock.

She roused slightly and changed her position, leaning her head into the corner between the seat and the coach's side wall.

Another dream held a tall, dark, threatening man who was saying to her father, "No, no, it's not this whey-faced female I want, with no spirit and no conversation. I want the other one, the pretty one, for my wife." Finally, when she escaped from a scene in which she struggled to free herself from grasping hands dragging her to the altar to wed an ancient, stooped, evil-looking man, she resolved to sleep no more.

"I was just about to awaken you," Lady Gifford said, as Phaedra tried to ease the stiffness from her neck. "We will halt shortly for luncheon. Tidy your hair and put on your bonnets, girls."

There was a moan from Chloe. "Do not speak of food. I shall die!" She was huddled in a corner of the coach with a shawl wrapped around her head.

"Chloe, I declare if you would not so indulge yourself, you would feel much more the thing," Lady Gifford scolded. "When you have taken some weak tea and toast you will feel much the better for it."

Another moan was the only answer to these unsympathetic remarks. But the girl had little longer to suffer, for the carriage soon drew up to the inn, where the landlord unctuously escorted them to a comfortable private parlor. Chloe was tucked into a soft chair, with her shawl still wrapped about her shoulders, and given her mother's smelling salts. She looked pale and wan, and her usual sparkle was missing.

"I could not eat or drink a thing," she whimpered, when their mother once again mentioned tea.

"Yes, you shall, miss," her mother said. "'Twill do you no end of good."

Lady Gifford and Phaedra did justice to the fluffy omelette and freshly baked bread that soon arrived. Chloe sipped reluctantly at her tea and nibbled her dry toast. She did look less unwell, however, after eating, and pronounced herself able to face the remainder of the journey. But only, she reminded them in long-suffering tones, because they were on their way to London.

THE SUN WAS NEARING THE WESTERN HORIZON WHEN THE SOUND OF POUNDING hooves, the rattle of harness, and frantic shouts woke the Hazelbourne ladies. Their coach swerved violently, as Jem Coachman worked to halt the team.

Phaedra leaned from the window to see what was happening. Ahead of their team and very nearly under the leaders' noses, another equipage sat askew of the roadway. A man was grappling with its harness, trying to calm the rearing horses. She opened the door and jumped to the ground. Her mother protested and Chloe cried out in alarm, but she ignored them and hurried toward the other conveyance, noting as she did so that it was a perch phaeton of uncommon elegance.

Jem Coachman was just behind Phaedra as she reached the heads of the rearing horses. They both grabbed for the harness. With three people working to soothe the animals, the pair was soon quieted. Jem wrapped the reins around a nearby tree trunk and kept a good grip on them. The horses stood nervously in the road, snorting and twitching. Their driver, a short, bandy-legged fellow in rough clothing, ran practiced hands over their sweating coats and checked their legs before speaking.

"I'm that obliged to ye, my lady, and you too, mister," he said, somewhat breathlessly. "If your man could just help me get turned and past your coach, my lady, I'll be back to see what harm me master ha' taken."

"Your master?" said Phaedra. "Do you mean someone was thrown from the perch?"

"Aye, that he was, my lady. And he must ha' been hurt, else he wouldna' let go the ribbons," the groom replied, as he gathered the reins.

"Then you must, by all means, return to seek him. We will follow, to offer such assistance as we can. Jem, get our coach moved as soon as possible, and turn it to follow this man until he finds his master. We must discover how serious his injuries are."

Jem Coachman held the pair while the other man mounted to his perch, and then climbed to his own seat and began moving their coach off the road. Fortunately there was a level, grassy verge, so he was able to pull completely out of the way. The phaeton was quickly turned, although Phaedra could see that the driver was challenged to manage the still restive pair.

As soon as she clambered into the Hazelbourne coach, she was bombarded with questions.

"Why are we turning?"

"Who is that person?"

"What happened?"

"One at a time." She pleaded, laughing in spite of her concern. "I have no idea who he is—a groom, whose master was thrown from his seat. We are going back to assist him in the event his master is injured."

"But why—"

"Of course, we must—"

By the time her explanations were finished, their coach was bowling along the road in the wake of the phaeton. Lady Gifford commended Phaedra's thoughtfulness, agreeing that they must discover what assistance they could provide the probably injured man.

Chloe moaned quietly beside her mother, as their speed was much greater than their usual traveling pace and the coach rocked quite violently. Phaedra thought that they had traveled about two miles before the coach slowed.

Jem had barely pulled the team to a halt before she jumped from the coach. Lady Gifford commanded Chloe to remain where she was and recover from her nausea, then she, too, climbed down. Jem secured his own team before he hurried to the heads of the phaeton's pair, while Phaedra followed the other driver to the side of the road where a body lay sprawled. The groom was touching the outflung arms and legs with much the same care as he'd given the horses' legs. Not quite sure what to do, Phaedra watched, her lower lip caught between her teeth.

The groom sat back on his heels. "He don't seem to have broken anything, my ladies." he said, As Lady Gifford joined them. "But the way he landed, all limp-like, makes me think he must ha' hit his head. Though he moaned when I first laid hands on him, he did."

Lady Gifford knelt and laid her fingers on the pulse in his wrist. "His heart is strong," she said after a moment. "I do not think he is seriously injured," She released his wrist. "Jem, do bring me the flask of water, and one of the rugs, I think. Perhaps if we bathe his head he will come round."

Phaedra, meanwhile, had knelt at his head, and now she examined his scalp with gentle fingers, parting the thick, dark hair. As she felt for cuts and scrapes, she said, " A bump behind his ear seems to be the most serious injury." She moved, to settle his head more firmly on her knees. "Oh! Here is blood upon my skirt. Where is he bleeding?"

"His wrist is cut," Lady Gifford replied. "But it does not appear too deep and has almost stopped bleeding. Let me tear the cravat in half, and I will clean and bind it up. Oh, thank you, Jem," she continued, as her coachman handed her a flask of water. She dampened both pieces of the torn cravat, handing one to her daughter.

The two ladies cleaned and bandaged the injured man. As they worked, his groom spoke.

"Master, he was tryin' out this pair before he bought 'em. I told him that they was too fresh and not properly trained, I did, but he wanted to give 'em a try. Drives to an inch, the master does.

"We musta' hit a rut or a stone in the road, for the rig gave a big lurch to the side and he was throwed. Hung on to the reins, as he shoulda', and that's when the barstards—'scuse me ladies—the horses bolted.

"Master, he was throwed out still a'holdin' to the reins, and I couldn't do nothin' to stop the horses. Soon's I saw master had loosed the reins I knowed he was hurt, so I jumped onto the off horse's back and did me best. 'Twasn't 'til I got me feet on the ground and was drug a spell that I was able to slow 'em. Your coach bein' in the road is probably why I got 'em stopped. It and the tall shrubberies along the road slowed 'em enough that I got me a good hold on their heads."

As he finished his recitation, his master's eyelids fluttered under heavy black brows and he groaned. "Ouch, stop that, damn you, Biggins. My head's hurting like the very devil. Stop poking at it!"

Phaedra lay off dabbing at his forehead with the damp cravat. As his eyes opened completely, she saw that they were even darker than her own.

"Who're you? What happened?" He groaned again, and closed his eyes for a few seconds. "Oh, yes, I was thrown. The horses? Biggins, the horses!" He tried to sit up, but Phaedra held him firmly by the shoulders.

"The horses are fine," Biggins assured him. "Just a bit winded, you might say. These ladies helped me stop 'em and came back to see if you was hurt. You just stay there, master, and get your senses back."

"Yes, young man," Lady Gifford said soothingly, "you must sit quietly for a while. You were quite unconscious for a spell. Do not worry yourself." She turned to her coachman. "Jem, if you please, fetch the hamper. We will pour this young man some wine, which, I am sure, will make him feel much more the thing."

Phaedra resumed dabbing gently at his forehead.

"Stop that, girl!" he demanded. "You're only making it hurt worse."

"You are an ungrateful man," she retorted, pulling her hands away, "I was only trying to get some of the dirt off your face so we could see if you had any other cuts or bruises. It would serve you right if you had, and they became infected, and you died of them."

"I promise you I won't die, unless you knock me out again with your ministrations," the young man replied. "I am feeling better by the minute. I do appreciate your assistance, but, as you can see, I am not seriously injured." He attempted to sit upright but failed; his head fell back onto Phaedra's knees.

His eyes closed again briefly and his lips tightened. After a few moments, he said, "I shall just rest here a moment, and not trouble you more. Biggins can see to me, and we will shortly be able to return these accursed horses to their owner." He attempted a laugh, but failed miserably. "He'll continue to be their owner, too, after this fiasco."

Lady Gifford held the cup to his mouth. "We will remain until we are certain that you are recovered from your fall. Here, see if you can swallow some of this wine."

He raised his head slightly and sipped. The effort seemed to exhaust him, for he relaxed back onto Phaedra's knees. As he lay there, she observed that his body, clad in buckskins, a fine linen shirt, and a well-fitted riding coat which, though torn and dirty, was of the finest fabric, was well muscled and trim. Fearing from his stillness that he had again fallen into unconsciousness, she placed her hand on his brow. His dark eyes flew open at her touch.

"Will you stop pounding on my head, young woman! I have hurts enough without you adding to them."

She snatched her hand away and opened her mouth to voice an angry reply. Before she could find sufficiently cutting words, a shake of her mother's head prevented her from speaking. Lady Gifford asked the young man to try again to sit upright. He succeeded in doing so, though he was forced to support himself with one arm for a few moments. Finally he was able to sit alone. He shook his head.

"Ow! That hurts like the devil!" Then, as if suddenly aware of the company, his mouth twisted. "Your pardon, my lady. An aching head is no excuse for swearing. Thank you for helping me, but I believe I can manage now. Please do not let me delay you further."

"Very well, young man. You do not seem to have taken any lasting injury. Only let us remain until you feel that you can hold your seat on the phaeton. Jem will assist you in mounting it before we depart. Now, do take a bit more of this wine. I am sure it will make you feel much more the thing."

The young man drank the wine and had soon lost much of his paleness. Jem Coachman held the horses while Biggins helped him mount to the perch. Biggins took the reins, over his master's half-hearted protest, and he bade a grateful farewell to the ladies.

They watched the phaeton move rather too rapidly away. "Well, at least the horses are probably too tired to bolt again," said Phaedra. "What a rude young man."

"I doubt you would be in the best of manners if you had been thrown about as he has. I am so glad that he was not more seriously injured. He could have been killed." Lady Gifford finished replacing the flasks in the hamper. As she walked back to her coach, she spied her elder daughter, who was dangling from the window and watching the phaeton out of sight.

"Chloe, what are you doing, hanging out of the coach like a hoyden? Get yourself back inside this instant."

Resettling herself in the coach, Phaedra found her weariness considerably abated. The light activity of assisting the injured gentleman had eased the stiffness in her joints and banished her drowsiness.

"Mama, who was he? What happened?" Chloe demanded, as the coach jerked to a start.

"Why, do you know, we did not learn his name," Lady Gifford said. "How peculiar, to be sure."

"I heard Jem tell Biggins who we are. It doesn't matter, though. He is a rude man whom we do not wish to know." Phaedra brushed dirt and debris from her skirt.

"You are being unfair. He was injured and no doubt in pain. One cannot hold his rudeness against him under these circumstances. Besides, he did say you were hurting him."

"Well, I thought he was handsome as anything, from what I could see, and his phaeton looked very expensive," Chloe said. "Perhaps we will meet him in London, and he will ask me to dance. Do you suppose he is wealthy, Mama? I wonder if he is married."

Phaedra shook her head in exasperation. "Chloe, you think of nothing but parties and dancing and catching a rich husband. You may never see him again, and I am not sure but what that would be desirable,"

She deliberately changed the subject. "How far is it to London, Mama? Do we make any more changes before we arrive?"

"Yes, I believe we do, and very soon, I imagine," Lady Gifford replied. "Chloe, how is it that you were so unwell until we stopped, when you suddenly became well enough to make a cake of yourself, hanging out the window? And if you were that recovered, why did you not come to our assistance?"

"I was much better as long as we were not moving and it did not upset my stomach to look out of the window," Chloe replied defensively. "I feel distinctly unwell now, though, and wish you would not scold. I shall try to sleep until we reach London." She pulled the shawl about her head again and lay back against the squabs.

Lady Gifford gave a ladylike snort. Phaedra suspected her mama was not misled by Chloe's stratagems. As for herself, she suspected her sister made too much of a good thing out of her motion sickness.

THEY GRATEFULLY ARRIVED IN LONDON SHORTLY AFTER EIGHT IN THE EVENING. All three were chilled through and thoroughly tired of traveling, though Phaedra had found the long drive through London the most interesting part of the trip. At one point, she had seen a great domed structure in the bright moonlight. Upon pointing it out to her mother, she was informed that the building was St. Paul's Cathedral, designed by the legendary Sir Christopher Wren.

The house the Hazelbournes had taken for the Season was just north of Grosvenor Square, in an unexceptional but not highly fashionable neighborhood. In the past Lord and Lady Gifford had stayed at the Duke of Verbain's town house when they visited London. This year, with two daughters to be presented and plans to remain through the month of June, they needed a house. While Lord Gifford was far from under the hatches, his fortune was only modest. He had gratefully taken advantage of an offer from a distant relative of Lady Gifford's who was willing to allow them the use of his London residence for a fraction of what a larger and better-located one would have cost.

It was barely commodious enough for the Hazelbournes, but there was a small rear garden giving onto a detached mews where the coach could be stabled and convenient for the ladies' use. The house was furnished with a partial staff, augmented by Hazelbourne servants sent up from the country.

Much to Chloe's dismay, there was no ballroom. She made unkind comments about this serious lack until she was reminded that she and her sister were to make their come out at a ball given by their great-aunt, the Duchess of Verbain.

The ladies were met by the assembled staff, headed by Edgemont, their butler from Gifford Court, who had come to Town a week ahead of them to make the house ready. Parsons, her ladyship's personal servant, hovered in the background. Lady Gifford, in the manner that had made her beloved of her servants all her life, greeted each of them and said a kind word to even the lowest tweenie.

"Now, my lady, you will come into the parlor and have a nice cup of tea," Parsons said, as the introductions were finished.

She bustled ahead of the three, leading them upstairs and into a large room off the central hallway. It was high ceilinged and papered above dark wainscoting with Chinese silk in a red and gold design. Gold velvet draperies covered two large windows overlooking the front of the house. Three red velvet upholstered sofas, several chairs with gold brocade seats, and half a dozen small mahogany tables were placed in stiff lines along three walls. An enormous fireplace with an ornate mantelpiece dominated the wall opposite the entrance, and a worn but still attractive Oriental rug in red, gold, and black covered most of the polished floor. There were several portraits in gilded frames on the walls, including one of Lady Gifford's maternal grandfather.

Lady Gifford and the sisters gaped at the room's overpowering redness while Parsons fussed. "You must be particularly exhausted. Why, we expected you an hour ago. Did you have trouble on the journey? Here, sit down, this chair looks most comfortable. Miss Chloe, you get a pillow for your mother's back. Miss Phaedra, pour her a cup and let her rest. Poor thing, jogging along all day in that coach, with two chattering magpies for company. Why..."

"That will do, Parsons," her mistress said. "I am only a little tired, and the magpies did not chatter. I am chilled, I will admit. We were delayed because we came to the assistance of a young man who had had an accident, but the delay was less than an hour. It was really a very easy journey. No, Chloe, I do not want another pillow behind me. I just want to sit here and drink my tea quietly. Do not fuss!"

The dresser sniffed. "And it was helping the young man that you got your skirt all dirty, I'll warrant." She frowned at the blood and grass stains on the skirt of Phaedra's blue wool traveling dress. "And you too, Miss Phaedra. I declare, you get out of my sight for one day and your clothes are all rags. It will take a bit of scrubbing to get those stains out of your dress, but I don't mind, I'm sure."

"Do let Mama rest a bit," Phaedra told the dresser. "We will sit here quietly for a few minutes, and then I will send Mama straight to her bed. Would you go up and prepare it, please, Parsons."

"Thank you, dear," Lady Gifford said, as her dresser stalked from the room in outraged sensibility. "She does tend to mother me over much." She turned to Chloe. "Are you feeling better, my dear? You have more color, but you are so quiet."

"Yes, Mama, I am feeling much more the thing. This house does not move, you see." Chloe smiled. "I was silent because I was thinking about that handsome young gentleman we met this afternoon. Do you think he will come to call?"

"I doubt it. We only told his groom that we were traveling to London and our names. We did not give our direction," her mother replied. "Besides, offering assistance along a roadside does not constitute an introduction. It would be the height of impropriety if he were to call without one."

"Perhaps he will write and express his gratitude. I truly would like to make his acquaintance." Chloe sighed. "He was so very handsome."

"Stuff!" Phaedra said. "He was not handsome, when you saw him at close range. He was swarthy and scowly. You are romanticizing, again, Chloe. You will probably never meet him again. Or, if you do, you will find, as I did, that he is rude and overbearing." She began to walk about the room, inspecting it.

Although somewhat bare, lacking the usual porcelain figurines, vases of flowers, and other decorative touches, its furnishings were quality pieces, if ever so slightly shabby. Phaedra fingered the velvet draperies, noting that they were slightly faded along the folds. Moving to stand before the fireplace, she examined the careful craftsmanship that had gone into the construction of the beautifully carved mantelpiece. "Do you know, Mama, it is really outside of enough that this room is so very red. In any other color, it would be truly lovely. As it is, one is overwhelmed."

"It does lack something of good taste," her mother agreed. "I am reminded somehow of Carlton House, the Prince of Wales' residence. It also is decorated in this style of overstated and tasteless opulence."

"Do you mean 'Prinny', Mama?" Chloe said.

"Yes, Chloe. But I beg of you, do not use that name for him. It is not polite in you to do so."

"I have heard you and Papa call him that," the girl protested.

"What is acceptable for your father and me to do is not necessarily so for a young girl in her first Season, so mind your manners."

"Yes, Mama," Chloe said, with a pout.

"Are there really rooms at Carlton House like this one, Mama? I cannot believe that our future king would be so lacking in good taste," Phaedra said.

"You will find, dear, that there are rooms in Carlton House that make this one seem plain and colorless," her mother replied dryly.

"Will we go to Carlton House, Mama?" Chloe clapped her hands. "Will we meet the Prince of Wales? Oh, I should like that above all things!" At her mother's cautious admission that an invitation might come their way, she bounced in her chair. "Oh! I do want to go there! Just think, Phaedra! To be invited to the Prince of Wales' palace. How wonderful it is to be in London at last!" She looked around. "But how can you criticize this beautiful room? It may be just the tiniest bit shabby, but it is so elegant, so royal in appearance."

Both her mother and Phaedra laughed. "As you say, Chloe. It is much more your style than mine, though." Phaedra barely restrained a yawn. "You should know, however, that the prince's residence, though it has the reputation of being very ornate and expensive, is nothing approaching a palace. Do you never read the newspapers, goose?"

She rubbed her temples. "I am so tired. Let us go to bed." Suiting her actions to her words, she rose and walked to the door. "Coming, Mama?"

"Yes, dear," Lady Gifford answered, as she stifled a yawn. "Come, Chloe, you must get some sleep. Tomorrow will be an exciting day, for we must begin organizing your wardrobe."

I shall not close my eyes," Chloe vowed. "We are truly here! We are in London! She twirled in the center of the room, narrowly avoiding a collision with a sofa. "I shall be a *succes fou*! I feel it in my heart." She patted her bosom.

"The feeling will cure easily with a cup of warm milk," Phaedra said, too tired to be amused by her sister's dramatics.

CHAPTER TWO

THE FOLLOWING DAYS WERE A WHIRL OF SHOPPING AND FITTINGS. ALTHOUGH she enjoyed watching her daughters discover the joys of shopping, each evening found Lady Gifford prostrate with exhaustion. Chloe had constantly to be restrained from choosing fashions and accessories far too dashing for a girl in her first Season. Phaedra, on the other hand, had to be sternly ordered to select frivolous bonnets and dainty slippers, her taste being much more for practical headgear and serviceable shoes.

Lady Gifford had her hands full at the Pantheon Bazaar, where Chloe invariably fell in love with unsuitably garish fabrics, while Phaedra selected those which would have had her labeled a drab. All was finally resolved, however, and both girls, while not completely satisfied with their growing wardrobes, would be clothed in a manner fitting their ages and station.

Unused to spending all of her days indoors and relatively inactive, Phaedra finally rebelled against the constant round of shopping and fittings. During a rare afternoon at home, she jumped to her feet, cast her needlework from her, and stated, "I am going for a long walk. My body is stiff and aching from too much sitting, standing or riding in carriages. I need fresh air and exercise."

"Of course, dear. Just remember to take Betty with you, for I need your sister's help to hem her primrose gown."

Phaedra and Betty strolled along the streets toward Green Park. Although she wished Betty were more inclined to stride along at a good pace, Phaedra was content just to be out of doors. "Phew. I almost wish I did not have to breathe," she said, wrinkling her nose. "How do you stand the odors, Betty?"

The young maid who had come with the house raised her brows in puzzlement. "Odors, miss? I don't smell nothing out of the ordinary." She sniffed. "Well, maybe a sort of moldy, nasty smell, but that's all."

"That's damp earth," Phaedra told her, shaking her head in defeat. Perhaps the denizens of London were so used to the scents of horse and smoke and the other, less pleasant, odors of humanity crowded densely together that they never noticed.

Once in the park, she said, "If you would prefer to rest here on this bench, you may. I intend to get some exercise."

Betty sat, with a grateful smile. "It feels good to sit, miss. The sun's so nice and warm."

Phaedra made two energetic circuits of the park before her need for activity was satisfied. As she returned to the bench to retrieve her maid, she spied a group of half a dozen stylish gentlemen approaching on an intersecting path.

One of them, a rotund fellow in a too-tight coat and trousers far better suited to a smaller man, peered at Betty through a silver-rimmed quizzing glass. "Well, well. What have we here?"

Phaedra ignored him. "Come, Betty. It is time we were returning." She tugged the girl to her feet, but before she could drag her along the path, a second man stepped into her way."Housemaids, I imagine. Ripe for the plucking." His voice was smooth, deep, and somehow hungry sounding.

Phaedra stepped around him, followed closely by the maid, who offered no resistance and, in fact, hung on tightly.

A third man said, "Here now, don't run away. We won't harm you." He blocked the path with outspread arms.

"No indeed," the first promised with a giggle. "We are harmless gentlemen. Wouldn't hurt a fly." General laughter agreed with him.

Dodging around a shrub at a half run, Phaedra and Betty almost collided with a tall man.

Instead of stepping aside, he caught Phaedra by the wrist. "Hold there. What are you running from?"

She recoiled. He was older than the others and dressed to the nines. "Release me, sir, if you please." Instead he captured her other wrist and soon had them manacled between long, strong fingers.

The other men caught up. "Ah, Dervigne, you caught our little housemaids. Good man!" The speaker slipped his arm around Betty's waist. "Give us a kiss then, sweetling." He bent his head.

Betty squealed, a sound that was abruptly cut off as the man kissed her.

"Let go of her!" Phaedra tried to wrench herself free, but the older man had a grip of iron. As the men surrounded her and Betty, she felt real terror. "I am a lady, sir. She is my maid. You have no right—"

"A lady? Dressed that way? Not likely," the deep-voiced one said. "Here, Dervigne, I'll take her."

Her captor appeared to study her features. "No, I think she's telling the truth." He pulled Phaedra closer, ignoring her struggles. "A toll, then, and I'll release you."

As his face approached hers, Phaedra gave up trying to wrench her hands free and kicked out instead. Her foot connected with his shin.

"Damn you!" He released her.

"Run, Betty," Phaedra cried, and swung her reticule at her maid's captor. It hit him full in the face. Betty took to her heels, with Phaedra right behind.

Fear leant strength and speed to their flight. Although several of the men pursued them with laughter and cries of "view halloo", she and Betty emerged from the park before they could catch up. Once among the crowds on a busy street, Phaedra looked back. The men were standing at the park's edge, laughing together.

Both girls walked rapidly along the street, with frequent glances over their shoulders. At last Phaedra found her voice. "We are only a block from home. I will be perfectly safe. Go on ahead. I will be along in a few moments."

Betty gave her a tremulous smile. "Thank you, miss. I was that scared, I couldn't move."

"So was I. Go now, and try to avoid being seen until you've tidied yourself." Phaedra watched the maid duck into the servants' entrance as she walked more slowly, needing time for the shaking of her hands and the butterflies in her stomach to subside. When Edgemont opened the door, all signs of her fright and her flight were well hidden, and she was able to give him a bright smile as she commented upon how exhilarating her walk had been.

Two weeks after their arrival in London, the Hazelbourne ladies returned from a brief shopping trip to find a note awaiting them from Lord Gifford's aunt, the Duchess of Verbain. It announced her arrival in Town and contained an invitation to call the next morning. Chloe was excited, because she took the invitation as the first step in her successful Season. Phaedra was less so, because she still dreaded the next few months. She remembered the Duchess as a commanding, regal woman, having no patience with girlish high spirits.

Their Graces' home in Portman Square was imposing, as was the Duchess. Even Chloe was subdued as they entered and were divested of their outer garments. The Duchess, stern faced as ever, embraced Lady Gifford with affection, and then turned to her daughters. She looked them up and down through a quizzing glass, her haughty stare made even more intimidating by the magnification of one faded blue eye.

"Well, now, you've grown into passable looking chits, I must say. The last time I saw you must have been four or five years ago. You'd spots and freckles, flyaway hair, and no bosoms. But you'll do now, I think. No beauty, but passable, quite passable."

Her mother's quick glance stifled the imprudent reply on Chloe's lips.

Her Grace continued, "Now which of you is which? I used to tell you apart, but you've grown to be amazingly like one another. Well, speak up gels, which is which?"

Lady Gifford quickly made the introductions, and both girls curtsied politely. The Duchess nodded curtly and snapped her fingers behind her back. "Come here, Mary, and become reacquainted with the Hazelbourne gels."

Chloe remembered The Duchess' granddaughter, Lady Mary Follansbee, as a quiet, shy little girl with enormous green eyes and a mass of freckles marring her face. On their rare visits to Verbain, she had never entered into their play, but had clung to her mother's skirts. The slender young woman with strawberry blond hair who came to stand beside the Duchess was clear of skin and lovely enough to arouse a small pang of envy in Chloe's bosom.

"Now you gels go over there in the corner and get to know one another again. I want to talk to Isabella."

Lady Mary smiled and said, "Do not let Grandmama put you off. Her bark is ever so much worse than her bite." She led Phaedra and Chloe to a cozy corner where four chairs were set in a comfortable grouping. "I do hope we will become great friends. I envied you so when we were small. You seemed to have such fun. I often wondered what it would be like to not be a lady, for just one afternoon."

"I disliked you intensely," Chloe admitted. "Mama always told us that we should learn to behave as you did, in a ladylike manner."

"Perhaps you can teach me to have fun now. I would like that."

Lady Mary's smile was so entreating and so sweet that Chloe could not resist returning it. "And perhaps you can be a good example for me. I still sometimes forget I am supposed to be a lady."

"I would rather you would show us London," Phaedra said. "So far all I've seen is shops and parks."

"Oh, I wish I could, but I am a stranger here, too. We must endeavor to explore it together. Now, tell me what you have been up to since we last met. You have grown so much alike. You are Phaedra and you are Chloe, is that right?"

"No, I am Chloe," she said with a laugh. "Phaedra is the serious one. I am never serious."

"Why are you serious, Phaedra?"

"What calumny. Just because I would rather collect and study plants than peruse *La Belle Asemblee*, my frivolous sister calls me serious." It was an old and affectionate dissention, one both she and Chloe had long indulged in. "Chloe merely flits about and never does anything practical. She sings well, though, so she is not entirely useless."

"Unfair!" her sister cried. "Just because I am more interested in parties and dancing than I am in scholarly pursuits!" All three girls laughed.

Their conversation was interrupted by the entrance of the butler, announcing Mr. Reginald Farwell.

The gentleman paused in the doorway, his wavy, golden brown hair, styled in an extreme Brutus, barely clearing the opening. He was dressed in the height of fashion, with collar points up to his cheeks and a lavender cravat folded into an intricate pattern and pinned with an enormous sapphire. His royal blue coat with enormous silver buttons looked as if it had been assembled directly upon his body. It partially concealed a waistcoat of extravagant stripes of scarlet and purple. Yellow pantaloons fitted snugly over long, slim, but well-shaped legs, and any number of fobs hung from his waistcoat. His shoes had narrow red heels all of two inches in height. Deep-set gray eyes were outlined by the longest, thickest lashes Chloe had ever seen. He coolly scrutinized the assembled ladies through an ornate quizzing glass. The other hand held a lacy handkerchief.

At last he moved, strolling languidly across the room. "Ah, your Grace, I find you as beautiful as ever," he said in a pleasant baritone drawl as he bowed over the Duchess' hand.

"Piffle," she responded. "Reggie, you know Mary. Let me make you acquainted with Lady Gifford and her daughters, Miss Hazelbourne and Miss Phaedra Hazelbourne."

"Lady Gifford, I believe we met some years past, but to be in your charming company is always pleasing to me," he said, lifting her hand to his lips in quite the most elegant gesture Chloe had ever seen. "And Lady Mary, you are, as always, the most perfect pocket Venus of my acquaintance," he continued, with a graceful bow in her direction.

Lady Mary merely smiled and said, "Hullo Reggie."

Turning in the sisters' direction he again raised his glass. Silently he inspected them, obviously paying close attention to their fashionable walking gowns as well as to their physical appearance. Chloe contained her irritation at being so closely inspected. She simpered and looked coyly at him from beneath lowered lashes. Her sister, clearly resenting his scrutiny, lifted her chin and glared at him. Finally he spoke vaguely to the space between them. "Miss Hazelbourne and Miss Phaedra, one of you would be ravishing; the two of you together is nothing short of breathtaking."

Chloe smiled widely and gave him her hand. He bowed over it, his lips not quite touching it, and murmured, "Such charm. Such style. I am overwhelmed. You are the elder, I take it."

"I am, sir, and am most pleased to make your acquaintance. You are the first gentleman whom I have met in London." Chloe cast a melting look into his face.

He turned to Phaedra and she grudgingly extended her hand. Chloe would have pinched her if she could have done so surreptitiously. Again he bowed, elegantly, gracefully. "Disapproval, Miss Phaedra? Or shyness? You interest me." He received no response, nor did he seem to expect one.

For the next several minutes, the conversation was general. Mr. Farwell shared several gossipy tidbits with them, mentioning names Chloe had often seen in the *Gazette*. Her mother and the Duchess laughed with him at tittle-tattle that held little meaning for Chloe. She decided he was someone to cultivate, however, because he seemed so completely at home in the *ton*.

Eventually her mother signaled that it was time for their departure. As Chloe and Lady Mary were finalizing their plans to meet in the park the next afternoon, Mr. Farwell stepped between her and her sister.

Phaedra took a half step back as Mr. Farwell loomed over her. He was so very tall. Somehow he had separated her from everyone else in the room. Leaning slightly towards her, he murmured, "Were you refreshed by your exercise the other day, Miss Phaedra?"

She stared.

"A good dash across the park is so invigorating, is it not? You did run quite a distance, however, and I feared you might have been quite exhausted." His eyes gleamed with amusement.

Oh, no! Of all people to see me. Oh, well, there is no help for it. "I had grown quite stiff and sleepy from sitting that day. Do you not feel that a good run often clears away the cobwebs and invigorates one?"

"Quite, Miss Phaedra. Quite." His smile faded and the drawl was suddenly missing, although his voice remained nearly inaudible. "A word of warning, however. In the future, you might consider your appearance before stepping out of doors. Had you appeared more the lady of quality, that small contretemps might have been avoided."

Before she could do more than gape, he stepped away and spoke to the Duchess.

Torn between anger at his impudence and embarrassment that he had evidently seen the entire episode, Phaedra resolved to ignore him as much as possible in the future.

The Duchess's parting words enhanced her resolve. "Pay no attention to this fop. He fancies himself God's gift to the fashionable world. Reggie, do you amuse Mary with your piffle while I have one last word with Lady Gifford. Now, Isabella," she continued, "you will be ready to begin going out by Monday next, will you not? Wednesday we go to Almack's. I have the vouchers for all of us.

"Sit down, Reggie, I cannot bear to have you towering over me like that," Phaedra heard the Duchess say as they exited the saloon.

"What a peculiar and affected gentleman," she commented, once they were in their waiting coach. "Have you ever seen anything so outrageous as that waistcoat?"

"Yes, he does somewhat overdo the foppish mode, "her mother replied, "but he does it so well and with such panache that it is no wonder that he is everywhere received."

"Well, I thought he was perfectly grand," said Chloe. "And such elegant manners. I vow, I have never received so gracious a compliment."

"Piffle, the Duchess called it, and piffle it was," Phaedra responded. "Mama, you wanted me to remind you to stop at Mlle. Hortense's to pick up Chloe's new bonnet."

Lady Gifford and her daughters were in the sewing room, industriously occupied, the morning following their visit to the Duchess. They were surprised to receive a huge bouquet of roses, addressed to Lady Gifford and Miss Hazelbourne. Accompanying it was a note expressing, in gracious and flowing periods, the gratitude felt by Herne Bradburn, Viscount Wilderlake, for assistance rendered.

"Oh, my, Mama, a viscount," Chloe enthused. "And what lovely roses. But who is he?"

"I believe he is the young man who took a header from his fancy phaeton,"

Phaedra said. "Don't you think so, Mama?"

"I do indeed. I must write to thank his for the roses." She went to her writing desk. "See, girls. He is not the rudesby you thought him. I'm sure his gruffness that day was merely due to his injury." She stroked the quill's end across her lips. "Wilderlake? I'm not familiar with that title. I wonder...well, the Duchess will know. Remind me to ask her what she knows of him."

Chloe clapped her hands. "Oh, I do hope that we will meet him soon. Surely he will be at Almack's or at one of the parties to which we have been invited. Perhaps he will dance with me! Mama, may I have one of the roses for my bedchamber? See, there are too many for the parlor. They are, after all, addressed to me as well as to you."

"No, indeed, they are not. He never saw you. It was Phaedra whom he wished to thank."

"But see, it says 'Lady Gifford and Miss Hazelbourne' on the card. I am Miss Hazelbourne. If he meant Phaedra, he would have said so."

"Perhaps he did not know that Phaedra had an older sister. No Chloe, you may not have a rose. You have enough imagination without a rose to feed your romantic fantasies. We will place them in two vases in the parlor, so that we all may enjoy them." She left the room, carrying the bouquet.

"Was not Mr. Farwell ever so handsome and suave, Phaedra?" Chloe said, after they had stitched and sketched in silence for a few moments. "I declare, his garments were so elegant, not like those plain ones the boys at home were wont to wear. And his manners, so gracious. I did like him. Surely, with his friendship with the Duchess and Lady Mary, we will see much of him. I wonder if Lady Mary is interested in him."

"She did not seem so," Phaedra replied. "Her greeting was not one of a young woman to a gentleman for whom she had a tendre."

"Well, so much the better. I would not want to flirt with someone who was already taken. Such a waste of energy. I wonder what his fortune is. It is too bad that he has no title."

"Chloe do not even think such thoughts, Do you wish to be considered mercenary?"

"I am not mercenary, just practical. After all, you would not expect me to marry a poor man, who could not afford to clothe me in the first rank of excellence, would you?"

"Yes, if you truly loved him."

"Pooh! You are overly romantic. Here, look at these sketches. What do you think? Would that gown not suit us for our presentation at the Queen's

Drawing Room?"

"No, it would not, Chloe. You know Mama said that the gowns deemed suitable as Court gowns are hopelessly old fashioned, with hoops and all."

"I suppose you are right. Still, this is a beautiful dress. Perhaps I will save the sketch for after I am wed and may dress as I please. It would be elegant, made up in a deep rose silk. Definitely not in muslin. I hate muslin!"

CHAPTER THREE

THE NEXT MORNING AT BREAKFAST THEY WERE JOINED BY MAMA'S COUSIN, Louisa Arbuckle, who had arrived very late the night before. Lady Gifford had earlier warned them to expect her. "I invited Louisa to be a companion to you, for I know you will often desire to attend different events."

Phaedra greeted her cousin with perfect good cheer, but Chloe made it perfectly obvious that she was not best pleased.

Cousin Louisa twinkled at Phaedra. "I'm sure we'll have many interesting adventures together," she said, reminding Phaedra of their botanical and ornithological expeditions in years past.

Phaedra allowed herself to hope that the next few months wouldn't be a complete debacle. Surely she could persuade Cousin Louisa to accompany her to the occasional lecture or museum.

Although their formal come out would not be for another fortnight, the Season truly started for the sisters on the following day. During the remainder of the week before their first attendance at the subscription ball at Almack's, they were invited to a tea party and a musicale. They also spent one afternoon viewing the Elgin marbles, an outing much enjoyed by Phaedra but not by Chloe, who nonetheless had stared quite avidly at the male bodies so meticulously depicted in marble.

One afternoon their mother took them driving in Hyde Park at the fashionable hour of five, where they made the acquaintance of several other girls and quite a few gentlemen. But none of the gentlemen, complained Chloe later, came even close to the sort she wanted to meet. "If this is all there is to a Season, why have we bothered coming to London? We could have gone to Bath and met gentlemen as unexciting as those we encountered today."

"There is no Almack's at Bath," Mama reminded her. "Have patience, Chloe. The Season has hardly begun, and Town is still thin of company. By this time next week, you will be besieged with gentlemen callers. Soon your head will spin with the number of invitation you receive."

Phaedra groaned inwardly. She could do without a siege by the sorts of gentlemen she had met so far—silly fops whose only topic of conversation was the style of their cravats or the patterns of their waistcoats, not to mention Corinthians of the first stare whose conversation was limited to sporting jargon or mildly scandalous gossip.

WEDNESDAY FINALLY ARRIVED. CHLOE SPENT THE ENTIRE AFTERNOON TRYING ON different gowns and complaining that they were all so insipid. By five o'clock she had worked herself into a state bordering upon hysteria. Every gown was crumpled and in need of pressing. She had scattered ribbons and silk flowers and slippers and petticoats about her room until the place resembled nothing so much as a particularly untidy dressmaker's establishment.

Phaedra had hidden herself away in the library, wishing to gather her energies for the evening's ordeal. Lady Gifford had retired to her chambers to rest. Chloe's anxiety increased until a tap on her door came, late in the afternoon.

Her mama opened the door and peeked in. "What in the world!"

Chloe started, and then burst into tears. "Mama, it is too much! I have nothing to wear that is suitable! This horrid girl has mussed all my dresses and will not press them. I cannot go to Almack's tonight. My life is ruined!"

"Stop that wailing this instant, Chloe. What is this mess? How did your clothing come to be strewn about in this manner?"

"I was choosing a gown to wear tonight. The pink one you said I was to wear is too dowdy. So are all my other gowns." She hiccupped. "Betty is useless. Why did we not bring Peggy? She is so much more helpful."

Her mother frowned forbiddingly. "Betty, return belowstairs. Edgemont has tasks for you."

The servant departed.

"Now, miss, let me have an explanation of this nonsense."

When Mama spoke in that no-nonsense tone, Chloe knew tears were useless. Still, she tried. "Well, I wanted to see how the pink muslin would look with my gloves and pearls and the white silk rose in my hair. When I got it on, I looked in the mirror and realized that it would not do. I appeared a silly young innocent with nothing to distinguish me. So I tried on my other gowns and they looked equally drab. Nothing I could do, no matter which ribbons or jewelry or anything I chose, would make me look less than young and simpering. Why can I not have Grandmother's diamonds? You know they are to be mine! And that stupid, stupid girl. All she could say was 'You look fine, miss.' She even objected to buttoning me. You must let her go, Mama. She will not suit at all."

"Betty is not your dresser, and even if she were, it is not becoming in you to keep her for what must have been hours catering to your whims," Mama replied as she busied herself with sorting through the pile of gowns on the bed. "She has other duties, you know.

"Now then, enough of this. You will wear the blush and pink gown tonight, or you will remain at home. I will tolerate no more excess of sensibility. You will be all that is correct in a young girl making her first Season. And you will behave yourself, young lady, or you will remain at home for the rest of the Season. Furthermore, you will treat Betty and Cousin Louisa with more courtesy."

Chloe summoned up tears to shimmer in her eyes. "Mama—"

"Enough, Chloe. Cousin Louisa is your relative, not your servant. I expect you to render her the courtesy you do me."

"But—"

"Chloe!"

When her mama used that particular tone, Chloe knew enough to leave off her pleading. "Yes, Mama."

"I shall take the pink gown to be pressed. You will, without assistance, return all your dresses and other garments to their proper places. No, do not object; I am quite out of patience with you. If your room is not restored to order by dinnertime, you will not go to Almack's this evening. Do I make myself clear?"

"Yes, Mama," she said again. As soon as her mama had pulled the door closed, she hurled the slipper she held with all her might. It made a loud thud when it hit the door. *Oh, dear, I hope Mama did not hear.*

Apparently she had not, for Chloe was left alone to put her gowns back in order.

Lady Gifford returned to her bedchamber where Parsons had laid out her own gown. "I must ask you to assist me in keeping a watch on Chloe, I'm afraid, Parsons. Betty is unable to resist her demands, and indeed, only encourages Chloe in her distempers."

"Of course, my lady. I'll keep an eye on her."

"Do not assist her to dress. It will do her good to be forced to do so without assistance for once. If she wants buttoning, she can always come to me."

"What about Miss Phaedra? I don't believe she's even come upstairs yet."

"Oh, dear! Please ask Mrs. Arbuckle to hurry her along, will you? She can assist Phaedra while you and I oversee Chloe. That girl!" Not for the first time she wished they had not been forced to delay Chloe's come out. Well into her nineteenth year, she was too conscious of being older than most of the girls being presented this Season. Her mother worried that she would be overly anxious to find a husband.

What a coil. With one daughter overly eager to taste life's spicier flavors and the other wishing only to be left to her studies, she was likely to be driven to distraction at least once daily. *If only George had come with me, instead of delaying. Thank goodness Cousin Louisa was able to join us.*

Chloe meekly came to her mother to ask to be buttoned and, equally meekly, requested Parson's assistance with her hair. When she descended the stairs for dinner, she did so demurely, and she remained unusually quiet throughout the meal. So did Phaedra, but Lady Gifford secretly thought hers was the quiet of dread. *I hope Louisa can lend Phaedra the support she so desperately needs. Otherwise, this Season could be a complete catastrophe.*

She displayed a deliberate insensitivity toward both of her daughters throughout the meal, instead chattering brightly to Cousin Louisa about the delights of other Seasons.

Cousin Louisa, whose own Season had been cut short by the death of her father, urged them to enjoy their own without anxiety about finding husbands. "By the time I was done with mourning," she told the girls, "I had met my dear Kenneth and had no more desire for the delights of Town. Sometimes I wish..." Her smile was at once wistful and tender.

Lady Gifford remembered how happy Cousin Louisa had seemed with Mr. Arbuckle. Such a tragedy, his dying so young.

The ladies retired to put the last touches on their ensembles before departing for Almack's. When the girls again came downstairs, Lady Gifford and Cousin Louisa were awaiting them in the foyer. Lady Gifford watched her daughters descending with a lump in her throat. They looked so lovely and so grown up.

Chloe was clad in a pink muslin gown with a blush overdress, embellished with white silk rosebuds at neck and hem. Matching pink slippers could be seen peeping from beneath her skirt. Immaculate white gloves covered her bare arms. The pearls around her neck were scarce paler than her own creamy skin, and the pink silk rosebuds in her hair set off its shining darkness.

Phaedra was equally lovely in an ice yellow gown without an overdress but bearing a slight train. Her mother's amber necklace circled her throat above a slightly scooped neckline—Lady Gifford had not been able to convince her younger daughter to expose even a fashionably decent amount of bosom—and a matching bracelet enclosed one white-gloved wrist. Her dark hair was threaded with white and pale yellow ribbons.

Lady Gifford sighed. So young and so innocent. Her mother's heart ached for her daughters, for she knew they were both somewhat out of the ordinary. Their Season could be a disaster if either of them was allowed to behave naturally.

"Well, girls, you both look charmingly," she said. "Now, Chloe, you must remember to behave with decorum and do not let your high spirits lead you into hoydenish actions. And Phaedra, please attempt to converse with your partners. But do not, in any event, bore them with your botanical pursuits. Gentlemen are not fond of young ladies who prattle too much of themselves. You may mention your interests, but be sure and ask them about theirs. If all else fails, you may discuss the weather." She ignored the quickly repressed giggles.

"Most important, you must recall that you are not to waltz until you are granted permission. I do not expect either of you to obtain such permission tonight. Generally, the patronesses like to observe unknown young ladies for several weeks before deciding that they are well enough behaved to be allowed to waltz."

A knock cut short these motherly admonitions. Edgemont opened the door and announced that Her Grace's carriage was without. She and her granddaughter, Lady Mary, awaited them.

As soon as all were settled, the Duchess turned to Phaedra and Chloe. "You gels had better be on your best behavior tonight. I was just telling Mary that to be accepted by the patronesses at Almack's is the only way a gel can have a successful Season. Silly situation, but that's the way the world is. If you lose their approval, you can just whistle down the wind for a fashionable husband. Be sure you don't waltz without their permission.

"No, you be quiet, gel," she said as Chloe opened her mouth to deliver a sharp retort, "I've seen more Seasons than your mother has years, and know whereof I speak. You follow my advice and you'll do, I tell you.

"Louisa, I fear your voucher is just as a chaperone. I could not persuade that stiff-rumped relative of yours, Mrs. Drummond-Burrell, to do more than let you in the door. So you'll have to sit in the corner with the other chaperones, I fear."

Cousin Louisa nodded. "Just as well. I have no desire to take my place in the Marriage Mart, Your Grace."

"Hmph. You should." She cocked her head and studied Cousin Louisa, who was looking almost dowdy in a dark gray gown that did not become her. "Or perhaps not. No sense in running against this year's field."

Chloe heard Her Grace's words with disbelief. Could Cousin Louisa still be a candidate for marriage? Surely not. She was *old.*

For the rest of their short journey, the Duchess interrogated Mama about the situation at Gifford Court. "What George does with his inheritance is no concern of mine, but I can't help being curious. He's always had an odd kick to his gallop. I tell you, Isabella, there is a frivolity about your husband I cannot entirely approve."

To Chloe's amazement, Mama did not dispute the Duchess' words. How could she allow anyone, even Her Grace, to disparage Papa? Even that thought was driven from her mind as the carriage slowed.

Chloe was speechless with excitement as they entered the assembly hall. There was no time for her to do more than gape briefly at the plain, unfestive appearance of the fabled Almack's. Mama immediately led them to a haughty woman whom she introduced as the Countess Leiven.

The countess gave the sisters a chilly smile, but spoke cordially to their mother. "It is too bad that you must play the gooseberry this year, Isabella. Is your charming husband to join you?"

"Yes, but he had obligations to keep him at home these past weeks. He will arrive in a few days."

"So nice," the Countess replied. "If you can escape from your maternal duties, please come to tea some afternoon."

Lady Gifford murmured her agreement and led the girls away. "Hush," she hissed as Chloe opened her mouth to speak. "Do not even think unkindly of the Countess. She can be a deadly enemy. I do hope she will take a liking to you, as much as she can like any girl with the freshness of youth."

The next patroness to whom they were introduced barely gave them time to greet her before she started speaking rapidly. She spoke of their appearance as if they were not present, but was, on the whole, complimentary. As they moved away from her through the crowd, Lady Gifford told her awed daughters, "You see why Sally Jersey is called 'Silence'. She is a terrible gossip, but she is also kind. I quite like her better than any of the others."

On being presented to Mrs. Drummond-Burrell, Chloe was amazed. How could such a top-lofty, ugly woman come to be so important? She was appropriately polite, remembering her mother's warning that this woman, on a whim, could do them great damage.

No other patronesses were present, but the introductions continued as they strolled. Mama was obviously well acquainted with and well liked by most of the *ton*. Chloe's head was swimming with names and faces by the time they had completed their circuit of the room.

Before the first set had ended, each girl had been asked for dances by gentlemen to whom they had been introduced. When the next set was made up for a country dance, both she and Phaedra had partners. Hers was Mr. Martin, a wispy youth in the extreme of fashion. Although he was pleasant enough, Chloe could not warm to him, for he bore no resemblance to the man of her dreams.

The third dance was a waltz. The sisters remained at their mother's side, watching the dancers swirl about the room.

Chloe suddenly sat up straighter and laid her hand on her sister's arm. "Look, Phaedra, over by the door. Is that not the gentleman whom you helped along the road?"

She turned to look. "I do not believe it is. This gentleman is older and, I think, somewhat taller. Do not stare, Chloe. It is rude."

"Well, he is excessively handsome, all the same, and I am sure that I have seen him in the park." She raised her hand as if to wave to him.

"Chloe!" Phaedra caught her elbow. "Behave yourself. You have not been introduced to the gentleman. You may not claim acquaintance on the basis of a chance encounter."

Mama turned to look questioningly at Chloe. Phaedra quickly explained. *The traitor.*

"Chloe, that is exactly the sort of behavior that I warned you against," Mama scolded. "You must not give in to these unladylike urges. If the gentleman wishes to make our acquaintance, it is up to him to do so. To wave at a gentleman anywhere in public is not at all the thing. Here, at Almack's, it is unthinkable."

Chloe clamped her lips together and covertly watched the dark haired gentleman as he surveyed the room with his quizzing glass. As his glance came to her, she quirked her lips in a small smile. His glance passed on with no sign of recognition. She continued to watch the door. Soon another familiar face appeared. She started to raise a hand to catch the gentleman's attention, but remembering her mother's admonition, restrained herself.

The familiar visage was that of Mr. Reginald Farwell. Although not the sort of gentleman Chloe could consider for a husband, he was attractive enough. Dare she attract his attention? She became aware of her mother's vigilance, and did not attempt to do so.

Mr. Farwell threaded his way amongst the dancers to make his bow to the Duchess. Chloe could not hear his words, but they obviously included Lady Mary. She saw him write his name on the girl's dance card.

He then moved to bow in front of her mother. "Ah, Lady Gifford. How pleasant to see you again."

He appeared to stifle a yawn. "And the Misses Hazelbourne. Are you enjoying Almack's? Delightful. So lovely to encounter you once more." He moved on without ever actually looking at either of them.

Chloe's mouth fell open. Then she shut it with a click of teeth and her expression hardened.

What a rude man.

THE EVENING DRAGGED ON. HER DAUGHTERS HAD PARTICIPATED IN MOST DANCES, but were obviously not the toast of the *ton*. Even Chloe was quite ready to leave when Lady Gifford suggested it. She had watched her elder daughter closely after Mr. Farwell's snub. She expected an explosion, and wished to get the girl at home before it occurred.

Her expectations were realized. Chloe gave way to a grand fit of hysterics as soon as they arrived home. She accused her mother of dressing her like a dowd, of refusing to introduce her to any eligible men, and of wishing to keep her an old maid for the rest of her life.

Nor was her sister spared. Phaedra, Chloe cried, had given her partners such a bad impression that she had ruined all Chloe's chances.

Lady Gifford calmed her eventually, saying that this was only their first introduction to Almack's and that subsequent weeks would see both girls achieving a moderate success.

"I do not wish to be a success at such a stuffy place." Chloe retorted. "Why can we not attend more lively entertainments?"

Only the threat of being sent back to Gifford Court for the rest of the Season at last quieted the distraught girl and convinced her to retire. Lady Gifford wished her husband were in London. Chloe would never let her father see her in such a state, obtaining her way with him by cajolery and manipulation.

Cousin Louisa, always the peacemaker, reminded her that George would arrive in a few days.

"I can hardly wait," she said, with a sigh.

In Chloe's bedchamber Phaedra opened her budget. "I will not have Mama made miserable by your tantrums, sister, you may be sure. If you do not moderate your behavior, I will endeavor to do exactly what you said of me and give all my dancing partners a disgust of me. Then where will you be? They will wonder if I am so detestable, why so might you be. I will behave as the most veritable bluestocking, which if the truth be known, I should chose to do anyway."

She paused, to unfasten the tiny pearl buttons at the back of Chloe's gown. "I have promised you that I will attempt to be all that is charming and amiable, so as not to hurt your chances to fulfill your dreams of your Season. So I shall as long as you do nothing to distress our parents. But harken to me, Chloe. I will not keep my promise if you do not attempt to moderate your behavior and to be more courteous to Mama and to Cousin Louisa.

"Oh, Chloe, do you not see how your present behavior is not to your advantage?" she continued, becoming more calm. "Whether you wish it or no, the *ton* has its rules for girls making their come out, and you must adhere to them. You would not be admired should you dress as you would chose, but rather be thought fast. And if you behave immodestly, the Prince Charming of your dreams will take you in such dislike that he will snub you."

"He would not!"

"Indeed he would. Had you behaved as you wished tonight, any true gentleman would assuredly have taken you in disgust. Furthermore, you have driven Mama to the brink of tears."

Eventually Chloe ceased her stormy weeping and seemed to listen. "Truly, Phaedra, I do not mean to distress Mama, nor to go against Society's rules, even though I think them excessively silly. But when I see other girls being sought after and waltzing and being the center of the gentlemen's attention, I cannot contain myself. There is so little time. I must marry this Season. I could not stand it if I were to be left upon the shelf."

"Then confine yourself within the rules of our society. If you wish to marry within it, you must live within it, both now and after you are married. While an excess of sensibility and an appearance of selfishness might be acceptable in an older woman, they will never make you popular with eligible bachelors or with their parents." She gave Chloe a nudge toward the bed. "Go to sleep now. Tomorrow will be better, and you will soon achieve the popularity which you so desire." She kissed her sister's cheek and tucked the quilts about her.

In her own room, Phaedra admitted to herself that she was not as optimistic about their social success as she had appeared. So many of the girls at Almack's tonight were far wealthier or more beautiful than she and Chloe. Their manners were all that were charming, their poise perfection. It was the latter that gave Phaedra pause. In company she tended toward silence, an onlooker rather than a participant. Chloe, fortunately, was more outgoing, but she was adventuresome and somewhat spoiled, though fundamentally good and kind. Hedged about with all the rules of the *ton*, might she not rebel? If that occurred, would anyone ever see the real Chloe?

Phaedra did not mind the strictures placed upon maidens of the *ton*, for she was much more of a serene disposition and had not built up the Season into something impossibly promising. Indeed, she still was convinced that she would return to Gifford Court at the end of the Season, still unpledged to any man. Quickly she buried the small twinge of regret that thought caused. Surely somewhere there lived a man who could appreciate her for who she was, not how well she conversed, flirted, danced.

What troubled her more than her own future was her sister's. She doubted her own ability to keep Chloe out of trouble, and could hardly wait for their father to arrive in London. With constant diligence, she might keep Chloe on her best behavior for the next few days. After that, her father's influence might prevent the sort of storm that had occurred this evening. But would even his presence hold his favorite daughter to the line, should she be disappointed in her expectations?

Phaedra hoped so.

CHLOE'S SPIRITS WERE RECOVERED BY THE NEXT MORNING. WHILE MAKING A PRETTY apology to her mother and to Cousin Louisa, she blamed her unstable nerves on the excitement of attending Almack's at last, and assured them that she would behave more circumspectly in the future.

Phaedra suspected that while neither lady believed her entirely; both seemed willing to give her the benefit of the doubt. Her sister chattered throughout breakfast, commenting on one or another of the gentlemen with whom she had danced. Some of her comments were derogatory, as when she ridiculed Mr. Martin's appearance.

Phaedra called her to task for this, reminding her that appearances were often misleading. "You must know I found Mr. Martin polite and thoughtful. Indeed, it was most evident that he was quite taken with you. All he could speak of as we danced was your charm, your beauty, and your graciousness. I felt myself quite abused, you know."

"Oh, he is nice enough, I suppose," Chloe said airily. "I think I shall keep him, for I think he will be quite attentive."

"Until someone better comes along, I suppose," Phaedra retorted. "Chloe, you are sometimes not a very nice person. I hope that you will not come to regret your attitude some day."

"Enough, girls," Lady Gifford interrupted. "You still have sewing to finish, so do stop dawdling. Chloe, Mr. Martin is a very nice young man and you shall treat him with kindness. It is not his fault that his appearance is less than pleasing. He resembles his father greatly. Do not trifle with his affections."

"I shall not encourage him to offer for me, if that is what you mean, Mama. He has no title, after all." Chloe glided from the room in an exaggerated walk, her aristocratic nose in the air.

Lady Gifford and her younger daughter exchanged rueful smiles.

"I hope, when my sister receives her comeuppance, it does not totally devastate her," Phaedra said.

"So do I, my dear, but I am not at all hopeful." Her mother sighed.

SEVERAL OF THE GENTLEMEN WITH WHOM THE SISTERS HAD DANCED AT ALMACK'S called that afternoon. Lady Gifford was somewhat taken aback when a person she knew only slightly arrived, her daughter in tow. The slim, languid Mrs. Graham was dressed all in black. Her blonde, rather plain daughter wore a beribboned and beruffled puce gown that became her not at all. The girl looked to be somewhat younger than Phaedra.

"My dear Lady Gifford, so happy to see you again. Why, I was elated to see you at Almack's last evening. And such beautiful daughters. So sure to make a splash in society. Sarah so enjoyed meeting them last night and positively insisted on our coming to renew our acquaintance this morning."

All this was spoken in a faint voice as Mrs. Graham settled herself upon a sofa with every appearance of staying there forever. "Sarah, do go and chat with the Misses Hazelbourne. I'm sure you girls will become great friends."

Mrs. Graham continued to gush about the Season and the Duchess and her daughter's glowing prospects until Lady Gifford gave up trying to respond and simply nodded appropriately. She sat back let the woman's word flow past her. *Louisa, why did I send you to the Pantheon Bazaar this morning? I need you.*

Chloe and Phaedra apparently were finding themselves with quite the opposite problem. After whispering a polite good morning, Sarah Graham simply sat and gazed upon their faces. Her response to Phaedra's politely interested questions was a silent blush. When Chloe ventured to compliment her on her really quite hideous morning dress, she simpered in confusion. The

Grahams left after an interminable twenty minutes. Lady Gifford relaxed back into her chair and breathed a sigh of relief.

Cousin Louisa entered a few moments later. "I met your callers on the steps," she said with a smile. "I wasn't aware you were acquainted with Mrs. Graham, Isabella."

"I was not," Lady Gifford replied, still feeling somewhat exhausted from being overwhelmed with words, "and I must confess that I wish I were not now."

"I was warned about her before I came to Town." Cousin Louisa seated herself on the sofa beside Lady Gifford. "In a way, her visit this morning might be seen as a good omen. It seems she has married off three daughters already, merely by attaching them to more popular girls and letting them pick up the leavings."

"Do you mean that she actually came here because she wanted her daughter to follow mine about and meet all their beaux? How common!"

"Oh, yes. She is very good at insinuating herself and her daughters into the crowd surrounding the Season's more popular young ladies. She shows an uncommonly astute sense of which of them will become successes. I should warn you that she is also an accomplished gossip who relishes even a hint of scandal."

"But how do you know this, Cousin Louisa, when Mama did not?" said Chloe. "You have not been in Town these past four years, you said".

"Oh, I have several friends with whom I have kept in touch. Ask the Duchess to tell you of the woman's past adventures. The most likely reason for your mother not being acquainted with the woman is that she has never had daughters to present before. She would not have encountered Mrs. Graham in the ordinary course of events, for the woman does not generally travel in the first circles of Society.

"Furthermore, I'll warrant that, once she has insinuated one of her daughters into a household, she becomes ill and plaintively requests Lady So-and-So to take pity on her poor health and please, take the poor child along to this fete or that. And Lady So-and-So, poor sympathetic fool that she is, does so, thus saving Mrs. Graham the exertion of chaperonage."

Lady Gifford shook her head with some vigor. "She will certainly not try that trick on me. Thank you, Cousin Louisa, for giving us warning. I hope, girls, you did not encourage Miss Graham? It would not do for you to become friends with her, I think."

"No, Mama, not a bit of it. Under other circumstances, however, I should not mind doing so," Phaedra said. "Poor girl, so sadly lacking in confidence.

And so unsuitably dressed. I wonder how she feels about her mother's methods."

"How could one be friends with a nonentity such as that? She spoke no more than five words during the whole visit," Chloe added. "But I pity the poor girl, nonetheless. Even riding on another's skirts, she will not marry this Season, I think. Not unless she overcomes her terrible shyness."

"Yes, she must be quite unlike her older sisters, from all reports. They, I am told, combined the incredible brass of their mother with a liveliness and prettiness that made them almost acceptable. If this one is less lively, she must resemble her father who, I am told, was a studious, quiet man," Cousin Louisa said.

Just then Edgemont opened the door to announce Mr. Reginald Farwell. Phaedra saw Chloe stiffen in her chair.

Mr. Farwell was a vision in biscuit inexpressibles, a green and yellow flowered waistcoat, and a pale blue coat. The high red heels of his shoes made him seem even taller. He minced into the room and bowed gracefully over the hand extended to him by Lady Gifford.

"So pleased, Lady Gifford," he murmured. "And your lovely daughters, too." His collar was so high that he was required to turn his entire upper body to look at the girls.

"Good morning Mr. Farwell," Phaedra said with as much cordiality as she could master.

Chloe repeated the greeting, but less cordially. Phaedra was tempted to pinch her.

"I fear I was remiss in not requesting the pleasure of your company in one of the sets last evening," he said, aiming his words to the empty air between them and somewhat above the level of their heads. "It is so fatiguing. I could not bring your names to mind and did not wish to appear discourteous in admitting I had forgotten them. But this morning, oh, quite early, I called on Her Grace and she was kind enough to made them known to me. Please accept my abject apologies. I shall not forget them again."

Phaedra bit her lip to keep from laughing aloud at this unbelievable excuse. She suspected he was testing them in some way, but for the life of her, she could not understand why.

Her sister visibly preened herself and fluttered her lashes until Phaedra feared she would be blown away. "La, sir," Chloe almost simpered. "I will forgive you this time. But if you should forget again, I will not be able to forgive the second lapse."

"How could I ever again forget?" he said. "Miss Hazelbourne, you have my word that your name and your face are engraved on my heart. As are yours, of course, Miss Phaedra," he continued, turning to her and waving a lace-edged handkerchief just under his chin.

"I am impressed you arose so early, merely to ascertain our names," she responded tartly. "Was it an arduous task?" Instantly she felt her mother's frown directed her way.

He appeared oblivious to her insult. "Not at all. How could I resist learning the identities of two such very different and lovely young women."

Phaedra fell silent then, letting her sister carry on a flirtatious conversation with the gentleman. Chloe and Mr. Farwell did not seem to miss any contributions she might have made, for he and her sister continued to exchange pleasantries, most of them comprising fulsome flatteries from him and flirtatious responses from her. Phaedra wondered how anyone could converse thus, if conversing it could be called. *Piffle. That's what it is. Just piffle.*

Her attention, however, was caught when Mr. Farwell said, "And do you have great expectations of your Season, Miss Hazelbourne?"

"Oh, yes, I do, Mr. Farwell," Chloe replied before Phaedra could interrupt. "My intention is to become an incomp—Ouch! Phaedra, why did you pinch me?"

"I thought I saw a spider on your arm."

"You never did, not in Mama's parlor!"

"Well, it looked like one. Tell me Mr. Farwell, are you interested in the theatre?" she said, in an attempt to distract Chloe.

"I am, Miss Phaedra. And you?"

"Oh, yes, and I am so looking forward to seeing the great Kean in Hamlet. But I am very curious. Have you heard the rumor that Mr. Shakespeare did not really write his plays?"

"I have heard that rumor, yes. But I consider it a great calumny. The immortal bard should not be so impugned."

"But do you not think that the evidence is great that at least some of the plays might have been written by someone else? Roger Bacon, for instance. Or Sir Christopher Marlowe."

"I beg of you, Miss Phaedra, do not endeavor to involve me in a literary argument. it is all so fatiguing." He yawned, patting his mouth with the handkerchief. "Have you attended the opera yet?"

"No, but we are to go tonight, with Her Grace and Lady Mary," Chloe interjected. "Do not mind my sister, sir. She is sometimes overly interested in intellectual subjects. Tell me about the opera house. Is it indeed as grand as I have heard?"

Mr. Farwell spoke of the beauties of the Covent Garden Theatre for the remaining few minutes of his visit, before punctiliously taking his leave. As the parlor door closed behind him, Phaedra rounded on her sister.

"Chloe, how could you!" she demanded. "You almost told him of your ambitions, and you know Mama says you must never speak of that subject in public. What would he have thought of you?"

"Phaedra, you promised not to be literary with callers. Oh, how could you? He will think we are all bluestockings!"

"That will be enough, girls," their mother told them. "Neither of you went beyond what was proper in your speech, but you both came very close to it. Please keep a better watch upon your tongues, or you will disgrace yourself. And Phaedra, next time do not accuse me of harboring spiders in my parlor, if you please. You will quite ruin my reputation."

"I am sorry, Mama, but it was the only excuse I could think of for pinching her," Phaedra replied, laughing.

"Yes, and I am sure that you have bruised me."

"No more than you would have bruised your own reputation, had you continued in the direction you were taking," Lady Gifford said. "Reggie Farwell is quite the pink of the *ton* and is received everywhere. If he were to take you in dislike, your future in Society would be blighted. Chloe, when you are as old as Lady Jersey and as famous, you may speak your mind. For the nonce, keep a damper on your tongue."

The entrance of two of their dancing partners of the evening before put a stop to their bickering. Mr. Martin, Chloe's earnest admirer, immediately gravitated to her side and Mr. Werthing, an older gentleman with whom Phaedra had enjoyed serious conversation, came to sit beside her and tell her of his studies of Roman antiquities in Dorset. After those gentlemen departed, other callers arrived.

They spent the rest of the afternoon conversing or sewing between calls. Neither disgraced herself again.

That night the Hazelbourne ladies were the guests of the Duchess, who had rented a box at the opera for the Season. None of the young ladies had ever attended an opera before, though all were familiar with some of the more popular arias.

Although she was not musically inclined as Chloe was, Phaedra was enthralled with the drama. She was sorry to see the end of the first act. When the house lights went up, she was surprised to find that one could see the occupants of most of the other boxes. She and Chloe and Lady Mary amused themselves by trying to find people whom they knew.

Mr. Martin came in to visit during the intermission, again devoting his attentions strictly to Chloe. She blossomed under his adoring gaze, fluttering her eyelashes and waving her fan flirtatiously. Lady Gifford joined their conversation, asking about his mother who had recently been ill.

Mr. Farwell appeared and invited Lady Mary to join him in a short walk in the corridor between acts. Cousin Louisa volunteered to accompany them in the interests of propriety. Phaedra felt a pang of envy. She was used to more activity than this day had offered. She continued looking around the theatre.

A young man who seemed familiar sat with an older woman in a box directly across from theirs. "Your Grace," she said, startling the Duchess out of a doze, "are you acquainted with the gentleman in the box opposite?"

"What? Who? Great heavens, gel, I can't see that far in this light. Describe him"

Phaedra did so. "He may be the gentleman whom we aided on our way to Town. Lord Wilderlake."

"Black haired and swarthy, you say? Could be Wilderlake. If you had to rescue him, he may be like his father, a ne'er-do-well."

"We did not exactly rescue him." She gave the Duchess a more detailed account of their encounter with Wilderlake. "I do not believe his driving was at fault, Aunt Verbain, only that the team was poorly schooled."

"Hmph. Well, he's got some manners, at least. Should have. His mother, Elizabeth Summers that was, was a charming woman. Should have had her head examined, marrying Wilderlake. But her family pushed her into it, I'll not doubt."

"Could that be his mother with him, Your Grace?" Chloe said.

"Tell me what she looks like and I'll tell you. Could be his fancy piece, just as likely, though."

Chloe described the faded but still attractive woman who shared the box with Lord Wilderlake. Her Grace allowed as how it might be Lady Wilderlake, but she would have to see her up close to be sure. "Tell you what, I'll send 'em an invitation to your ball. Then, if she comes with him, she's his mother. How does that please you?"

"Oh, Your Grace, you need not do that. I was merely curious."

Phaedra concealed her smile at the lack of sincerity in her sister's protest.

"Well, and so am I. Knew the old viscount, his grandfather, pretty well when I was young. Bit of a rake he was, but a charming one. I always had a soft spot for him. Married some dowdy chit with a fortune, took her off to the wilds of somewhere in the north, and wasn't seen for a few years. When he came back to Town, he...no, never mind that. Would like to see what this young sprig is like. Haven't heard a word of him since his father died eight or ten years ago. He's either been out of the country or he's been up north tryin' to hold the estate together. In that case, you don't want to be bothered with him." She closed her eyes.

Phaedra resumed her visual exploration of the theatre. Such an interesting hodgepodge of people.

Mr. Farwell, who had remained in the box at Lady Mary's invitation, was found to be asleep when the next intermission occurred. The Duchess expressed no surprise. "He's more apt to be asleep than awake. Let him alone. He'll wake soon enough if anything interestin' happens."

Phaedra kept her disapproval to herself, wondering why she cared enough to feel censorious.

Lady Mary moved to the chair beside Phaedra. "We have hardly had a chance to visit. I hope the entire Season will not be this hectic."

"I, too. Mama says that some days one can expect to be invited to attend three or more events. I cannot imagine maintaining such a frantic pace for more than a short while without having hysterics."

"Nor can I. I have told Grandmama that I will not let her wear herself out during this Season. Not that she will listen to me. I expect that I will have the headache quite often in the coming months."

"And I have convinced my mama that I am sure to disgrace myself if I am forced to be on my best behavior more than once each day. She has agreed that I need not gad about with my sister all of the time." She shared a conspiratorial grin with Lady Mary.

"Your sister is very spirited, is she not?"

"She is, but she is also spoiled," Phaedra replied. "It comes from being able to twist our father around her littlest finger from the cradle. Mama has tried to discipline her, but Papa always says she is such a darling and it would not hurt her to attend just one assembly or to have her own horse before she could reach the stirrups or to picnic unchaperoned with the Squire's son or whatever it was that she wanted."

She put a gloved hand to her lips. "Oh, dear. I do sound like a jealous cat. Do not mistake me. I love my sister, but I am not blind to her faults. She has a most sweet, generous nature when she is not attempting to get her own way. It is just that she has such high spirits and such a zest for life that her emotions sometimes outweigh her good sense."

"Yes, I suspected something of the sort," said Lady Mary. "She is a most charming and animated girl. I did not mean to sound critical. I do like her, but I feel that you and I are much more of a kind."

"Oh, but you are not so serious as I," Phaedra objected. "You are able to converse charmingly and to be at ease in company. I am so wretchedly unsure of myself with strangers and I have no conversation."

"I think you underrate yourself. Reggie admires you, and he is a most discerning person."

"That fop!"

"Yes, Reggie does seem a fop. But there is more to him than meets the eye. He is quite my favorite honorary brother."

"Then you are not interested in him in a romantic way? My sister was wondering."

"Oh, my, no. Reggie and I are as comfortable together as if we were truly siblings. I could never love him as one should love a husband. But do not let his appearance blind you to his character. You see, he..."

The rest of her words were lost as the Duchess commanded them to hush their chatter and let a poor old woman hear the opera. Phaedra relinquished her seat to Cousin Louisa as the curtain rose for the final act.

Mr. Farwell still slept.

LORD WILDERLAKE FOUND THE OPERA TEDIOUS, DESPITE THE GLORIOUS MUSIC. His mother professed to be enjoying it excessively. Somewhat bored, he let his gaze wander over the other boxes during the intermissions. Soon he noted the presence of Miss Hazelbourne in the front row of the Duchess of Verbain's box. She was extraordinarily pretty. The young woman to her left was equally lovely. During the second act, he attempted to devise ways he might manage an introduction to his good Samaritan and her companions.

The Season was still young, he told himself sternly. There was plenty of time for him to find a wife.

CHAPTER FOUR

THE NEXT AFTERNOON SAW LORD GIFFORD'S ARRIVAL. HE ENTERED THE FRONT door just as his wife and daughters gathered in the foyer, ready to depart.

"Papa," squealed Chloe. "You're here! How wonderful. And just in time for Lady Everingham's Venetian breakfast."

"Well, miss, you're looking fine as five pence. London must agree with you." He pulled her arms from around his neck and turned to embrace his wife. "There my dear, have I caught you just as you were leaving? I missed you, love, and had hoped that you'd be free to spend the afternoon with me." He bussed her heartily.

"Welcome to London, my darling. And I have missed you, quite dreadfully. But no, I cannot spend the afternoon with you, unless you'd care to accompany us to Lady Everingham's?"

"Not my style, you know that, Isabella. Besides, I can't stand the old harridan." He turned to his younger daughter. "And how are you, Phaedra? Has London been as bad as you had feared?"

"No, Papa," she responded. "But then I have been fortunate to have Cousin Louisa's company and so have avoided being overwhelmed with gaiety"

"How do you do, my lord?" Cousin Louisa extended her hand to Lord Gifford. "It is good to see you again. Cousin Isabella, would you like me to accompany Chloe to Lady Everingham's Venetian breakfast? Phaedra and I can wait until another day to attend Mrs. Stewart's literary salon."

"No, Cousin, Phaedra has earned this afternoon with you. I will go with

Chloe, and my husband can rest or take himself off to his club. We will not waste away to be apart for one more afternoon.

"Come, Chloe," she continued. "We must be off if we are to be only fashionably late. Good-bye, my dear. I will see you at dinner this evening." She blew her husband a kiss as she hurried Chloe out the door.

"Poor Papa, for us all to desert you," Phaedra said. "Would you like to come with us?"

"To a Literary Tea? Not on your life." He chuckled as he patted her on the shoulder. "You go and enjoy yourselves. Though how you can enjoy a literary bash is beyond me. I'll just take myself off to my club after I've had a bite of luncheon. Renew old acquaintances and all that, y'know. Edgemont! Edgemont, you old reprobate, I'm like to faint with hunger. Is there anything in this house to eat, or have my wife and daughters spent all my funds on ball gowns and left us to starve?"

Phaedra laughed as the butler listened to her father's words with a disapproving expression. As she and Cousin Louisa exited, she told the older woman, "Papa so loves to get the best of Edgemont, who has never given up trying to train our family in what he considers proper behavior. Papa is equally persistent in attempting to deflate his pretensions. They both enjoy the game excessively."

Cousin Louisa replied with a smile, "Edgemont quite intimidated me when I first came to visit Gifford Court. Since then I have found him to be both kind and dependable under that so-very-proper exterior. Do we need a hackney, or shall we walk to Mrs. Stewart's? It isn't over a mile, and it is such a beautiful day."

Phaedra, liking exercise as much as her companion, voted to walk.

CHLOE WAS MUCH IMPRESSED WITH LADY EVERINGHAM'S HOUSE IN RICHMOND. IT was exceedingly grand and elegant. The vestibule boasted a magnificent crystal chandelier, and the twin curving staircases to the first floor were like nothing she had ever seen. The chamber set aside for the ladies' wraps was decorated with velvet drapes and green-and-rose flowered wallpaper. A maid was present to assist guests with repairing the ravages of the short drive from London.

So many beautiful things. Shelves and tables were laden with porcelains, paperweights, and assorted other knickknacks, as well as numerous vases holding fresh and dried flowers. *This is how my house will look, someday. Filled with priceless treasures in the first stare of elegance.* She moved slowly, letting her fingertips drift across polished table tops, hover above a finely detailed china shepherdess and her love. It seemed to her that the very air she breathed was rich and sweet.

In the sunken garden two large open-sided tents sheltered small tables. A third tent held a long table upon which rested platters, bowls, and trays displaying a rich variety of foods. In the midst of beds of daffodils and tulips stood a wooden platform upon which a small string quartet played music she recognized as being from the pen of a famous Austrian composer whose works she did not care for. Liveried waiters were everywhere, carrying trays of full and empty champagne glasses. *This is my world, the world I was destined to reside in.*

A large woman wearing a deep purple gown and a towering purple turban stood at the top of the wide marble stairway leading down into the garden. She inclined her head slightly as Chloe and her mother approached.

"My dear Lady Everingham," Lady Gifford said, "how kind in you to invite us. I wish you to meet my elder daughter, Chloe."

Chloe curtsied to Lady Everingham and murmured her pleasure at being invited. The latter looked the girl up and down and said, curtly, "Looks like her pa, more's the pity. Too bad she doesn't take after you, Isabella."

Before Chloe could speak, her mother said, "Considering how attractive you used to think my husband, Mathilde, we will take that as a compliment."

Lady Everingham snorted. "Your tongue's not grown any sweeter, has it? Never mind. I'm glad to see you." She looked down her nose at Chloe. "Here's my son, the earl. Make you acquainted with Miss Hazelbourne, Jeremy. Go on now and mingle, the two of you. Isabella and I have catching up to do."

Chloe held out her hand to the slender, colorless young man, only to find it clutched tightly. He smiled at her as he raised it to his lips and kissed it. She noticed that his teeth were slightly crooked and his nose overly long. But Lord Everingham was an earl. His appearance was unimportant. Furthermore, the maintenance of a house and garden like this one bespoke a large fortune.

"I am happy to meet you, my lord." She pretended to be thrilled at the kiss and suppressed the urge to wipe her hand upon her skirt.

"And I you, Miss Hazelbourne. May I say that your beauty can only enhance the delights of my mother's garden."

He is an earl, Chloe reminded herself. *A rich earl.* "Thank you my lord. Such a nice party, is it not?"

"I suppose, although my mother's parties are not usually enjoyable to me. Today, I believe I shall enjoy myself."

"Please, Lord Everingham, release my hand. People are beginning to stare."

"Your hand? Of course." Instead of releasing it, he tucked it into the crook of his arm. "Let me show you the remainder of the garden. But first, some champagne." He stopped a passing waiter and took two glasses from his tray.

Chloe had been firmly instructed by her mother to drink nothing stronger than lemonade, but she decided a single glass of champagne would not harm her. She had never tasted it, and was so very curious. She sipped—and sneezed.

"Are you quite all right, Miss Hazelbourne? Is it too chilly here?"

"No, I am all right." She sipped again from the glass. "I always sneeze at the first taste of champagne," she said, with all the sophistication she could muster. "It is so delicious that it is quite worth the discomfort of the sneeze."

Lord Everingham guided her into a shrub-lined path paved with mossy flagstones. They were soon hidden from the party by the masses of greenery.

"Miss Hazelbourne, no...no! I cannot keep calling you Miss Hazelbourne—it is too...too ordinary for such a beauty as you," Lord Everingham said, as the sounds of the orchestra grew ever fainter.

"My name is Chloe, but only when we are alone, my lord. Mama does not approve of too much familiarity on short acquaintance."

"A beautiful name, classical and poetic. And my name is Jeremy. 'My lord' is so formal. It keeps one at a distance, don't you think?"

"Oh, indeed, it does...Jeremy."

The two of them walked among the shrubbery for some time, Lord Everingham pouring forth extravagant compliments to Chloe and she positively glowing under the attention. Compared to the fulsome compliments bestowed upon her by the boys at home, Lord Everingham's remarks reeked of sophistication. *He is not all that unattractive*, she decided, peeping at him from under her lashes. *And he is an earl.*

The shadows were noticeably longer when she suddenly realized that they had been out of sight of the rest of the company for some time. "I must return, my lo—Jeremy. My mother will be worried."

"Oh, if only I could keep you here forever, my lovely Chloe." He pressed one hand over his heart. "Alas, I cannot. Come, this path will take us directly back." He led her along another path, nearly a tunnel among leathery-leaved shrubs and ivy-twined tree trunks.

When they emerged, Chloe saw her mother seated at a table under the nearest tent. Mama sent a speaking glance in her direction but did not summon her, so she followed Lord Everingham into a corner where he held a chair for her at a small table. At his gesture, a waiter came to them.

"Bring some of those little sweet puffs for the young lady, Egbert. I'll have cheese and bread. Champagne for both of us, and strawberries. Bring a big bowl of strawberries." He leaned forward. "I am particularly fond of strawberries, Chloe. Aren't you?"

Chloe opened her mouth and closed it again. He was an earl and he wanted to feed her strawberries. Why not? Surely two or three would do no harm. Besides, she would likely be at home before the hives emerged.

From where she sat, her mother was fully visible, and her frown unmistakable. Chloe mentally crossed her fingers that a mild scold would be her only punishment for disappearing. She really had not been aware of time's passage, but she knew that her unchaperoned absence from a party in the company of a young man was unacceptable.

The footman reappeared with a laden tray full of food. Between them, Chloe and Lord Everingham made a good meal. Several times he failed to place the food into his mouth and it fell back to the plate. Chloe giggled when a strawberry dropped to the table and rolled across, leaving a trail of pink spots on the cloth.

"But I am so overwhelmed with your beauty that I cannot take my eyes from your face, Chloe. Forgive my poor manners."

"So there you are, Jeremy!" someone behind Chloe said. "About time you returned."

Lord Everingham's shoulders drooped and his lower lip protruded. "We were only walking in the shrubbery, Mother."

"Faugh! You were trying to hide, as you always do. You are the host here. It is beyond rude for you to disappear as you do. Miss Hazelbourne, I hold you equally responsible. My silly son has no better sense than to go walking alone in the shrubbery but I cannot imagine your mother not cautioning you against it."

"I have indeed," Mama said. Her tone was far more moderate than her hostess's. "Chloe, you knew better."

"Please, all blame belongs to me," Lord Everingham protested. "I was thinking only of showing her the gardens."

"Faugh! You were trying to escape, as you always do, at every one of my parties. Go along, now. It's time you paid attention to other of our guests."

Lady Everingham rudely turned her back and stalked away.

"Lady Gifford, Miss Hazelbourne, I am sorry you were forced to undergo my mother's criticism. Her tongue is often sharp, but she really does not mean the half of what she says. Please excuse me, Miss Hazelbourne, for as my mother said, I must see to our other guests." He bowed gracefully before the ladies.

"Oh, Mama, I am sorry," Chloe said after he had left them alone. "I truly did not realize how the time was passing."

"I will not speak to you of your actions now, Chloe," Lady Gifford replied in a near-whisper. "I do not wish to create a scene, nor yet to allow anyone to see how distressed I am. You must realize that it was not how long you were alone with Lord Everingham, but the fact that his mother publicly called attention to your absence together that will cause gossip."

"She had no right—"

"Perhaps not, but as I warned you earlier, she is a force in the *ton*. Her approval could have been of great benefit to you, and now..." Her mama chewed her lip. "Well, we can only hope for the best."

"I did nothing untoward, I promise," she whispered, near to tears. "Please do not tell Papa."

"I must, for it would never do for him to hear of it as gossip. I shall also tell him that you drank champagne. He will be most disappointed in your behavior."

Chloe hung her head. Her mother gave her arm a small shake.

"Chloe, you must not look so. After Lady Everingham's loud comments, you must not act as if I had reprimanded you. It is only by behaving as if you had done nothing shameful that you might be able to avoid gossip about your actions this afternoon. Now smile."

Chloe smiled until her cheeks ached.

THE EVENING FOLLOWING HIS ATTENDANCE AT THE OPERA, WILDERLAKE DROPPED in to Watier's, more for lack of anything else to do than any interest in cards. He rarely gambled, knowing all too well from his father's example where gaming could lead. He was restless, aware of a curious sense of something being amiss but reluctant to recognize it. For days now, his mind had often held an image of immense brown eyes surrounded by short, thick lashes and a dimpled chin set with disapproval. He told himself that it was merely curiosity, but himself was not entirely convinced.

The club's library was practically empty. Most of those present were of an older generation and not well known to him. He made his bows to several, before catching sight of a familiar face in a corner. Wanting conversation, he walked that way.

"Hello, Reggie, am I interrupting your nap?"

The tall dandy opened his eyes and answered. "Not at all, Herne. Or should I call you Wilderlake, now you've the title? Haven't seen you for an age. I was drowsing out of boredom. Sit down."

"Thank you. I was suffering from the same affliction. Perhaps we can together stave it off." He pulled a comfortable chair into the corner and sprawled into it. "I see you haven't changed your style, Reggie. Still playing the fop."

"Of course. It suits me." He waved a lacy handkerchief under his nose. "But tell me, how is it with you? I can't remember the last time you came to Town."

"Ten years ago, shortly after I came down from Oxford. You weren't about that Season. To tell the truth, if the little I've seen is an example of how things haven't changed, I would wait another ten to return, if it weren't for my mother." A waiter came to take his order for brandy. Wilderlake relaxed, truly comfortable for the first time since he had come to London.

"You refer to the hopeful mamas and their darling daughters, I suppose. Gets a bit daunting, does it not?"

"It does, indeed. One would think that the stories of my father's excesses would serve to depress the hopes of the predatory mamas, but they have not."

Farwell laughed. "You are new blood. Fair game. Your father's sins occurred so many years ago that many of the *ton* have probably forgotten him. Gossip only lasts as long as the next scandal."

He raised a delicate quizzing glass and peered through it. "I see you follow the Beau's lead in style. How dull it is, all those somber colors and so little jewelry."

"By God, Reggie, you do that well. But I cannot believe that you've changed so—" A quick shake of his friend's head made him bite off the rest of his words. "Interesting waistcoat," he said, to cover the moment of silence. "I don't believe I've seen that particular combination of colors before."

"Puce and apricot? Lovely isn't it? I had it specially woven, from my own design."

"It's...interesting." Wilderlake wondered if his leg was being pulled or if Reggie had truly changed so much from the young man he remembered. He eyed the other's footwear. "The shoes are an especially good touch. One would not expect someone of your height to increase it even more with such heels."

Their drinks arrived. Each raised his glass in a silent salute to old friendship.

After a suitable pause in respect to the liquor's fine flavor, Reggie stretched a long leg before him and appeared to admire his fine leather shoes with their tall red heels. "Ah, my boy, should you breathe a word of my drab past, I shall call you out. I have no desire to be considered a potential husband by the insipid chits who flock to the Season. What mama would take me seriously, dressed as I am and with neither title nor fortune? I am the eternal dancing partner, the salon conversationalist, the safe escort for innocent young ladies. But I am not an eligible match."

"And do you garb yourself this way in the country?"

"At house parties, yes."

Aware his question had been only partially answered, Wilderlake contained his unsatisfied curiosity. "You almost convince me to adopt your style. Almost, but I fear I couldn't carry it off as you do. I would burst into laughter each time I saw myself in a mirror."

He thought Reggie's lips twitched, but the small motion—it there had been one—was so slight, so quick, that he might have been mistaken.

The two of them sat in comfortable silence, for several minutes. At last a thought occurred to Wilderlake. "Tell me, Reggie, when I had to leave Eton for a year, to pick up the pieces of my inheritance, you were speaking of going for the army when you finished your education. Did you?"

"I did not. Instead I took a position with a trading company in India, and lived to regret it. The place is hot and filled with nasty insects and snakes. No place for a gentleman, I tell you, particularly one with my delicate sensibilities. I vow, I spent four years fearing for my life and health, until my great aunt Charlotte died and left me everything. I sold out and came home as soon as I could."

"Wasn't she the one who wed the Nabob? The aunt you used to visit during the long holiday?"

"The very one. A formidable woman, but one with a good heart. I would have wished my deliverance to have come at a lesser cost."

"So you are a country gentleman. I cannot imagine you in that role."

"No need. I leave such bucolic worries to my agent. London is my milieu, except for the occasional house party" He yawned, a sure sign to Wilderlake that no more personal information would be forthcoming. Reggie had always been reticent about himself.

Wilderlake changed the subject. "You are probably acquainted with most of this Season's offerings on the Marriage Mart. Have you met a Miss Hazelbourne?" He waited tensely for the answer.

"I have. Were you wishing to make her acquaintance?"

"Yes, I am. Actually," he paused, "I have already met her under rather unpleasant circumstances. But it was not a formal introduction so I cannot claim an acquaintance."

"Aha! You're the chap they rescued on the road to London. You owe them a great deal. They have not breathed a word of your identity, except to the Duchess of Verbain, who told only me. If the *ton* only knew that a member of the FHC—you do still have your membership, I trust?—had been thrown from his phaeton. *Tsk tsk.* Now I know you will keep my secret, else I will tell your tale."

"My lips are sealed."

"As are mine." Reggie made an appropriate gesture and his eyes gleamed with laughter. "Have you an invitation to Her Grace's ball next week?"

"No, I do not."

"You will receive one, for she told me so last night. Do you make sure to attend and I will see that you are introduced to Miss Hazelbourne." He laughed aloud, but gave no reason for his amusement.

"What is the joke? Is Miss Hazelbourne a secret drinker, perhaps? Or is the family dirt poor and she hanging out for a husband of great wealth? Not that it matters. I should merely like to correct her impression of my rudeness. I was not myself when I regained consciousness after the accident."

"No, no. Miss Hazelbourne is all that is respectable. Rather a lively young lady, in fact. There is no joke; I am only amused by the vision of your lying broken on the roadside, only to be rescued by one of the Season's hopeful mamas and her darling daughter. What a perfect way to become noticed by the ladies."

Wilderlake snorted. "I think I will look in at White's and then make an early night of it," he said as he rose. "My mother has requested my escort tomorrow morning. I shall see you again soon, Reggie, and will be interested in viewing you in the role of eternal dancing partner. Good night."

"Good night, Herne." As Reggie spoke, his eyelids lowered and he seemed to fall immediately asleep. Wilderlake left him, chuckling to himself as he recalled stories about Reggie Farwell's sleepiness. He recalled one, which had never been confirmed but which he fully believed, about the time Reggie had been involved in a seduction. Apparently he had been well on the way to success when he fell asleep. While he slept, one of his friends had interfered and had won the fair Cyprian's favors for himself. Reggie had professed himself vastly disappointed, but had done so with a smile on his face. Scarce two months later, the friend had had to empty his pockets to buy himself free of what had turned out to be a ruinously expensive relationship.

There were other times at the gaming table, when he had fallen asleep just as he began losing, thus removing himself from the game without insult to other players—for everyone knew that Reggie Farwell was prone to uncontrollable sleepiness at all times and could not be blamed for his strange affliction.

Wilderlake stepped out into the cold night air. As he buttoned his greatcoat, he laughed out loud, sure as anything that his friend only fell into sleep when he chose to do so.

CHAPTER FIVE

THE EARLY SPRING DARK HAD FALLEN WHEN LADY GIFFORD AND CHLOE ARRIVED home from Richmond.

"No, my lady," Edgemont said, in reply to Lady Gifford's inquiry. "His lordship has not returned, nor have Miss Phaedra and Mrs. Arbuckle." He opened the door to the parlor. "Shall I send up a tea tray?"

"Please. Although the day was fine, I took a slight chill on the journey home. Come Chloe."

"Mama, I—"

"Not now. Let us relax until your father arrives. I am still out of patience with you."

Chloe curled into a wing-back chair near the fireplace, chewing her lip. Her mama was being unreasonable. She had done nothing wrong. Nothing at all. It was the earl's fault, for luring her into the shrubbery. If he was any sort of a gentleman, he would tell his mother so, and she would realize that Chloe was blameless. Tomorrow she would ask him; surely he would do what she asked.

The door opened and her father entered. "What is it, love? Edgemont said you appeared overset when you came in."

"As I should be. My lord, your daughter may have disgraced herself in the eyes of the *ton*, despite my many warnings. She absented herself from the party in the company of Lord Everingham for the better part of an hour this afternoon. Unfortunately, when she returned, that odious Lady Everingham called them both to task in a loud and penetrating voice. Everyone now knows about it, and many will believe the worst."

Her father turned a worried face to her. "Well, Chloe, you have landed yourself in a fine mess. Is there any reason for us to be concerned?"

"What do you mean, Papa?"

"Did that young idiot make advances to you?"

"Oh, no, Papa. He was entirely circumspect. I promise you we just walked about. He did compliment me on my appearance, but his behavior never went beyond what is respectable." She mentally crossed her fingers, remembering the way he had kissed her hand.

"I saw him holding your hand for an unconscionable time when you were introduced. Do you mean to tell us that he did not recapture it once you were alone?" her mother demanded.

"No Mama, he did not. And if he had tried, I would not have permitted it. You have taught me better than that. I did nothing I have not done at home. You have never scolded me for walking in the garden with our neighboring gentlemen. Why was this so different?"

"Chloe, I have attempted time and again to convince you that the *ton* is ever ready to believe the worst of a young woman whose behavior is even slightly questionable. The casual behavior in which you indulge at home will simply not do in London. Your behavior must always be all that is demure, circumspect, and ladylike." With a moue of distaste, she went on. "Lady Everingham is particularly high in the instep, and overly protective of her son. And not at all reticent about venting her opinion of what she deems unladylike behavior."

"How unfair!"

"It's the way of the world, pet," her father said with evident sympathy. "This is why I argued against giving you girls a London Season. Phaedra is as out of place here as a cow with skirts and you're already teetering on the edge of scandal." He shook his head. "What possessed you, Isabella, to take her to Everingham's? You know what an old harridan that woman is."

"The Duchess advised me that she is finally looking for a wife for her son. I thought—"

"Oh, Mama, you didn't—"

"He would be a very good catch, Chloe."

"Oh, Mama!" Chloe could not contain a small giggle. "He reminds me of a sheep. I doubt I could never fall in love with a sheep."

"Hush, Chloe. Never say such things, even in the privacy of our home." Her mother sat upon the sofa and leaned her head back, eyes closed. After a long silence she said, "What shall we do, George?"

"Nothing. Pretend it never happened. I'll warrant that most people will chalk any gossip up to the old harridan's dislike of any girl whose way her precious son casts an interested glance. Don't you remember last year, when she told everyone that Maribeth Fortescue had been casting out lures. It was all the talk for a week or so, and then it all died out when Miss Fortescue wouldn't even dance with him." He seated himself beside his wife and took her hand in his, patting it gently.

"Papa," Chloe said, after a moment, "did you really argue against bringing us to London?"

"I did indeed. You're too headstrong by half, pet, and your sister's too retiring. You would've been better off to make your debut closer to home, where one wrong step wouldn't have spoiled any hope of making a match. For tuppence, I'd take you back—"

"Oh, no, Papa! Please! We had to come to London. I would not marry any of those silly boys at home for anything." Her eyes filled with tears she could not hold back. "Have I really ruined myself?"

"Of course not," he said heartily. "But you may be the center of gossip for a week or two and some of Society's busybodies will watch you forevermore. Best be on your mettle, pet. And listen to your mama. She's up to every rig and tow in Town."

"I will, oh, I will. I shall be the model of propriety from now on. Only... Lord Everingham did ask me to go driving in the park tomorrow. Might I not do so?"

Her mother's eyes flew open "Absolutely not. Have you heard nothing I've said to you? For the next week, you will accompany me on afternoon calls, and will accept no invitations to ride or drive in the park. We will attend Lady Applemore's musicale tomorrow night, rather than the Heywood's ball. I think a visit to the Royal Academy as well, and perhaps you might attend Sophia Larrimore's literary salon with your sister on Friday."

"Oh, Mama," Chloe groaned.

"Hush, Chloe. You have brought this upon yourself. Furthermore, I must warn you, if Lady Everingham expresses her opinion to any of the patrons of Almack's, you will not be given permission to waltz tomorrow night. Without that permission, you may not waltz at your own ball."

"I will waltz at my ball. I must!" Chloe stamped her foot.

"You will not, unless you have the permission at Almack's. And if you do not, perhaps it will bring home to you, as my words have obviously not done, the fact that you have already placed a cloud upon your reputation. You must now endeavor to convince everyone that this afternoon's incident was a momentary lapse of judgment."

The tears that had threatened earlier filled and overflowed Chloe's eyes. Her father gathered her in his arms. "There, my pet. You must not cry. It will all come about, you will see. Just follow your mother's good advice. Now, get you to bed. Tomorrow will be better."

"Yes, Papa. Good night. Mama, I will truly try to behave." She made her way slowly from the room and up the stairs, feeling exceedingly put upon.

It was not my fault. He was so charming, even if he does look just like a sheep. How could I resist him?

CHLOE'S MANNER WAS SUBDUED AT BREAKFAST THE NEXT MORNING. PHAEDRA, ON the other hand, was still excited about the literary salon she had attended the day before. She had met several aspiring authors and poets, and had learned that Lord Byron sometimes attended Mrs. Stewart's salons.

"And while I think his poetry is pretentious and silly, I would like to meet him, if only to see for myself if he is as beautiful as everyone says."

Her mother interrupted her chatter. "Phaedra, I am sorry to disappoint you, but I will require that you accompany your sister and myself for the next week or two. She has narrowly avoided disgracing herself. I will depend upon you to keep her under your eye for a while."

"Disgraced herself? Chloe, what have you done?"

Lady Gifford related Chloe's activities of the day before. Chloe sat silent, a sullen expression upon her face.

"Oh, Chloe, how careless! And how unfair too, that one woman should be have such influence that she could blight a girl's hopes."

"Life is not—"

Both girls finished their mama's familiar statement. "...always fair." The mood of gloom momentarily lifted. Unwilling to let it descend again, Phaedra said, "I had planned with Cousin Louisa to visit Astley's Amphitheatre this afternoon. Chloe could accompany us." She pretended not to see her sister's grimace.

"Not today. We will require your presence in the parlor. There will undoubtedly be a number of callers, many of them bent on obtaining more fuel for their gossip."

"Very well, Mama," Phaedra replied, with a long-suffering sigh. "And I suppose that I must accompany you to tea parties and whatnot for a while."

"I am afraid you must. But only for a sennight or so. Can you bear it?"

"I can if I must. Chloe, I must confess that I am quite out of charity with you. How could you so forget yourself?"

"Stop it, stop it!" Chloe cried. "You are all acting as if I had done something criminal. I only walked in the garden with Lord Everingham. He was quite tiresome, too, although you probably would have enjoyed his conversation, Phaedra. He introduced me to nearly every shrub and flower we passed, just as you sometimes do."

Leaning forward, Phaedra said, with great interest, "He is a horticulturalist, then?"

"I suppose so. I found it quite odd, an earl speaking of gardening as if he were common. I am not sure I care to encourage his interest."

Phaedra could not resist asking, "Why not?"

"You know I have no interest in horticulture. Besides, I would never let a gentleman who looks like a sheep go beyond what is proper."

"A sheep? Tell me more," Phaedra said, interested in spite of herself.

"He is not very tall." She gestured with her hand, about three inches above her head. "His hair and eyebrows are pale, so that he looks washed out, like clothing that has faded in the sun. But he is very *au courant* in his dress, his manners are quite unexceptional, and he is an earl. He must be rich. The Everingham house is elegant beyond anything I have ever seen. He seemed quite taken with me."

"And his mother, was she also taken with you? It did not sound like it."

"No, she was quite horrid. I hate her!"

"So you were merely practicing your wiles on this unfortunate young man, as you do upon poor Mr. Martin. It is most unkind in you to do so. You do not find Lord Everingham attractive, but you do nothing to discourage his attentions. What will you do if he has developed a tendre for you?"

"Oh, I shall enjoy it. And I am sure he has, Phaedra. If you could only have seen him gazing at me like a lovelorn ewe while he poked himself in the chin with his fork. I do believe I have made a conquest."

"What an interesting comparison. Is he effeminate then?"

"Oh, you know what I meant. He is masculine enough, even though he is slender and his shoulders are narrow and his voice is a light tenor. I am sure I could fall in love with him, should I choose."

"Chloe, I have a terrible feeling you are living in a dream world. Just be sure you do nothing to compromise yourself."

"With Everingham? How perfectly ridiculous. But one should always have something to fall back upon, you know."

"You would not be pleased if your admirers acted thus towards you, I think." Seeing blank incomprehension on her sister's face, Phaedra threw up her hands. "Never mind. I will go up and help Cousin Louisa. She is embroidering silver oak leaves on Mama's gray silk gown."

"Oh, how wonderful. I will come with you."

The sisters, their minds diverted to something other than their social life, went companionably upstairs, to sew and gossip until the hour for callers to arrive.

THE HORDE OF CALLERS DID NOT MATERIALIZE. MRS. GRAHAM AND HER PAINFULLY shy daughter arrived first. Chloe practically snubbed Sarah, but Phaedra, feeling sorry for the girl, attempted to converse with her. As before, it was a failure. The girl again sat with her eyes fixed upon Phaedra's face and did nothing but nod or shake her head and occasionally giggle softly. Phaedra was relieved to hear Lady Mary Follansbee announced. She had run entirely out of topics to introduce.

Instead of coming to her rescue, Lady Mary sat down next to Chloe, leaving Phaedra to muddle along with Miss Graham until her languid mother said it was time for them to leave. Only then did Miss Graham speak.

"Oh, Miss Phaedra, I cannot tell you how much I appreciate your kindness. I know that I have no conversation. Everyone else ignores me, but you always take time to speak with me. And you are so amusing." She subsided into a painful blush, but pressed Phaedra's extended hand gratefully.

Well! Perhaps Miss Graham is not so insipid after all. She may be overwhelmed. I believe I would be, with a mother like hers. It is nice to be appreciated. She crossed the room to join Chloe and Lady Mary.

"How unkind you are, Mary. Could you not see that I was in need of assistance? I vow, trying to converse with Miss Graham is most exhausting. I find myself answering my own comments, quite like our nurse at home who never needs a second person with whom to carry on a conversation."

"I am sorry for you Phaedra, but I felt that Chloe was in greater need."

"So the gossips are at it."

"Oh, yes, we had three callers this morning, one after another, who told us of Chloe's *shocking* behavior yesterday." She smiled to show her opinion of the opprobrium.

"And who were they?"

"Two of them were old biddies who do not matter greatly, for they have little influence. But the third does matter. Lady Everingham."

"That harridan." muttered Chloe.

"Never say that where you might be overheard, Chloe," Lady Mary warned in a barely audible tone. "Harridan she may be, but she has incredible influence among the *ton*, and she also is very possessive concerning her precious son. Grandmama told me that she has in the past encouraged him to play the gallant with the debutantes, but has pulled him up short in no uncertain terms if he seemed serious about anyone. Grandmama is certain she has spread untrue rumors about several girls. Even though she has said publicly that it's time he marry, I wonder if she will ever allow him to. She certainly does not seem to intend that he should become well enough acquainted with anyone to develop a tendre for her."

Just then Edgemont announced Lord Everingham. Chloe blushed and Phaedra looked to the doorway with curiosity. The slight young man who entered had a high forehead and a long nose. She could see where Chloe had conceived the notion of a sheep, even though his appearance was not displeasing. His clothing was in the first style of elegance.

As Lord Everingham was making his bow to Lady Gifford, Edgemont reappeared to announce Mr. Farwell.

"Good," Lady Mary said softly to Phaedra. "I asked Reggie particularly to come today. I thought he might cheer her up." Phaedra smiled her gratitude, but was unable to respond because Lord Everingham had joined them.

Chloe held out her hand. "Good afternoon, Lord Everingham. Are you acquainted with Lady Mary Follansbee?"

"I have that honor. So happy to see you again, Lady Mary." He turned back to Chloe immediately. "Miss Hazelbourne, I had come to take you driving, but your mother tells me that you are unable to go with me. Are you unwell?"

Instead of replying, she said, "May I introduce my sister, Miss Phaedra Hazelbourne?"

This time his acknowledgement was just short of rude. "Miss Hazelbourne, please—"

Chloe was clearly unwilling to allow him to suspect she was anything less than perfectly happy to stay at home. "I beg your indulgence, my lord. I have decided to rest this afternoon so I will be fresh for our attendance at Almack's tonight. Do you attend?"

"I had not planned to do so, but knowing that you will grace the premises, how could I be absent? Your presence will light Almack's as no chandelier could, and the very floor will rejoice with the touch of your slippers upon it."

Phaedra was biting her lip to keep from giggling at his stilted, flowery compliments. She interrupted. "Lady Mary, Chloe, if you will excuse me, I will join Mama and Mr. Farwell. Lord Everingham, it was a pleasure to meet you." She suspected he hardly heard her, so intently was he gazing at Chloe.

What a coil. He seems well and truly enamored of her.

She extended her hand to the tall, slim gentleman, resisting with difficulty the impulse to laugh aloud at his choice of garb. "Mr. Farwell, how good of you to call."

As she led him to a neutral corner, he spoke in a tone for her ears only, "You sister is playing with fire. His mother will do everything in her power to separate them. She has her eyes set much higher than the daughter of as minor baron."

She smiled as if he had said something amusing. "Of course she has, if she will allow him to wed at all. Papa may be the nephew of a duke, but he is not in line for the title." With a gesture indicating he should seat himself, she took the chair in the corner. "Lady Mary told me you came to cheer up my sister, which was kind in you. As you see, she is not in need of anything except some common sense. And you, I am sure, cannot offer her that."

"My dear Miss Phaedra, are you so unkind as to insinuate that I lack common sense?"

"Not at all. Or yes, perhaps I do. You must know that your piffle does not go well with me."

"Ah, but my piffle is of the highest quality. I am quite the favorite with hopeful mamas, and young ladies quite adore me, for I never require that they stretch their poor little minds with political or intellectual conversation."

"No, you prate of fashion and parties and indulge in light gossip. Do you never, Mr. Farwell, have a serious thought?"

"Never, Miss Phaedra. Why if a serious thought should enter my head, I would cast it aside as I would a soiled handkerchief." The lacy scrap of fine linen in his hand fluttered in illustration.

"What a waste. There is much more to life than balls and fashion."

Phaedra awaited his reply. When none was forthcoming, she looked more closely at him. His eyes were closed. Extravagantly long lashes lay against his cheeks. *I would give my soul to have lashes like those.* She shook him by the shoulder. "Mr. Farwell, I may not be a sparkling conversationalist, but this is outside of enough. If you prefer to nap, you should retire to your rooms to do so. How rude you are!"

"But serious conversation always sends me to sleep, don't you know. Now, let us piffle, and I promise you I will remain awake."

"I have no talent for piffle. You may go ahead, and I will sit here with an expression of interest on my face. I would not be so impolite as to fall asleep while you are speaking."

"No, but you would bore me with your intellectual pretensions."

"Pretensions? How dare you?"

"Well, are they not? You claim that you do not enjoy the fashionable life, yet you partake of it. You profess to despise parties and balls, yet once there, you give every appearance of enjoyment. I have heard you condemn Almack's as a bride's auction—yes, I did, when you were not aware I was present—yet you, I'll wager, are willing to allow yourself be auctioned off in the Marriage Mart. If you did not, why did you come to London? Surely there are prospective husbands in the country? Miss Phaedra, you are only pretending to be above this social life that your sister and I choose to lead."

"I never claimed to be above it. But I find so much of it a waste of time. And yes, there are young men at home. But they are all so...so uninteresting."

"Of course it is a waste of time. But a pleasurable one that every member of the *ton* chooses to enjoy. You cannot have it both ways. Either you are a part of the *ton* and participate in its life style, or you are not, and you should not claim the benefits it offers. Your choice, Miss Phaedra."

"I would have rather stayed in the country, Mr. Farwell. I do not enjoy this frivolous life," Phaedra insisted, furious at his attack upon her attitudes.

"Do you not?" he retorted. "Then you are a very good actress."

"Oh, very well, I do enjoy some of it. But not so much, and not all of the time. I cannot spend my life living like this."

"No more can I. But for three months each year, is it so bad?"

"That is too much. If I could have a month of it, as my parents have often done, I would be content. I am a country girl, Mr. Farwell."

"As for your uninteresting young men in the country," he said, as if she had not spoken, "had it occurred to you that they would be less dull for a bit of Town bronze?"

"Perhaps," she was forced to admit.

"You may be certain. One cannot reap the benefits of Town without paying the price."

"What do you mean?"

"Why Town is where the arts flourish, where life is varied and exciting, where one may experience the highest intellectual stimulation. Here is the opera, the theatre, the art galleries. These are as much a part of the fashionable life as are Almack's and the Duchess' ball and your presentation at Court."

"No, they cannot be. The *ton* is all that is silly and wasteful. Those other things are meaningful. They give value to life."

"And who do you suppose supports them? Would we have the fine music or the Elgin marbles without the wealth and influence of members of the *ton*? We are not all fribbles, you know. There are many of the nobility who are engaged in intellectual or artistic pursuits, but that does not prevent them from enjoying society as well."

"I had not thought about it quite like that," Phaedra admitted reluctantly.

"Well, if you are a true intellectual and honest with yourself, you will think about it. Now, I have been serious quite long enough. What will you think of me? Miss Phaedra, has anyone ever told you that the dimple in your chin is an invitation to kissing?"

Phaedra was speechless for a moment. "Mr. Farwell, I will not listen to such nonsense," she said when she found her voice.

"No, you wish only serious conversation, I recall." He sighed feelingly, a hand pressed over his heart. "Forgive me, Miss Phaedra, I am capable of no more. I shall, as you suggested, retire to my rooms for a nap." He rose and bowed his farewell.

After he left, Phaedra sat and thought about his words. She grew angry as she did so. How dared he call her a false intellectual? A hypocrite? She had always been the practical, sensible sister. She was well-educated. She could read Greek and Latin, was knowledgeable of scientific principles, and knew a little about art and music. Cousin Louisa said she was far better educated than most young ladies of her age and station.

Mr. Farwell was nothing but a fop, a silly, vapid fribble. She would avoid him whenever possible, from now on.

I am not a hypocrite.

CHAPTER SIX

PAPA WAS STANDING AT THE BOTTOM OF THE STAIRS WHEN THE SISTERS came down the following Wednesday evening. He appeared far more distinguished than Phaedra had ever seen him, for he never wore full evening dress in the country.

"What a lucky fellow I am," he said, and smiled widely. "I'll be the envy of all when I walk into Almack's with my lovely ladies."

"Thank you, Papa." Chloe curtseyed. Her eyes sparkled as brilliantly as the small sapphire in her necklace, a gift from their late grandmother. Her sky blue gown was trimmed with gold tissue ribbons that fluttered softly from a bow just under her bodice. Matching ribbons were twined to hold her hair in a deceptively loose cluster of curls at the back of her head. Phaedra could not recall seeing her sister look so fine.

Her own gown gave her a sense of uncommon confidence. It was an unusual combination of apricot muslin with a sheer peach overskirt. Tiny green satin leaves trimmed the hem and were scattered along the too-low neckline. Although her mama pronounced it perfectly modest, she felt exposed.

"Save me a place on your dance cards, girls. Once the bucks get a look at you, I won't have a chance."

"Oh, Papa, you will always have a chance with us," Chloe said, and slipped a red rosebud into his lapel. "I would rather dance with you than anyone else."

Phaedra wished she had thought of giving Papa a rose. Coquettish gestures did not come naturally to her as they did to her sister.

Chloe chattered throughout the short drive to Almack's. Phaedra was just as happy to be silent, for she continued to be troubled over Mr. Farwell's accusation. She did enjoy some parts of Town life, but it still seemed terribly superficial. Her ruminations were cut short when the carriage pulled up at the doors to the assembly rooms.

She hesitated before stepping through the sacred portals, for she had a sudden premonition of disaster. *Nonsense. Too much has been made of a small lapse in judgment. With Mama and Cousin Louisa and me to keep an eye on Chloe, how can she do anything scandalous?* With fingers crossed, she walked into the room beside her mother, a determined smile on her face and trepidation in her heart.

Lord Everingham, who had been standing just inside the doors, quickly came to Chloe's side with a request for as many dances as she would give him. At her mother's nod, she allotted him two. A few other gentlemen came up to request dances, but again neither Hazelbourne sister created any particular sensation.

Phaedra's partner for the first set was a young man whose name she could neither remember nor read upon her dance card, so poor was his handwriting. He was pleasant company and danced well, so she enjoyed herself well enough. When he escorted her back to her parents, she thanked him prettily, and immediately forgot about him. As she acknowledged her mother's introductions to the ladies and gentlemen with whom she had been speaking, Phaedra felt her heart leap into her throat. Here, within the respectable walls of Almack's, was the nasty creature who had captured her in Green Park.

He looked perfectly respectable, so why did her skin crawl when he looked at her? Why did she feel her virtue was at risk?

Silly! He saved you from those others. Just because he tried to steal a kiss, you've made him out a villain.

Nonetheless, a shudder of distaste scrabbled its way up her spine.

Did he recognize her? His smile and bow were all that was correct as he smoothly requested her company for a set. Wishing for the first time she were so popular that her dance card had filled immediately upon her entrance, Phaedra reluctantly allowed him to sign his name. Her reluctance was noted by Chloe who quizzed her about its cause when they were briefly alone a short while later.

"I cannot explain why I do not wish to dance with Mr. Dervigne," she whispered, "but I will admit he makes me uncomfortable."

"You are being excessively silly, Phaedra. Such polished manners he has, and such presence. I vow, he puts all the younger gentlemen to shame. I was quite impressed with him and allowed him two sets, you know." She smiled at an approaching gentleman. "You are too particular in your likes and dislikes, sister," she concluded, just before laying her hand on the proffered arm. "Why Sir Harold, I have been looking forward to this moment for quite the past hour."

The next hour flew by as Phaedra found herself enjoying herself far more than she had expected to. Then Mr. Dervigne came to claim his dance. It was a country dance, so there was little opportunity for conversation, but she still found herself ill at ease. His low-voiced compliments when they came together were not so warm as to approach impropriety, yet they edged ever so slightly beyond what was pleasing. When he took her hand in the figures, his grasp was more firm than was comfortable. At the end of the dance, he escorted her back to her parents. When he bowed over her hand, he pressed a moist kiss upon her palm.

She snatched it away, wiped it upon her skirt.

Ignoring her obvious distaste, he said, "Miss Phaedra, such a pleasure. May I request your company for a drive in the park tomorrow? I have a new phaeton. Having you accompany me on its maiden run would give me great pleasure."

"I am sorry Mr. Dervigne. My mama does not allow me to go driving in phaetons, for there is no place for my chaperone."

"Oh, but surely, your mother will agree to such a harmless pastime. I promise you that all the best young ladies are seen in phaetons these days."

Rather than argue with him, she said, "My mother's rules are quite strict. You may ask her, but I am certain of the answer she will give you. Thank you for the dance, Mr. Dervigne." She curtsied. *I cannot like him. He does not exactly frighten me, but I would not choose to be alone with him.*

Mr. Dervigne, she noted, did not approach her mama, but instead went to Chloe to claim his dance with her.

Chloe had watched Mr. Dervigne with Phaedra and wondered why her sister seemed less than flattered by his attentions. Within a few minutes of the beginning of the next set, she decided she liked his polished manners and obvious interest. She responded to his compliments, offered each time the figures of the dance brought them together, with the demure smiles and fluttering lashes she had practiced well before her mirror. When the music stopped, she accepted his offer of punch and accompanied him to the refreshment tables. He provided her with a cup of Almack's overly sweet but flavorless punch before drawing her aside from the crowd.

"Miss Hazelbourne, I must confess that I find you a most fascinating young lady. I wish we could have a less public opportunity to get to know one another."

"Why thank you Mr. Dervigne. I should be glad to have you sit with me during the next waltz." Lord Everingham's name was on her dance card for that event, but she hoped Mr. Dervigne would catch the hint and obtain permission for her to dance the waltz. Lady Mary had told her that the patronesses sometimes yielded to an established gentlemen's request before they would ordinarily grant permission to a young lady. "Unless, of course, I receive permission to waltz with someone else."

The gentleman was oblivious to her hinting. "Unfortunately, Miss Hazelbourne, I am already engaged for the waltz. I had in mind something more, ah, private."

"Like what, sir?"

"Perhaps you would care to drive in the park with me one day soon. I have a perch phaeton, you know."

"Oh, how marvelous! I love perch phaetons." Chloe had never ridden in one but thought them terribly dashing. "I would be pleased to drive with you, Mr. Dervigne."

"The park is so crowded, though," he said slowly, as if in a quandary. "One cannot really appreciate a phaeton at the slow speeds permitted there. Perhaps you would prefer a short drive in the country?"

"Oh, yes. I would like that above all things." Chloe clapped her hands. Now here was a gentleman to cultivate. He offered something more exciting than the bland pastime of driving sedately in Hyde Park. "I am free on Monday next. Shall I expect you then?"

"At two, I think. That should be early enough," he told her with a smile.

Chloe returned his smile, excited at the prospect of driving with an experienced, older man. Mr. Martin, arriving to claim his second dance, interrupted their conversation, greeting Dervigne with cold politeness.

"Has that fella been sayin' anything impolite to you, Miss Hazelbourne?" he said as soon as they were out of earshot.

"Why, no," she answered, puzzled by his question. "Why do you ask?"

"Just wondered. Not the sort a girl like you should know. Bad man."

The movements of the dance separated them before she could find the words to defend Mr. Dervigne. She decided Mr. Martin must be jealous of the older man's poise and consequence and chose to ignore his words.

Reggie had been speaking with Lady Jersey throughout the country dance, but was keeping his eye on one of the participants. Her apricot gown stood out among the whites and pinks that were so much more common. As it ended he said, "Now, Sally, will you give permission for the Misses Hazelbourne to waltz?"

"No, I will not," that lady replied. "There has been too much talk of behavior that was less than acceptable, but the accounts differ as to which of them is guilty. I would not be doing my duty if I were to encourage such carryings on by appearing to condone them."

"You have been listening to gossip again."

"Of course. I always listen to gossip. How else am I to amuse myself? No, Reggie, you must find someone else to waltz with. Now, there is that poor, shy Miss Graham. She has done nothing to disgrace herself. I would allow you to waltz with her, though I should not, for her mother is the most pushing female that I have ever met."

"I will dance with her later, Sally, if you will first give me permission to waltz with Miss Phaedra Hazelbourne. In fact, if you will grant permission for both the Misses Hazelbourne, I will dance with Miss Graham twice. Come Sally, do not be so stiff-necked."

"No, Reggie. And do not put on that pleading, little boy expression. You will not get around me that way. Besides, if I were to give the Misses Hazelbourne permission to waltz, the guilty one would next waltz with Lord Everingham. And while I would like to see his mother confounded with his finally showing some backbone, I do not want to anger her."

"I will tell you which one behaved injudiciously—for that was all it was, I believe—if you will give the other permission. As a matter of fact, I believe that neither has behaved in a way to deserve your disapproval, no matter how her actions appeared."

Lady Jersey chuckled. "For shame, Reggie. No one likes a tattle-tale." She cast a flirtatious glance upwards. "You will continue to pester me until you achieve your aim, will you not?"

"Of course," he said, wafting his handkerchief gracefully. "You know me well enough."

"Well?"

"I would like to waltz with Miss Phaedra Hazelbourne," he said. Lowering his voice, he added, "Just remember, I told you nothing more than the name of the young woman I wish to waltz with."

She snatched the handkerchief from his hand and pretended to swat him with it. "Honestly, Reggie, you are a caution. Come, then. I will need you to let me know which of the two she is."

Reggie assumed an expression of innocence as he followed Lady Jersey across the room. He indicated which of the sisters was Phaedra with a slight nod of his head.

"Miss Hazelbourne," said Lady Jersey to the surprised girl, "I would like to recommend Mr. Farwell to you as a partner for the waltz."

Phaedra could barely find the words to thank her, so astounded was she. She looked at him with consternation as he took her hand to lead her out.

"But, shouldn't you be dancing with Chloe? I mean..."

"No Miss Phaedra, I should not."

"It is not right that I should be granted permission to waltz before my elder sister," she protested.

"You may give me credit for attempting to obtain permission to waltz with your sister first, for to do otherwise would be a lapse of good *ton*. But I was unable to do so, and so I settled for you as my second choice." He smiled down on her. "You do waltz, do you not, Miss Phaedra? It is not too unintellectual for you?"

Phaedra's distress disappeared with a rush of anger. "Yes, but I am surprised that you would lower yourself to dancing with one who bores you to sleep. You need not, Mr. Farwell. I can return to the chairs and relieve you of this onerous chore."

"Don't be stupid," he said, pulling her into his arms. "I am waltzing with you because I chose to. Now, will you engage in polite conversation, or must we brangle throughout the dance?"

Phaedra had only waltzed previously with her father and sister, so she found herself required to concentrate on her steps for the first few moments. When she finally felt confident, she smiled up into his face.

"Mr. Farwell, you dance beautifully."

"That is much more the thing, Phaedra. Now if we can manage to get through this dance without ripping at one another, I will feel the evening has been a success." His arm tightened about her waist slightly and he swung her into a sweeping turn. "Are you excited about the Duchess's ball?"

"Oh, yes, even though I know it is considered hopelessly provincial to be so," she answered breathlessly. Waltzing with Mr. Farwell was so much more spirited than with Chloe. "But I do love to dance, and the Duchess' ballroom is so much nicer than Almack's."

"More comfortable, too. And the food and drink will be edible, unlike the stale cake and weak punch which they serve here."

"Yes, but don't you see. If Almack's were to serve food and drink to please the palate, we would all stuff ourselves and then be too lethargic to dance."

"Is that what you intend to do at your ball?"

"Why of course. I am told that there will be lobster patties and buttered crab and ices and everything. Papa has told Mama that we are to be allowed to drink champagne, too, since it is our ball. It has always been forbidden us before. I tasted it once and must confess that I quite enjoyed it."

"So you will not only stuff yourself into lethargy, but you will also drink yourself into insensibility. And you are the serious sister. I shudder to think what Chloe will do."

Phaedra had started to chuckle at his partaking of her nonsense, but at his criticism of her sister, she stiffened in his arms.

"My sister's behavior is none of your concern, sir."

"Oh, come now, Phaedra, I meant no insult."

"I will thank you not to make free of my name, sir."

"My sincere apologies, *Miss* Phaedra." His teeth gleamed whitely as he grinned down at her, clearly unrepentant.

She was not mollified and thereafter answered his attempts at resumption of the silly repartee with monosyllables. She was relieved and in no good mood when he escorted her back to her mother. Her "Thank you, Mr. Farwell" was polite, with nothing of friendliness in it.

She realized something was amiss as soon as she sat beside her sister. Mama's lips were compressed and her brows lowered. Chloe glared from behind her fan.

"What has happened?"

"You—you traitor," whispered her sister. "How could you accept the waltz with Mr. Farwell. I should have been given permission before you. I am the elder. You should have begged off."

"Chloe, I told you to hold your tongue," Mama warned in a low voice.

"I will not. Phaedra knew that she had no right to waltz before me."

"She had every right. The patronesses of Almack's are the sole judges of who shall be given the permission to waltz here. They obviously felt that Phaedra had shown herself to be a properly behaved young lady."

"But she could have refused. She knew how important it was to me."

"Yes, Chloe, I could have refused," Phaedra told her, "and I am sorry I did not. Mr. Farwell was horribly rude."

Phaedra's head began to ache after Chloe's attack. As a result, she had little enjoyment of the rest of the evening, despite waltzing twice more, once with Mr. Martin, who was a surprisingly good dancer, and once with Lord Wilson, a very young but extremely handsome man. Chloe sat both waltzes out, trapped between her parents on the sidelines.

Papa took himself off to his club after handing them into their carriage. "I've need of some manly company after doing the pretty all evening," he told them, seemingly oblivious to the currents of ill will swirling among the women. Phaedra knew that only the presence of their mama held Chloe in check during the drive home. Once they were alone she would receive the brunt of her sister's rage.

Mama took her aside as she started up the stairs and told her to lock her door against her sister. "For if you will refuse to listen to her hysterics, she will cry herself to sleep and you will not suffer."

"Oh, Mama, I must listen. If I do not, she will work herself into such a state that she will be ill for days. If I allow her to vent her spleen upon my head, we will all be the better for it. Then tomorrow she will be all smiles again and so much easier to go on with. And the Duchess' ball is the day after tomorrow."

The storm that broke over her head was the worst display of Chloe's temper she had ever experienced. Phaedra apologized and soothed and reassured, but to little avail. All that mattered to Chloe was that at her own ball she would not be allowed to waltz. Everything that had gone wrong this past sennight was, somehow, all her sister's fault.

Phaedra made the mistake of pointing out that Chloe had brought all her problems upon herself by refusing to follow her mother's advice. It did no good. For the first time in their lives, she and her sister went to bed without making up their differences. Phaedra consoled herself with the thought that she was in the right. Chloe should not be too much given her own way.

Even so, she slept poorly.

LADY GIFFORD, STILL DISTRESSED OVER HER ELDER DAUGHTER'S WILLFULNESS and ill temper, and knowing the ordeal facing her younger daughter, was determined to enlist her husband's aid, in keeping Chloe in line. The girl had always minded him in the past, no matter how upset she had been. She waited up for him.

He arrived a bit over an hour later and expressed his surprise at finding her still awake.

"This could not wait until morning, George," she said, "I must persuade you to take Chloe in hand. I can do no more, and indeed, am at my wits' end."

She sat up against her pillows.

"Nonsense, Isabella," he said as he removed his cravat. "She behaved nicely tonight. I'm sure she has learned her lesson."

"Oh, George, you know she has not. She was furious that she was not given the permission to waltz, particularly since Phaedra was. She is probably in Phaedra's room at this moment, making the poor girl miserable."

"You must not pay attention to their little tiffs, love. Chloe would not do anything to distress her sister. Oh, I know she is high spirited, just like you used to be, but she's a good girl and don't mean any harm by it."

"George, she has not been a good girl since we arrived in London. She has thrown tantrums at the least provocation and has made all of us miserable."

"I won't believe that of Chloe. She has such a sunny disposition."

"Only when you are present, love. When you are not, she is willful, stubborn, temperamental, and selfish. She is rude to the servants, and to Cousin Louisa she is more than rude, she is actively hostile. She closes her mind to everything I tell her. She flirts outrageously with everything in trousers."

When her husband paused in his disrobing to stare at her, she took a deep breath and attempted to moderate her voice, which had grown quite shrill. "Why, just this evening Robert Dervigne told me that she had agreed to drive with him in the park and he was sure that I would give permission for her to do so unchaperoned, for he drives a phaeton, you know."

"That rake! He will drive my daughters nowhere. And what were you doing, giving him permission to dance with them? I won't have him about!"

"One cannot refuse an invitation to dance from a gentleman who is accepted by the patronesses, you know that, George. I did tell him that under no circumstances would he be allowed to take Chloe driving without a chaperone. But you have changed the subject. Will you take Chloe in hand?"

He came to sit beside her, slipping an arm around her waist and pulling her close. "If you feel you cannot manage her, my love, I will. Certainly. But I cannot be with her every moment. I have business to conduct while we're in Town. Besides, a gentleman can't be a young lady's chaperone, not everywhere."

"No, but when you can be there, I believe your presence will be enough to keep her in line. Will you accompany us as much as possible for the next few weeks, please?"

"If only to keep Dervigne at arm's length. I don't want him hanging about the girls."

"That's all right, then. I feel so much better to know you will be there to help me. Good night, love," she said. "Blow out the candle."

A few moments later, her voice reached him in the dark. "George, do you know a Viscount Wilderlake?"

"Hmm? What's that? I was half asleep."

"I asked if you were acquainted with Wilderlake."

"Don't think so. Knew his father." A yawn interrupted him. "Man was a gamester, squandered his fortune, or at least what his father before him had not lost at the tables. Left the son with pockets to let. Why?"

Lady Gifford related their adventure on the journey to London. "He seemed like quite a nice young man, but we have never been in the way of meeting him. He did send a very nice note to thank us for our trouble."

"Adding him to your list of possibles for the girls, eh? Well, as long as he's not the wastrel his father was, that's not such a bad idea. Not wealthy, but a good family."

"Her Grace sent him an invitation to the ball. I want you to make sure we are introduced. He should do quite well for Phaedra, if he is serious. If Chloe can avoid destroying her reputation with her escapades, she will have no trouble finding a husband. But Phaedra is not appreciated as she should be."

"You worry too much, wife. Now come here and let me kiss you. I'm an old man and I need my sleep."

CHLOE CONTINUED TO FULMINATE AFTER RETURNING TO HER OWN BEDCHAMBER. She paced the floor and catalogued the acts of persecution and neglect inflicted upon her by her family for a good half hour. Eventually, her anger was exhausted and she reluctantly admitted that she should have followed her mother's advice, at least until she had been granted permission to waltz. But had she really disgraced herself? Of course not. Mama was being overly cautious. How could one woman influence the entire *ton*?

Convinced she would soon be forgiven any minor lapses of behavior, Chloe thought again of her mother and sister's scoldings. Perhaps she had allowed her temper to overrule her better judgment tonight, she admitted. But it was so unfair! Without permission to waltz, and at her very own ball, she would be miserable. What right did those horrible, high-and-mighty old women at Almack's have to decide whether or not Chloe Hazelbourne could waltz at a private party?

CHAPTER SEVEN

THURSDAY MORNING THE DENIZENS OF LONDON AWOKE TO RAIN THE downpour continued intermittently throughout the day, accompanied by blustery wind. Phaedra and Cousin Louisa braved the weather to visit Lady Mary in the afternoon. The Duchess' house was in a state of confusion with preparations for the ball Friday night. Phaedra offered their assistance and it was quickly accepted. They were set to supervising the washing of the crystal drops on the many wall sconces in the enormous ballroom while Lady Mary helped with those from the great chandelier which hung over the center of the room. All three were soon up to their elbows in soapsuds as they took over the washing themselves in an attempt to hurry the chore along. Servants were rushing everywhere, and tradesmen scurried in and out bringing plants, statuary and even a small fountain to set up in the ballroom, which was planned to appear as a sylvan glade.

As the two girls rested a moment while awaiting more crystal drops, Phaedra looked about her. The ceiling was painted with elysian scenes. On the two long walls were mirrors, divided into small panes so as to resemble windows. Deep green velvet draperies enhanced the resemblance and complimented the lighter green medallions on the ivory silk wallpaper. Gazing critically about her at the decorations being installed, she said, "Mary, I do believe that this will be an improvement upon nature."

"How so?" Lady Mary said.

"Why they are building a glade with an appearance of naturalness, but without all those portions which make nature so uncouth. Unless you are importing ants and worms and dirt and rocks. And snakes, we must not forget the snakes."

"Oh, do you think we should include them?" Lady Mary said in a serious voice.

"By all means. It would add to the authenticity of the setting."

"What a delightful notion. We must immediately order some snakes. They could be placed over there, under the musician's balcony. Or would they be better near the fountain?"

"I think the fountain would be better. Then they would feel at home. They prefer a moist setting, you know."

"Perhaps we could scatter ants over all the greenery, shaking them out of their bag like pepper," Lady Mary proposed, "to add spice."

Phaedra stifled a giggle. "Let me see, would that be better, or should we place them in the bower which will enclose the refreshment tables? That would enhance the impression of being on a picnic."

"What a marvelous idea. Ants. I shall add that to my list. And what more do we need? Would slugs be appropriate?"

Phaedra pondered. "Slugs would be very appropriate if placed in the foliage behind the row of chaperones' chairs." She tapped her chin with a forefinger. "Do you know, it is too bad that the ballroom will be so well lit. A few bats hanging from the chandelier might be a clever touch."

"Absolutely not. I detest bats. But perhaps I could convince Grandmama to send out for a dozen or two sparrows and perhaps some robins. Birds add so much to an outdoor setting, don't you think?"

"Oh, yes, and they offer so much opportunity for amusement. Just think what reaction there would be if one came and perched on the rim of Lady Everingham's plate as she was nibbling at her sweetmeats." They both dissolved in laughter.

Cousin Louisa called them to attention. "If you hope to get these drops washed today, you had better get busy. Look here, the maids have got so far ahead of you that they now have nothing to do."

Lady Mary told the grateful maids to rest a few moments. "I would imagine their legs are tired, with all that running up and down the ladders." She said as she immersed more crystal drops into soapy water. "So much more difficult than stairs."

"You are kind. So many mistresses would have set the maids to another task instead of allowing them to rest," Phaedra said.

"Kindness and practicality are frequently the same thing. The maids will work better and faster for a short rest, and they will not be so prone to drop the crystals."

Close to another hour passed before they washed the last delicate crystal prism. As they watched the maids replacing them, Lady Mary thanked Phaedra and Cousin Louisa for their help and apologized for letting them work when they had come on a social call.

"Nonsense," Cousin Louisa said. "The ball is for Phaedra as much as for you. It was the least we could do. Now, is there anything else we can help you with, Lady Mary, before we depart?"

"No, there is not. This was my last housecleaning assignment." She escorted them to the vestibule herself and let them out, repeating her thanks.

Phaedra dreaded going home, because she feared a repetition of the previous night's storms. Chloe had been quiet at breakfast and had not spoken to her. She was pleasantly surprised, therefore, to find that her sister's disposition had improved considerably through the course of the afternoon. Several gentlemen, it seemed, had called and had filled her head with flattery and poetical allusions. Lord Everingham had been particularly attentive and had brought her flowers and sweets.

"I do not know whether it was his obvious devotion or his gifts that succeeded in bringing her out of her temper, but which ever it was, I am grateful," Lady Gifford observed in an aside to Cousin Louisa. Phaedra pretended not to have heard it.

The following day was quiet, as Lady Gifford had refused all invitations and had required the sisters to remain at home and rest in the afternoon. They were to dine at the Duchess's mansion before the ball, in a select group of about thirty. Preparations for the evening began in the late afternoon, when the household staff began carrying hot water to all four bedchambers.

The only crisis of the day was brought about by Chloe's attempt to decide which of her four posies she should carry. Her mama settled the question by commanding her to carry the flowers her father had sent her. As the sisters joined their mother and Cousin Louisa in the foyer, Lord Gifford came out of the parlor and looked them over.

"My word, such a bevy of beauties! I'm a lucky dog, I am, to be escorting four such lovely ladies."

And indeed, they were all four in the best of looks. Lady Gifford had chosen a gown of palest gray. Its drifting silk gauze overdress was shot with silver and embroidered with silver oak leaves twining up the front of the skirt and over the bodice. Her prematurely grey hair shone silver in the candlelight, and a spray of diamonds holding two silver gray plumes in her coiffure matched the gems sparkling at her throat and wrists.

Cousin Louisa, forsaking her usual dark colors, had clothed herself in a silk gown of a color somewhere between lavender and gray. Although somewhat out of date in style, it was nevertheless elegant, with trimmings of jet beading. A matching turban was almost covered with jet beads, sparkling dramatically.

Chloe's gown of palest rose muslin was unadorned except at hem and sleeves, where pearls were sewn in a scroll pattern. The deeper rose ribbon covering the high waistline was held at the front with a matching rosette surrounded by leaves made of pearls. Her slippers matched her gown, as did her gloves. More pearls encircled her throat and were threaded through her brown hair, which was arranged *a la grecque*. Her posy was blush roses in a silver holder. Excitement had put color in her cheeks and a sparkle in her eye.

Phaedra was as lovely as her sister. She was clad in a gown of creamy white, a color very nearly matching her skin. The gauze overskirt was a slightly darker shade of cream, shot with golden threads. A golden rope encircled the high waist. Her jewelry was topaz set in a golden chain about her throat and dangling at her ears. Her hair was pulled to the top of her head by a golden comb and fell in ringlets down her back. The posy she carried was of white roses, their petals delicately touched with golden yellow, surrounded by feathery asparagus fern.

The Duchess's dinner party was unbalanced, for the ladies far outnumbered the gentlemen. Her Grace offered no apology for the uneven numbers. The ball was for the three girls, but this dinner party was for her friends. Chloe found herself seated between Lady Hortense Wimbledon and a rather deaf old gentleman. He examined her through his quizzing glass and pronounced that she was a taking little thing before addressing himself exclusively to his food. As Lady Hortense was far more interested in conversing with the person on her other side, Chloe found herself quite ignored. She could not decide whether to be outraged or relieved. To her considerable surprise, she had little appetite. Instead a cold lump of apprehension sat in her middle.

What would this night bring? Would she take? Or would she be judged merely acceptable, like so many girls who had to settle for less than their dreams?

No! I will not believe that. I must take. I must.

Lord Gifford was on Phaedra's right and Lady Jersey on her left. She found that she only had to nod and smile occasionally to converse with Lady Jersey. By the time the ladies retired, she felt as if she had been caught within a whirlwind.

The receiving line, which Phaedra had dreaded because of the numbers of people she would have to meet, was merely exhausting. So many curtsies, so many hands to shake, so many *how d'ye dos* to respond to, and so many names to try to remember. She found herself in a daze, until a vaguely familiar voice caught her ear. She looked up into nearly black eyes set beneath heavy, dark brows.

The Duchess greeted the older woman beside him. "Well, Elizabeth, it's about time you came back to Town. So this is your son. Cranky lookin' fella, ain't he? Make you both acquainted with my granddaughter, Lady Mary Follansbee."

Lady Mary greeted them graciously. Wilderlake bowed low over her hand, but he did not smile.

The Duchess's many-ringed had waved in her general direction. "Lord and Lady Gifford, and their daughters, Chloe and Phaedra."

The sisters had barely time to murmur greetings to Lady Wilderlake before her son bowed before them, saying, "And one of you was my good Samaritan, but which one? You are so very similar."

She had no chance to reply, for the next guests were close behind him. From the corner of her eye, she saw Chloe gazing after him. *Oh, dear. This could become complicated.*

Lady Mary was led out for the first dance by her grandfather, the Duke of Verbain, Chloe by Lord Gifford, and Phaedra by her mama's cousin. She had always liked her ministerial uncle, Godfrey Stevens. It was he who had encouraged her parents to allow her to become educated far beyond what was usual for a young woman of her position.

She appreciated his coming to Town just so she would have a male relative with whom to open the ball. He had arrived only that day, but would stay for a sennight. Phaedra engaged to go with him to the gardens at Kew the next day but one. Uncle Godfrey had long encouraged her interest in plants, and indeed, was acquainted with Sir Joseph Banks. She looked forward to the excursion with great pleasure.

The Duchess had planned that every fourth dance would be a waltz. Unlike most of her contemporaries, she enjoyed the dance and did not think it improper. Phaedra had reluctantly allotted the first waltz to Mr. Farwell, fearing that they would again argue. She was standing by her mother, waiting for him to claim her, when Lord Wilderlake approached her.

"Miss Hazelbourne, dare I hope that you are not engaged for this dance?"

"I am, sir, but I do not believe my sister is." It never occurred her to ask if he would be willing to sit out the waltz with Chloe.

"Then will you save another waltz for me? I wish to speak with you, which I cannot do in a country dance."

"I would be delighted."

He signed her dance card for the last waltz of the evening.

Reggie approached just then. "Trying to steal my partner, Wilderlake?"

"No, but to capture her for a later waltz." He bowed and left them, heading for Chloe who stood in the center of a group of young men.

As the music began, he set his hand at Phaedra's waist. "Well, Miss Phaedra, what shall we dispute this evening?"

"Why nothing at all, Mr. Farwell. I am so in charity with the world that I will not argue, even with you."

"Good." He pulled her closer and she did not resist. "At the risk of a setdown, I would like to say that I have never seen you looking lovelier. I am pleased that you chose to carry my posy."

"I had no choice. It so perfectly matched my dress, you see."

He whirled her about the floor. "It does, indeed. We fops are good for something, are we not?"

Phaedra only smiled. She was completely lost in her enjoyment of the dance. If only it could go on like this forever.

"Oh my God," he said suddenly.

"What is it? Did I tread upon your foot?"

"Your sister. She is dancing."

"Oh, no! How could she? And with whom?" She tried to see Chloe, but too many of the other dancers were taller than she.

"With Wilderlake. He could not know she was not granted permission last night."

"What can we do?" Phaedra was unsure why she imagined he could help the situation, but had no doubt that if anyone could, it would be he.

"Too late. Lady Jersey has seen her. No, do not pull away. You cannot stop her now, and if you were to fly to her side, it would only compound the problem. Smile, Phaedra, you are enjoying this dance with me. And you have not a care in the world. Come, now, let me see your eyes sparkle. Surely you are that good an actress."

She smiled, but her heart was not in it. They danced in silence until the music stopped, and she started to rush to her mother. He held her back and said, "Slowly, slowly. You must not act as if anything is amiss." They strolled across the ballroom. Mr. Farwell smiled and nodded at various ladies and gentlemen. Phaedra attempted to do the same, but her face was so stiff she wondered if her expression was not closer to a grimace.

As they approached, Phaedra heard Mama say, "Chloe, I do believe you have torn your hem."

Chloe opened her mouth to protest, but a quick frown silenced her. "Let us retire and I will see if I can pin it up. Phaedra, will you assist me? If you gentlemen will excuse us?"

As soon as they were in the corridor Chloe said, "Mama, my gown—"

"Hush, you silly child. Do not say a word until we are alone." Instead of turning toward the ladies' retiring room, she guided them into a small salon and closed the door behind her. "Phaedra, please stand here and see that no one interrupts us. Chloe, what have you to say for yourself?"

Chloe's lower lip stuck out, much as it had when she was a child and thwarted. "It is *my* ball, and I have the right to enjoy it." Her voice trembled ever so slightly.

"You have no rights except those you are given. And you were not given the right to waltz. You may never be allowed into Almack's again."

"I don't care! It is a stuffy place where they make you act like statues. I hate it! There will be other balls, anyway."

"There may not be, if you are not invited. You have once again showed society that you do not accept its rules. You could be ostracized for the rest of the Season."

"Mama, someone is approaching," Phaedra called softly from her position by the door.

"Very well," her mother said. "Chloe, I cannot force you to sit at my side for the remainder of the evening, for to do so would cause even more talk. But you will behave yourself or you will find yourself restricted to the house for the rest of the Season. Do you hear?" She rose to her feet. "There, I believe that I have mended it," she continued as footsteps paused outside the door. "Now move carefully and perhaps the hem will not tear again this evening."

"Thank you, Mama," Chloe responded dutifully, although her mulish expression belied her tone.

The door opened just then and the Duchess entered. She hardly glanced at Chloe and Phaedra. "Do you need assistance, Isabella?"

"No, I believe I have handled the problem for now. I may call on your influence later, however, when we have some idea of how severe the consequences are."

"Serve her right if she was ostracized," Her Grace said. "Foolish chit."

"I'm not—"

Mama held up a hand. "Hush, Chloe. Do not say one single word."

Phaedra saw the worry in her eyes, and tightened her lips. Poor Mama. She had been so determined that they would make good matches in London. For herself, Phaedra didn't care. She had never expected to take. But Chloe—

It's her own fault, though. Mama warned her. So did I.

When they returned to the ballroom, both girls were claimed by their partners. Unfortunately, the dance sets had already been made up, so they were forced to sit out. But they danced the next set and no one acted as if there was anything unusual in Chloe's behavior. She relaxed, certain her mother and the Duchess had exaggerated the situation's gravity.

Lord Everingham sat out the next waltz with Chloe, under her mother's watchful eye. "I cannot see why you will not dance this waltz with me," he told her, a trace of petulance in his voice. "You danced with Wilderlake."

"Oh, my lord, I am so fatigued. Besides, we can talk more comfortably here than on the dance floor."

"I cannot hold you in my arms, here," he retorted.

Chloe soothed his hurt feelings with soft words and promises of other times, other waltzes. When the music ended, he relinquished her to her next partner unwillingly but with good grace.

Mr. Martin was her partner for the supper dance, Lord Everingham having been required to take his mother in. The shy young man was pathetically grateful for the favor. Chloe, not wanting to be alone with his puppylike devotion, suggested that they join her sister and Lady Mary at their table.

It was a gay group. Reginald Farwell had engaged Lady Mary for the supper dance and Phaedra's escort was Lord Wainright, a chubby, happy-go-lucky young man. The conversation was anything but serious, and the group drew the attention of the adjoining tables with their hilarity. Lady Mary and Phaedra convulsed the group with their story of the proposed additions to the ballroom decorations.

Lord Wainright was particularly taken with the idea of the ants. "I say, they could have been placed in the shrubbery around the musician's balcony, don't y'know. Then we could have had a gay old time when they started crawling up the fiddler's legs. None of this slow music, but a jolly good romp." He chuckled at the image this evoked.

"A frog in the punchbowl would have been a good addition," Mr. Farwell contributed, sounding half asleep.

"Oh, yes," Phaedra agreed. "And he could have been trained to croak whenever someone took his third glass of punch. A sure cure for greed."

Several other suggestions were made, each more silly than the other. Chloe was less amused than the others, for she was still fulminating at how unfairly she had been treated. First those wicked old women at Almack's refusing to grant her permission to waltz, and then her own mama lacking all sympathy for her disappointment. Even her sister was against her.

Lord Wainwright's suggestion of goldfish in the champagne was quite disgusting, but she did not say so. Still, the others' laughter was contagious, so she enjoyed herself somewhat.

The last waltz was also the final dance of the evening. Mama had consented to dance it with Papa, leaving Chloe alone on a sofa with instructions to remain there with Cousin Louisa. Lord Wilderlake came to claim Phaedra. She watched them swing into the waltz and told herself that she didn't care. Not one little bit.

But she did. The unfairness of it all seemed to swell inside her, becoming a hot ball of resentment. She chewed a fingernail, and tried to ignore the whirling rainbow of color as everyone else enjoyed themselves.

"Miss Hazelbourne, there is an empty hallway just outside."

She looked up at man who had spoken so softly. "Lord Everingham. How good of you to come to keep me company."

"Actually," he said, with a sly smile, "I had something more interesting in mind. As I said, there is an empty corridor just outside that door." He pointed to her left. "The music is quite audible there. Would you care to accompany me?"

She glanced at the door, at Cousin Louisa, who was turned away, speaking to a woman on her other side, and then back at him. "My lord, I am afraid I do not understand—"

"Come dance with me, Miss Hazelbourne. As long as no one sees you, what difference can it make?"

She had already danced with him twice. Chloe remembered her mother warning her that to dance with any gentleman more than two times was tantamount to announcing their betrothal.

Lord Everingham, for all his wealth, was not the man of her dreams.

But it is the last waltz. And this is my ball, my come out.

She held out her hand and allowed him to raise her to her feet. A few steps and they were in the corridor. He pulled the door closed behind them. The music was, indeed, quite loud enough to dance to.

He might look like a sheep, but he was a superb dancer. She closed her eyes and let the music take her.

AFTER THEY HAD WALTZED IN SILENCE FOR A FEW MOMENTS, LORD WILDERLAKE smiled down at Phaedra and said, "Are you the sister who kindly came to my aid as I lay senseless along the road?"

"I am, my lord. I hope you have no lingering pain from your injury."

"None at all. I thought it was you, although the first time I saw your sister, I wondered. Are you twins?"

"No. Chloe is almost two years older than I, and far more outgoing. I am the family bluestocking, and tend to reclusiveness, I fear." As soon as the words were out of her mouth, she wondered why she had said them. "Chloe is lively, and thrives on company and conversation and gaiety. She is not exactly frivolous, you must understand. It is just that, compared to her, I am quite dull."

"So you claim to be sober and gloomy?"

"No, not gloomy. But my interests lie less with people and more with plants and art and literature."

"And music?" he said in a hopeful tone.

She laughed. "I have no talent for music. Chloe does, and takes it very seriously indeed. I cannot carry a tune, although I do enjoy listening."

As Lord Wilderlake swept her into a gliding turn, Phaedra spied Chloe and Lord Everingham slipping through a door. She stumbled. "Excuse me, my lord," she said as she recovered. "I fear I am tiring. It has been a long evening and I have never danced so much before."

The music went on and on. Desperate to discover what new calamity loomed, Phaedra began to wonder if she was doomed to waltz forever. At last the last notes dies away and the dancers spun to a halt. The ball was over. Wilderlake escorted Phaedra back to her parents. Chloe magically reappeared before Mama and Papa returned, slipping into a chair beside Cousin Louisa, who was deep in a conversation. Phaedra wondered where her sister had been.

Had anyone else noticed that she had been alone in Lord Everingham's company again? All the way home Phaedra fretted, unsure whether to tell her parents what she had seen. Chloe would surely view such an action as a betrayal of sisterly allegiance.

CHAPTER EIGHT

HOW MUCH DID SHE OWE HER SISTER? IF CHLOE HAD BEEN SEEN WALTZING with Lord Everingham, if tomorrow's most delicious *on dit* was how the wayward Hazelbourne girl had compromised herself at her own come out Ball... Should she wait and see, or warn Mama and Papa of the brewing storm? Phaedra chewed her lip and did her best to ignore the churning of her stomach.

What could their parents do to save Chloe from the price of her willfulness? Would they take the whole family back to Gifford Court? Phaedra found herself hoping they would not, for she was enjoying her Season much more than she had anticipated. But if they did not return home, how could they keep Chloe sequestered within the house in London? And even more to the point, how would they all explain doing so?

Lady Gifford bade her daughters a quiet good night as soon as they had arrived at home. "It is very late and we are all tired You will each go to your own room and retire. I do not wish to hear that you have disobeyed me."

"Mama..." Chloe began.

"You heard your mother, pet. Now get you both to bed. We will talk in the morning," Lord Gifford said firmly. The sisters went quietly up the stairs.

Lord and Lady Gifford went into the parlor and shut the door. "Would you like some brandy my love? You look as if you could use it?"

"Yes, George, I think I would. Heaven knows, I need something to calm me." She sank onto the sofa and kicked off her slippers. "How could Chloe be so foolish, after all my warnings?" She accepted the glass and sipped at its content.

"Are you certain she was seen, love? Might it not be possible that no one spied her with Lord Everingham.."

"I wish it were so, but I know it is not. That wretched Hermione Petersham was standing right beside Cousin Louisa when they came back in from the corridor. She knows they were out there unchaperoned. And you know what a busy tongue she has."

Her husband frowned into his glass, but said nothing.

"I fear Chloe's Season is at an end. Lady Mary might be able to spurn the dictates of Society and get away with it, for her rank and connections are high enough. We are neither so exalted nor so well connected. It is possible Her Grace might be able to convince Sally Jersey not to rescind the girls' vouchers, but she could never persuade any of the other patronesses. And without them, we will have wasted the Season." She heard her voice quaver on the last words. With a deep breath, she fought against the need to bury her head on her husband's comforting shoulder and weep her heart out. "I had such hopes," she whispered. "Such hopes."

"Nonsense! We'll come about. Society knows us for respectable folks. They'll know we'd never raise any but a lady."

"Even a lady may ruin herself. If Chloe has not, she has skirted very close to it. Since our daughters' portions are not large, their manners and social standing must be above reproach. A man might marry Chloe for her good name and her social worth and never mind that her portion is small. He would think twice if she shows that she thinks herself above Society's conventions."

"The more fool he. I wish I had never agreed to this Season." He scrubbed a hand across his chin. "I knew postponing Chloe's Season would cause trouble. Damned inconvenient, your mother and grandfather dying when they did." He clamped his mouth shut on the last word. An instant later, her said, "Damme, love, I didn't mean—"

"I know you did not. It *was* inconvenient." She let her sigh speak volumes. "Perhaps we should have taken them to Bath instead of bringing them to London. It might have been a more appropriate venue, for we both have many friends there who would assist in stemming gossip. Here in London we are, unfortunately, not so widely acquainted."

"I should have come up to Town with you. I could have managed Chloe. You and she do set each other's backs up, don't you?"

Lady Gifford sighed. "I am afraid we do. Even so I was certain she would heed my advice and behave herself. She is determined to marry well." She gave into temptation, and leaned against him. His arm pulled her close, secure and safe. "Oh, George, I am so tired of constantly fearing what she will do next."

"Well, if you want my advice, we'll just behave as if nothing has happened. The gossip will pass. Mrs. Petersham is well know never to have a good word for anyone."

"I am not so optimistic. Even if Sally Jersey were to ignore Chloe's behavior, Lady Everingham will not. When the word gets out that her son was the man with Chloe, she will add fuel to the fire. She has not approved of Chloe since that day at her Venetian breakfast. Lord Everingham has pulled himself from under her thumb and she does not like it one bit."

"Well then, just forbid her to see him," Lord Gifford suggested.

"That would not do, for then the odious woman would feel his consequence had been slighted. No, I am afraid she will not rest until she has completely ruined Chloe's reputation. We must do something that will not seem as if we are attempting to separate them."

"Too bad she can't come down with the grippe or influenza or something. That'd keep her out of circulation for a sennight or two. Maybe give this whole thing time to die down."

"George, what a perfectly marvelous notion. She can come down with influenza. Or seem to. That way I can keep her confined to the house, a punishment she rightly deserves, and without causing any gossip that would be detrimental to her reputation. Will you assist me in convincing her just how irresponsible her behavior has been?"

"Anything, my love. When I've had a little talk with her, she'll mend her manners, you can be sure. It's a pity she'll have to be confined to her bedchamber, though. She's such a high spirited little thing. It goes hard with me to be so unkind to her."

"She has earned a little unkindness. We cannot let her go unpunished, can we?"

Lord Gifford shook his head slowly. "No. I just hope this influenza notion will do the trick."

"So do I" Lady Gifford said, knowing she was wasting her words. She had a dreadful premonition that the next days would be difficult.

AT BREAKFAST LATE THE NEXT MORNING, HER MAMA INFORMED CHLOE THAT SHE was sickening for influenza.

"I certainly am not. I am perfectly healthy."

"On the contrary, you will pretend to be ill for the next fortnight. It will give the talk about your scandalous behavior time to die away."

"But Mama," she wailed, "Lord Everingham was to take me driving in the park today, and Mr. Martin said he would call and..."

"You will do nothing but remain in your chamber feigning illness. Furthermore you will continue to do so for at least a fortnight, or until I can be sure that you have learned to obey me," Mama said, in her do-not-defy-me voice. "Louisa, I must ask that you assist us in this deception. One of us will need to remain at home at all times, ostensibly to nurse poor Chloe, but in reality to make sure that she does remain in her bedchamber."

"Of course, Isabella," Cousin Louisa replied. She stirred her tea, a thoughtful expression on her face. After a moment she said, "May I suggest that the Duchess be told the truth. She may be of some assistance."

"Of course. I will call upon Her Grace this afternoon and beg her advice and assistance."

Chloe had listened to the exchange with growing disbelief and anger. "I am not ill! And I won't stay in my room for two weeks!" She burst into tears. "I will not be a prisoner in my own home. Oh, Papa, do not let her do this horrible thing to me!" She flung herself around his neck and sobbed into his cravat.

"Hush, pet. Two weeks won't seem so long. We'll get you all manner of books to read. Hush, now." Wearing a helpless expression, he patted her heaving shoulders.

"I cannot bear to be locked up and miss everything, Papa. Why tonight is Mrs. Stanfield's musicale, and she has asked me to play. Oh, please, Papa."

She felt his chest heave under her before he set her aside. "No, pet, you will obey your mother in this. You've been rather a naughty puss, and you must play least in sight until the talk dies down. But there, I'll come and visit you often. Teach you to play piquet, or something. Dry your tears now, do. Your pretty eyes are getting all red."

Chloe almost felt sorry for her papa, for she knew he was excessively softhearted where she was concerned. In a last bid for sympathy, she let her tears flow unchecked down her cheeks and managed a small quiver of her chin.

Papa only shook his head sorrowfully.

"Very well, I will consent to be incarcerated like a common criminal," she said in a broken, tragic voice. She stood and laid the back of her hand against her brow. "I shall now go to my cell and await my next meal of bread and water." She walked slowly out of the room, shoulders drooping. Just outside the door, she gave one last pathetic sniffle.

As soon as she knew those in the breakfast parlor could no longer see her, she stopped and stood quietly, straining her ears to hear what was said.

"Well, Isabella, that was more than enough," Papa said. "I still think you are being too hard on the chit, but you're her mama, so I suppose you know best. Think I'll go to my club. No hysterics there." His chair scraped across the floor as he rose.

Chloe dashed down the hall and up the stairs to her bedchamber. Once there, she made sure that the sound of her door closing was loud enough to be heard in the breakfast parlor. She didn't exactly slam it.

Phaedra almost could pity her sister as she left the breakfast room, dejection in every line of her body. Some of it was genuine, she was sure, but she rather suspected that Chloe was over-dramatizing the situation for her own benefit.

"Phaedra, would you mind receiving our callers this afternoon?" Mama said, after Papa had departed. "I do not think I can maintain my composure before what promises to be an excess of concern over my poor, sick child today."

"Of course, Mama," she replied. "Cousin Louisa and I will handle all the callers. Why do you not have a short nap before you go to enlist the Duchess's aid?"

"I believe I shall. I did not sleep well last night." She pushed her half full plate away and rose." Oh yes, please do not visit your sister. I cannot forbid her father to visit her, but his sympathy is all she will receive, if I have my say."

"I will cooperate in her incarceration, Mama." She left unsaid her relief at being freed from Chloe's emotional outbursts for a while. At the same time, she knew she would miss Chloe. They had been inseparable for so long.

Mama squeezed her shoulder in passing. "I do realize, you know, what you have to put up with from your sister. But if you will not prevent it, Phaedra, how can I? You should not let her abuse your good nature so, my dear."

"Mama, I have been witness to so many of Chloe's tantrums that I hardly notice them. And my audience prevents you and Papa from having them inflicted upon you. I do not mind, truly. At least not usually." *She is older than I; why can she not act her age?* Resolutely Phaedra banished the unworthy thought.

She and Cousin Louisa settled themselves comfortably in the sewing room after breakfast. "Do you believe Chloe's actions last night will have serious repercussions?" Phaedra wondered aloud.

"I wish I knew. Her behavior will reflect negatively upon you."

"Mama has always been strict with her, but Papa was lenient and so indulgent. She could always get him to give her what she wished. I used to be dreadfully jealous." She laid her embroidery in her lap and stared sightlessly into the fire. "Now I am happy I was not so indulged. My expectations are far more realistic than my sister's."

"I do not remember her so willful as a child."

Phaedra hesitated before replying. "I do not think she was, not really. When we were small, she was always pleasing to be with. She was generous to a fault. Oh, she always wanted her own way, but I could usually cozen her into giving in when something was important to me. It has only been the last year or two that she has become so determined to do just as she pleases. She was dreadfully disappointed when her Season was postponed twice."

"I'll warrant the change in her behavior first came about when the young men in your neighborhood noticed she was no longer a child. You did say she was the local belle, I believe. She must have been the recipient of an abundance of flattery."

Phaedra nodded. "The experience must have given her such a sense of her own importance that she now believes the world must revolve around her,"

"If that is the case, there is hope she will come to her senses," Cousin Louisa said encouragingly. "Or she will not, and she will continue to outrage Society and ruin her chances for a good marriage." She paused, but then went on, her tone less optimistic. "Perhaps this enforced solitude will cause her to reconsider."

"I hope so," said Phaedra, doubtfully.

SHE BECAME VERY TIRED, THAT AFTERNOON, OF TELLING GENTLEMEN OF CHLOE'S ill health. Prevarication did not set well with her, and she was distressed to have to elaborate upon her sister's symptoms. Lord Everingham was particularly distressed. He bemoaned the fact he would not see her for at least a fortnight and confided to Phaedra that he did not know if he could survive the deprivation.

Lord Wilderlake was among the callers that afternoon. He expressed dismay at Chloe's illness, and requested that Phaedra relay his greetings and concern. Phaedra imagined he showed more than a friendly interest. She wished Chloe had met him before Lord Everingham, for he seemed far more responsible and mature.

Mr. Farwell arrived shortly after Wilderlake. Today he wore a purple satin waistcoat richly embroidered with flowers and small birds, a golden-tan coat with exaggerated shoulder pads and wide, pointed lapels. His inexpressibles were the palest lavender, and molded to his legs almost indecently. She caught herself admiring the long, well-defined muscles under the knit fabric and quickly looked away as her face grew hot. He expressed sorrow at Chloe's becoming ill in the middle of the Season. She thought she saw the hint of a smile in his eyes, and suspected he was aware of the deception.

She had little chance to speak to anyone for more than a few moments that afternoon, so full was the parlor with Chloe's admirers. When they had finally all departed, with promises to send books or flowers to cheer up the invalid, she dropped into a chair.

"I am exhausted. Do you realize I have managed to be charming for quite three hours. It was a chore, let me tell you. Oh, how I wish I could remain at home this evening, rather than attend Mrs. Stanfield's musicale."

"I know, my dear. But your mother expressly wishes you to be seen in public for the next while, so everyone will believe your sister is truly ill."

"If you could only know how I wish she was. No, I do not mean that. It is just that I hate having to lie."

Cousin Louisa patted her hand in sympathy. "It is in a good cause. No one is being harmed by it."

"You are right," Phaedra said. "But if I have to be on my best behavior all evening, I shall probably scream the moment we arrive home."

" I pray you will wait until then, my dear. There are those who will be watching you very closely tonight, to see if you are behaving correctly. You are, unfortunately, going to suffer somewhat for your sister's sins."

Phaedra managed to behave the perfect lady that evening, but only by a tremendous effort of will. Many times she had to bite her tongue when someone made a disparaging remark about her sister. Several ladies cut her dead.

Even Mrs. Graham made a point of commenting on Chloe's absence. "My dear Miss Hazelbourne, I do hope your sister's, ah, excessive high spirits last evening were not a cause of her unexpected illness," the languid lady remarked.

"What do you mean?" Phaedra did her best not to bristle. *I do not like this woman. I believe she thrives on others' misfortunes.*

"I just wondered if perhaps she was being kept in her bed to recover from the strenuous exercise she had at the ball. Why, I distinctly saw her dance the waltz."

"Yes, Mrs. Graham, she did. I also danced the waltz, but am not exhausted."

"I did not see her waltz at Almack's last Wednesday, so I thought that perhaps she had some physical impairment that prevented it," the lady purred.

Phaedra opened her mouth, but her angry response was halted by Cousin

Louisa.

"Why Mrs. Graham, I do believe I saw your daughter looking for you in the refreshment room. If you will excuse us, I wish to introduce Miss Phaedra to an old friend of mine."

She pulled Phaedra away with an iron grip upon her wrist. "You must not let her cause you to say something indiscreet, my dear. She would repeat it all over Town. Come, I wish you to meet Colonel Peterson, who was a friend of my father's." She led the girl across the room to where an elderly gentleman with bushy white hair sat scowling upon the company.

To her surprise, the scowling face of Colonel Peterson hid a jolly spirit. She took him in immediate liking and they sat talking until the music began again. After the last pianist had performed, she sought out her hostess and took her leave, pleading sleepiness.

"I quite understand, Miss Hazelbourne," Mrs. Stanfield told her, shaking her hand. "I hear that the Duchess' ball did not end until three this morning, so you must be at the point of exhaustion. Please give my regards to your mother and tell your sister I hope she will recover quickly. Mrs. Arbuckle, so glad you could join us."

In the carriage, Phaedra and Cousin Louisa both breathed sighs of relief. "Well, we made it through one evening without catastrophe," the older woman said. "Only thirteen more to go."

Phaedra chuckled, albeit a bit wryly. "So we did. I thank you for preventing me from insulting Mrs. Graham. I vow, I wanted to slap her silly face. Why could she not just say right out that she had heard my sister had misbehaved?"

"That is not the way of the *ton*, my dear. All must be polite and gently spoken. A frontal attack would be unmannerly. You will no doubt be faced with much worse than Mrs. Graham before the fortnight is out. I overheard Lady Detweiler telling someone that Lady Everingham had called Chloe fast."

"How dare she!"

"Lady Everingham dares anything. And she has taken your sister in intense dislike, it seems."

"And I her. The old bat!"

"My dear, you will be hard pushed to keep your temper in the next two weeks. The Duchess has heard that Lady Everingham has vowed to her bosom bows that she will destroy Chloe's reputation. Your mother was vastly overset and threatened to return to the country tomorrow. It was only by convincing her that to do so would be to give up all hopes of either of you making good marriages that the Duchess was able to calm her."

"Poor Mama. So that is why she had the headache and did not come to dinner."

"Yes, and your father is out of sorts because she is. But that may be all to the good, for I think that if he sees how Chloe's behavior truly distresses your mother, he will be less forgiving with her."

"I hope so. She needs to learn a lesson." She bit her lip. "It is just so unfair! How can people be so unkind, when all my sister did was go against a few unwritten rules."

"Unfair it may be, but those unwritten rules have their uses. Society's strictures on behavior are intended to ensure that no nobleman marries someone unsuitable to be his wife and that there is no question about the paternity of his heirs. Once an heir is produced, many gentlemen actually encourage their wives to take lovers, you know."

"But those cannot be love matches!"

"Of course they are not. You, I am sure, will never find yourself in such a situation, because I think that when you marry, it will be for love. But do you really expect your sister to require love in addition to a title and a fortune? She seems almost desperate to marry soon."

"She is, for she found the delay in her come out difficult. She perceives that only married women have any sort of freedom of behavior." Phaedra could not refrain from giving vent to a heartfelt sigh. "I would prefer to believe otherwise, or at least hope so. Poor Chloe. To have her life ruined because she is impatient with convention and eager for all life has to offer. How can anyone really believe she has done anything immoral?"

"By the time Lady Everingham is finished spreading her lies and innuendos, some will have no doubt she is both fast and loose, I am afraid. There are always those who are ready to believe the worst of anyone. Even those who do not entirely believe the rumors will wonder if there was not, perhaps, some basis for them. Unfortunately, the gentlemen who will avoid Chloe are not the ones with whom we should be concerned," Cousin Louisa continued. "It is those who will be drawn to her by the hint of scandal who worry me."

"What do you mean?"

"There are gentlemen who would take advantage of a young girl, who would use her badly and then cast her aside. They do not seek wives, but conquests. Chloe will almost certainly become the target of some of these. She may already have come to their attention, in fact. She informed me today that she had engaged to drive with Mr. Dervigne on Monday, and asked me to send him her regrets."

"But Mama forbade her."

"Your mother forbade her to ride with him unchaperoned. I believe Chloe had convinced him to take her up in his landau, for the weather promises to be fair. Betty was to accompany her."

"I'll wager Mama knew nothing of this."

"Perhaps. Chloe may have intentionally misled both your mother and Mr. Dervigne. However, all is moot, for she will not be riding with him."

Phaedra screwed up her face, as she would when biting into something unpleasant. "I do not like Mr. Dervigne. His manner is not pleasing. One could almost call him oily."

"Neither do I care for him. I suspect, though with little basis for my suspicions, that Mr. Dervigne's intentions toward your sister are less than honorable. I have heard whispers about his misconduct with a young woman last Season. Unfortunately, the blame for the situation was laid entirely at her door, so that she was forced to retire to the country, her reputation in tatters."

"How terrible! We must not let that happen. How can we protect Chloe?"

"Your mother and I are prepared to select very carefully all who approach her once she is allowed to go about again. She will be forbidden to go anywhere with Mr. Dervigne, in particular, even chaperoned. Unfortunately, it will take Chloe's cooperation."

"I wish we had never come to London."

The carriage pulled up in front of their house just then. Once inside and divested of their cloaks, Phaedra sagged.

Cousin Louisa must have noticed, for she gave Phaedra a gentle nudge toward the stairs. "Do not let yourself lose sleep worrying. We will come through this, I am sure. Good night, my dear."

"Good night, Cousin Louisa. Oh, how good my bed will feel tonight. I am so tired." She mounted the stairs slowly, stopping at the top of the first flight to lean over the banister. "What will we do if Chloe will not heed us?"

"Let your mother and father worry about that. You are not Chloe's keeper, you know. Go to bed."

"No, but sometimes I think I am her conscience," Phaedra whispered to herself as she entered her bedroom. "And I wish I were not."

CHAPTER NINE

CHLOE, LOCKED IN HER BEDCHAMBER AND DEPRIVED OF HER SISTER'S COMPANY, spent the first two days of her incarceration alternately weeping and pacing the floor in rage. She had broken all the vases in the room the first day, throwing them one by one against the door that kept her confined.

Mama, seeing the shards, merely said, "How unfortunate. Now you have nothing to hold your admirers' bouquets," in a bored tone, and commanded Betty to bring a broom. She had not required the maid to clean up the mess, however, nor had she caused the vases to be replaced. Chloe therefore received none of the many bouquets which were sent to her. Mama described them in great detail, thus providing her with another source of anger and resentment.

Papa attempted on several occasions to jolly her with teasing, promises of many parties to come, and affectionate pats and hugs. Believing her father an unwilling accomplice in her imprisonment, she was somewhat more responsive to him. She could not entirely forgive him, though. If he truly loved her, he would order Mama to release her from imprisonment.

After two days of simmering resentment, Chloe's mood had calmed enough so she could accept that her mother truly did believe she was acting in her best interests. *But Mama does not understand. She has forgotten, if ever she knew, how miserable it is to be an unmarried girl and have to watch one's every move.* She thought of several ways to convince her parents to release her, but discarded each after admitting that Mama would not be fooled for an instant.

By the fourth day, Chloe was desperate. Time was slipping away. Time she could have been using to fix some gentleman's interest. Time that postponed the day when she would have the freedom of being a married woman.

She had not yet received an offer, a fact that worried her only a little. She was confident either Mr. Martin or Lord Everingham could be brought up to scratch whenever she desired. Perhaps even Lord Wilderlake, of lesser rank than Jeremy, but so much more handsome. He had shown interest at her ball. As she fretted about the time she was losing, Chloe finally had an idea.

PHAEDRA DAILY DID HER BEST TO IGNORE THE SNUBS SHE ENCOUNTERED WHEREVER she went. When asked about her sister's health, she painted a doleful picture of Chloe's illness. Having suffered the influenza the previous winter but one, she was able to describe such symptoms as Chloe was supposed to be undergoing. Lord Everingham offered to send his mother's personal physician. Lord Wilderlake sent books and music to cheer her up and always inquired closely about the progress of her illness.

Mr. Farwell also frequently inquired about Chloe. His inquiries were more a matter of form than sincerity, she decided, not liking the hint of mockery she fancied she heard in his tone.

Chloe's incarceration had been in force for five days when the Hazelbournes again attended Almack's. Their vouchers had not been rescinded as Lady Gifford had feared. Phaedra faced the evening with reluctance, fearing that Lady Everingham would be present. She and her chaperones wore their most ravishing gowns, as if armored for battle.

Lady Mary and Mr. Farwell were sitting with the Duchess when they entered the hallowed halls. Mr. Farwell promptly rose and bowed, saying, "Ah, Miss Phaedra. I have been awaiting you. I wished to petition you for the first waltz." He took her dance card from her hand. "And a quadrille."

"And I for the second," came a voice from behind her. Lord Wilderlake stood there.

She smiled. "How nice you both are. I had not thought to waltz this evening, but..."

"But nothing, Miss Phaedra. I have been looking forward to this evening since your ball," Wilderlake told her. "May I also request the first country dance?"

"Of course." She smiled and handed him her dance card.

Colonel Peterson joined them just then. "Came to see if you wished to give me a dance or two, young lady. Enjoyed your conversation the other night. Wanted to continue it," he said with a scowl.

"Why yes, Colonel. I would enjoy it."

Several other gentlemen came up just then. Before she knew it, her card was full and she had to refuse Lord Everingham a second set. She could not believe that she had become so popular and told herself it was because Chloe was not present. Had she been, the gentlemen would have all preferred her company. To her surprise, none of them asked about Chloe except Lord Wilderlake and Lord Everingham.

Mr. Farwell claimed her for the first waltz. "You seem to be enjoying yourself," he said, as he spun her into the dance. "Could it be that you can relax, now that you do not need to wonder what outrageous act your sister will commit next?"

"Of course not. I am enjoying myself because I have had every dance claimed and everyone is so kind. This past week..."

"This past week has been hellish for you hasn't it Phaedra?"

"How silly you are, Mr. Farwell" she replied, airily. "It has been rather enjoyable. Of course, I have been worrying about my sister, but Mama has said that I must not let her illness inhibit my social life."

"False coin, my dear. You have been snubbed and forced to turn a deaf ear to hints of scandal. I'll wager that your sister is no more ill than I am."

She was silent through several more turns. When she looked up into his face, she saw none of the usual ennui, no scorn. Only sympathy. "It has been horrible" she admitted. "How did you know?"

"I have eyes and ears. And I saw your sister's actions at the ball. But come, let us not dwell on it. You have many friends who will stand by you. Forget your sister and enjoy this evening for yourself. Be happy."

"I would like that." She attempted to relax and enjoy the dance.

Later Phaedra danced with Mr. Martin and with Lord Everingham, who several times when the pattern brought them together cleared his throat as if he was about to speak. Afterward he escorted her back to her mama's side. As he bowed over her hand, he said, "Miss Phaedra, I wonder if—" The rest of his words were lost as Lord Wainwright joined them.

That young man was inclined to be heavy-footed, especially upon his partner's toes. When the set ended, Phaedra wanted nothing more than to sit a while and rest. Instead she waltzed with Lord Wilderlake next, finding him light on his feet but somehow less exciting to dance with than Mr. Farwell.

As they circled, he informed her that he would be away from Town for a few days. " Please tell your sister I hope she will be recovered by the time I return to Town. I will call on her then."

"I shall. I, too, hope she will recover soon, but Mama thinks it will be at least another week before she is able to have company."

To her great relief, the next set was promised to Colonel Peterson, who asked her if she would mind sitting it out so they could converse. The Colonel offered to fetch her some punch to drink while they chatted and she gratefully accepted his offer. While she awaited his return, she noticed Lord Everingham approaching her. His determined expression brought a certain character to his sheeplike countenance.

Oh, no, I cannot listen to more of his concern for Chloe. But the young lord's path was blocked by Mr. Farwell, who grasped his arm and held him while he spoke. Judging by Everingham's glare, he did not care for what he was hearing. When he pulled away and attempted to move in her direction once again, Phaedra realized that Mr. Farwell was forcibly restraining the earl from approaching.

She watched with some curiosity as Mr. Farwell forced Everingham into a chair and stood over him speaking with some emphasis. The Colonel returned just then, and Phaedra was constrained to give him her full attention, little as she wished to.

Reggie knew Phaedra was watching his encounter with Everingham. A good thing she was seated far enough away that she would not hear them. He leaned close to the earl, keeping his voice low. "You young fool. You have already caused enough trouble for that family. You danced with Miss Phaedra once, and that is enough. I will not have her the object of your mother's vicious rumor mongering!"

"But I just wanted to talk to her about Chloe. There is no harm in that. My mother would not mind." Everingham attempted once again to approach Phaedra.

"We are not going to take the chance." Reggie tightened his hold and forced him into a nearby chair. "Sit down, my lord, and listen to me." He repeated some of the gossip he had heard just that evening.

"I say! No one would believe—"

"You think not? Perhaps you should listen more closely to what is being said here tonight. Even in the clubs this afternoon, I heard Miss Hazelbourne's name bandied about. I have no doubt that her behavior at the Duchess' ball was a delicious tit-bit in many a drawing room, and will continue to be the center of a storm of gossip until a new scandal replaces it."

Everingham attempted to stand, but Reggie held him in the chair. "You young fool! It is to your thoughtlessness that is to blame, as much as Miss Hazelbourne's *naïveté*."

"I have done nothing wrong!"

"Perhaps not, but I have no doubt your mother was the source of most of those rumors. Although, to give the devil his due, there are many in the *ton* ready to embroider what they hear. They will continue to do so, until Miss Chloe Hazelbourne's reputation is in shreds." Seeing a stubborn denial on the younger man's face, he demanded," Who took her into the shrubbery, out of sight and unchaperoned?"

"We only walked in the garden. All perfectly innocent."

"I don't doubt it. But your mother saw more than innocence, and had no compunction about saying so publicly. You then compounded the problem by dancing with her three times at the Duchess' ball. Worse yet, you waltzed with her, a move of incredible stupidity. You knew she hadn't permission to do so."

"But—"

"You know the rules, Everingham. You have been on the Town these past three years, You must be aware of how the *ton* relishes even a hint of scandal. Miss Hazelbourne is in her first Season and has never been in Society. She is the veriest innocent. If you did not mean ill by her, you should have better protected her name. Now go away. I want to take a nap." He sat in the chair next to Lord Everingham and let his chin fall to his chest.

From under lowered lids, he watched Everingham return to his mother's side, wearing a thoughtful expression. Whatever he said did not please her. The glare she cast in Phaedra's direction was hot enough to scorch.

AFTER HER FAMILY ABANDONED HER TO DISPORT THEMSELVES AT ALMACK'S, CHLOE realized she was to be incarcerated forever, and would never be given another chance on the Marriage Mart. The next morning she took matters into her own hands.

ALL WAS SILENT AS SHE SAT IN HER ROOM, WATCHING THE HANDS OF THE CLOCK creep around the dial. A note, delivered to her by a conspiratorial Betty, had informed her that rescue would be waiting in the mews at two o'clock in the morning. If she could not escape from the house without being detected, she was to set two candles in her window. On seeing the candles, her hero would depart, but would return each night until she was able to meet him.

She was practically quaking with anticipation. Her own note, smuggled out by Betty, had described in great and inspired detail how her parents had imprisoned her, were feeding her on the poorest table scraps, and had signified their intention of setting her free only after the Season had ended. Would not dear, kind Jeremy please come to her rescue? She had even managed to squeeze a few tears out of her eyes, to leave their stains upon the note.

Her parents and sister had returned from a soiree shortly after midnight, and now Chloe was waiting for the household to become quiet. She had the candles ready, but hoped she would not have to use them. A small portmanteau was packed with extra clothing, in case she would be able to put her plans into effect. For Chloe, believing that her mother was right insofar as she said that Lady Everingham's gossip had cast serious doubts upon her innocence, had resolved to elope with Lord Everingham.

Revenge, she was certain, would be sweet.

The household had been silent for some time when the clock struck the quarter before two. She opened her door, glad that she had rubbed butter from the bread served her at supper upon its hinges. She had more butter, wrapped in a twist of paper, to apply to the kitchen door and to the gate that opened onto the mews.

Chloe crept quietly down the servants' stairs and into the kitchen. The door opened quietly after she had liberally smeared its hinges, and she passed into the small moonlit garden She hesitated a moment before crossing the open space, and then hurried to the back wall. Again she applied butter to hinges and, this time, to the lock as well. Her actions were rewarded, for the gate opened silently. She slid through, pushing the gate closed behind her, and hoped no one would notice it was unlocked until well into the morrow.

The mews was dark. She started when a horse stamped and shivered at the rustling of mice in the straw. Her heart leapt in fear when a shadow detached itself from beside the stables. The next instant, she breathed a sigh of relief as Lord Everingham stepped into the moonlight. He held out his arms and she ran into them, dropping the portmanteau with a soft thud.

"Let us go elsewhere so we can talk. Is your carriage nearby?" she whispered.

"No, I took a hackney to the next street over. I did not wish to arouse anyone with the sound of my coach." He lowered his head and kissed her cheek, a gentle, undemanding touch of warm lips.

Chloe relaxed against him, wondering if she should return his embrace. "Let us go to it at once. We must not risk anyone's finding us here."

He hesitated.

"Please, Jeremy," she said, in a low, tremulous voice. "I must speak with you and we dare not risk being heard."

He led her along the shadowed street to the hackney. Handing her into its shabby interior, he commanded the driver to take them to Hyde Park.

"In the middle o' the night?"

"Do as I tell you, my man. There will be an extra something in it for you if you'll take us to the park and just drive around until I tell you otherwise," Everingham promised.

"Oi'll wager that the watch'll not leave us be, in the park and all," the man protested.

"Oh, very well, just drive around somewhere. Get to it, man." Lord Everingham pulled the door closed as he entered, cutting off what little light had reached the interior. "Now, my dear Chloe, what is it you wished to tell me? Why were you incarcerated? Are you quite sure that you have recovered?"

She hated the suspicion in his tone. "I was never ill! My wicked family locked me away because I was becoming more popular than my sister. She has always been my parents' favorite. They did not like it that all the gentlemen were paying more attention to me than to her. So they locked me in my room until she could attach a serious suitor," she concluded, with a heartrending sob.

"How wicked. Your mother seems such a nice lady."

"Oh, she is nice enough. It is my sister who is wicked. Mama and Papa will do anything she asks of them." She reached out and clasped his hands. "Jeremy, dear Jeremy, will you not save me from my evil sister?"

"I would do anything to prevent your tears, my sweet Chloe," he vowed. "But I cannot take you away from your parents like this. They could have the law on me."

"Jeremy, you could take me from them, and the law would have nothing to say about it."

"How?"

Although she could see his face only as a pale oval in the darkness, Chloe could imagine the bewildered expression on his sheeplike countenance. "Why, we could elope. If I were your wife, my parents would no longer have control over me. And I would be from under the terrible domination of my wicked sister."

"But my mother!" His voice was irresolute, as if he was having difficulty breathing. "What would she say?"

"You are of age, are you not? Does she hold the purse strings?"

"Well, no...but...but I could never marry without her blessing."

"Why not?" She withdrew her hands from his. "Are you afraid of your mother?"

If he was, she knew he would never admit it. "It just seems such a shabby trick to play on her," he said, with some hesitation.

Chloe was convinced that no trick was too shabby to play on the nasty Lady Everingham. She said nothing, only sniffed and let a small sob escape.

"Oh, Chloe, do not cry. Please."

"I will stop now," she replied, with a hiccup. "I will be strong. You had better return me to my house, because if you will not assist me, I must try to steal back inside before the servants are astir."

"I want to help you. It's just that..."

"I understand, Lord Everingham. You care more for your mother than you do for me. And you were so convincing when you swore eternal devotion." Again she reached tentatively to touch his hand. And sniffed.

"Oh, please, Chloe. Do not cry again. Please." He captured her hands and put them to his lips.

Chloe found the soft pressure of his mouth pleasant, but vaguely disappointing. Surely she should be thrilled.

He tightened his clasp. "Confound it, I'll do it!"

"You will? You really will?"

"Yes. But I must fetch my coach and prepare for the trip." His voice strengthened.

Now that her eyes were becoming accustomed to the near-darkness inside the hackney, she could see that his chin had gone up and his shoulders back. He was determined, at least. But would he be able to carry through with such a daring plan?

"How will you obtain your coach without your mother knowing? How will you explain your absence?"

She rather imagined that he would have strutted had be been elsewhere. "My mother knows that I plan an early start tomorrow—no, it is today, now. I will visit a friend of mine in Hertsfordshire, and attend a mill the day after tomorrow. She will not be surprised if I take the coach, rather than my curricle. And Smith, my groom, will drive us if I bribe him to do so."

"Oh, marvelous. What shall I do while you are fetching your coach?"

"You will remain in this hackney. I shall require him to take you toward the edge of town. You will be perfectly safe, since I intend to reward him amply for his cooperation." Now that he was in command of the situation, Lord Everingham showed surprising enterprise.

When Chloe said, with a melting look, "Oh Jeremy, you are so clever," his chest expanded and his chin went up a notch. She leaned forward and kissed his cheek, finding the action not at all unpleasant.

Their hastily made plans were carried out forthwith. It was scarce four o'clock in the morning when the elegant coach belonging to the Earl of Everingham met an anonymous hackney on the north side of Regents Park.

CHAPTER TEN

PHAEDRA WAS BUSY ALL MORNING, HAVING FALLEN BEHIND IN HER CORRESPONDENCE with other amateur botanists. Her mama and Cousin Louisa had gone shopping. Papa was also away from the house, gone to Tattersall's with an old crony. So when Edgemont came to her with word that her sister's bed had not been slept in, it was well past noon. By the time Mama returned home, she and the staff had searched the entire house, with no success. Chloe was gone. There was no note or anything to indicate where she had gone, with whom, or when she had departed.

Upon being questioned, Betty had stammered forth a disjointed explanation. All she knew, she insisted, was that she had delivered Chloe's note to the doorman at a club with a brass plate having letters that matched those on the note. "I don't read so good, mum," she wept, when pressed for the club's name. "No'm, I didn't wake her this morning. She told me not to."

Lady Gifford scolded her roundly for carrying the note, but shook her head when Edgemont asked if he should let her go. "I suppose I cannot really blame her," she admitted to Cousin Louisa and Phaedra when the grateful but still weeping maid had returned belowstairs. "Chloe can be very convincing."

"She probably bribed the girl" Phaedra said. "It would not be the first time, but always before what she asked was harmless—extra care with her garments, or a sweet before bedtime."

"I wish you had told me," her mama said.

"Mama!"

"No, I can see that you would not. You've never borne tales against your sister."

Feeling guilty as well as angry, Phaedra retired to a corner of the parlor and picked up her embroidery. She would rather have been out searching for her sister, but where would she go? After picking out the same flower three times, she gave up and paced the floor.

After a while, Mama returned with the news that Chloe's hairbrush and toothbrush were missing, as well as her nightdress, a morning dress, and the white and pink ball gown. "All of her jewelry is gone, too."

Edgemont came to the door. "Perhaps a portmanteau is also missing, my lady. However, the box room is so crowded that I could not be sure without taking everything out and counting."

"So she has indeed run away. Where can she be?" Mama's voice was almost firm, although her lip trembled.

"With one of her suitors, I'll warrant," Phaedra said. "She would never be foolish enough to travel about London unattended or unescorted. She has made no female friends, so she must be in the company of a man."

"But which one, and when did she leave?"

Seeing her mama very near tears. Phaedra knelt before her and took her hands. "Mama, please attempt to calm yourself," she said quietly. "We will find my sister, you know. I am certain we will learn she has been safe ever since she left this house."

Mama sipped tea, choked. When she had done with coughing, she said, "What if she has been in some gentleman's company overnight?"

Cousin Louisa handed Mama a glass of brandy. "There is nothing else to do. She will be compromised and he must marry her."

Phaedra had a terrible notion. "Perhaps that was all along her motive."

At these words, Mama did burst into tears. Phaedra pulled her into a close embrace. "Mama, please do not cry. You know how she was determined to marry as quickly as possible. Perhaps she was able to convince one of her court to elope. She could have concocted some outrageous tale of persecution and the poor besotted fool would have been honor-bound to rescue her."

"Have Betty back in here," suggested Cousin Louisa. "Perhaps she knows more than she is telling us."

Betty was summoned and questioned again. While the inquisition was underway, Papa burst into the room.

"What has happened? Isabella, love, are you all right? I came as soon as I had your note." He enfolded his wife in his arms.

Lady Gifford wiped her eyes. "Oh, George, it's Chloe."

"What's Chloe? Has she again done something to upset you?"

"She is disappeared."

"What?"

Phaedra handed him a glass of brandy which he immediately drank down. "Please sit down and listen, Papa." She gave him a gentle push toward the sofa. "Mama, drink your brandy, too. You will feel more the thing." If only she dared take a glass of the potent spirits herself, but someone had to remain calm.

"Will someone tell me what is going on?" Papa demanded when Mama's disjointed explanation faltered.

"Chloe's disappeared, but no one knows how or when." Cousin Louisa related how they had discovered Chloe's absence and what they had done since then.

"We fear she convinced one of her suitors to elope with her," Phaedra added, when Cousin Louisa faltered. "Chloe could well have convinced herself that she would not be permitted to marry this season."

At first Papa refused to believe that his favorite daughter's actions might have been less than above reproach. Only when Mama agreed that an elopement was the most likely scenario did he finally become convinced.

"What time was she last seen? Did you say good night to her, Phaedra?"

"Yes, shortly after we came in last night. I did not go into her bedchamber, but she replied to my knock. That was nearly midnight."

Papa paced the length of the room and back. "I'll contact the Watch, ask if a respectable young woman was seen abroad during the night."

"Perhaps we should send a note to your Aunt Margaret. She may be able to help us," Mama suggested.

Papa dispatched his note and ordered Edgemont to confine all servants to the house so they could not gossip abroad. The butler returned a little later to inform them that Jem Coachman, while searching the garden and mews for any clue to Chloe's disappearance, had discovered an unlocked gate.

Papa paced. Mama sat on the sofa and wrung her hands. Phaedra was taken thoroughly aback at the change in her parents, who were usually the most calm and confident people she knew.

At least cousin Louisa seemed calm. "Our first task is to find out who she is with, if for no other reason than to relieve your parents' minds."

Nodding, Phaedra said, "It would help if we knew when she left the house."

Papa stopped his pacing. " If it happened last night, we might as well wait for them to return," he said, his voice breaking on the last few words, "for they'll have too great of a head start for us to catch 'em"

"Many of her most faithful suitors may be away from Town," Phaedra contributed. "Lord Wilderlake told me he was to attend a mill somewhere to the north. Mr. Martin mentioned it as well, as did several others of her usual dancing partners."

"None of those gentlemen were at last night's soiree," Cousin Louisa said. "She could be with any of them."

The clock struck two. Mama made a small hopeless sound and Papa slammed his fist onto the desk. "They've been gone at least twelve hours. We'll never catch them."

Just then the Duchess was announced. When she entered, Mama wailed, "Oh, Your Grace, I am so glad to see you. You must help us. Chloe has eloped!"

Her Grace's mouth dropped open and she stared for a moment before recovering her usual *sang froid*. "Headed for Scotland, I'll not doubt. The silly chit! I was afraid she would do idiotish, when I saw how willful she was. Isabella, that one was too often unspanked as a child."

"I know that, but it is now too late. What are we to do?"

The Duchess settled herself in a comfortable chair. "First thing, stop that caterwauling. You might as well resign yourself that the chit's to be wed. 'Twould be nice to know the identity of your son-in-law-to-be, though."

Mama's sobs increased in intensity and Papa pressed a comforting hand upon her shoulder.

Cousin Louisa related the conclusions they had reached.

"Good God! That does complicate matters," the duchess said. "No way to know who she's with if all her suitors are out of Town."

"My lord," Edgemont said from the doorway, "here is news. A stableboy saw a cloaked figure stealing from the mews sometime after midnight."

Papa went with the butler to question the lad further. The women waited in worried silence. Phaedra wanted to offer her mama words of hope, but found none within herself. When Papa returned, all looked expectantly at him.

He shook his head.

Papa paced. Cousin Louisa embroidered. Mama sat with her embroidery in her lap, but instead of plying a needle, her fingers plucked nervously at the cloth. Phaedra forced herself to sit still, although she wanted to go outside and run as far and as fast as she could. The silence went on for an intolerable time. At last it was broken by loud knocking at the front door. Again they waited.

Hoped.

Edgemont entered, holding a silver salver, after a few minutes. "This note just arrived, my lord. 'Tis from the Master of the Watch."

Papa unfolded it with a shaking hand. "Thank God!" he said, after a moment.

"What is it, George? What does it say?"

"It seems a young man hired a hackney to bring him here, or rather to the next street over. The hackney waited while the man disappeared for some minutes. When he returned, he was accompanied by a woman, hooded but the driver swears she was young.

"They drove around for nearly an hour, before the young man was dropped in St. James Street and the young woman was taken to Regents Park, where she waited in the coach for nearly an hour. Eventually a coach with a crest on the door met them, and the pair departed in it. That was around four this morning. The driver did not recognize the crest, but he was able to describe it well enough that the Master recognized it." He pursed his lips and frowned. "Everingham. He's not whom I'd have chosen, but at lest he's respectable."

Phaedra sat mute as the others babbled. *Poor Chloe. She'll be well paid for her foolishness. Her life will be uncomfortable, to say the least, with Lady Everingham as a mother-in-law.*

The Duchess called them to order after a few minutes of confusion. "Four o'clock this morning. It is three of the afternoon now. You've little chance of catching her, George. Isabella, I suggest you start planning a wedding."

Mama's expression was woebegone as she looked across the room at Phaedra. "Oh, darling, I am so sorry."

"Sorry? Why?"

"Enough, Isabella," the duchess said. "We'll come about with no great harm done, as long as the silly chit marries. I do wish you will allow me to send for Reggie Farwell, though. He may be able to assist us."

"Oh, your Grace, how could that fop be of any help?" Phaedra said.

"I do not like it, Your Grace," Papa protested. "What is the guarantee that he will not broadcast the story at his club? I've a poor impression of that overdressed fribble and do not want my daughter's escapade to become the latest *on dit* of St. James Street."

"Reggie is a very resourceful young man," the Duchess told him. "He will not tattle, George. You may rest easy on that score. Fetch a footman, Phaedra," she said, and went to the small escritoire in the corner.

A footman was dispatched with Her Grace's hurriedly written note. Again the family waited, but now the Duchess directed the conversation along other paths. She related several humorous tales of minor scandals among the *ton*, and generally kept their minds off of their problems for as much as two or three minutes at a time.

By the time Mr. Farwell arrived, rain was falling heavily. He entered, shaking droplets from his greatcoat. As Edgemont helped him off with it, he was quickly informed of the situation.

"I am amazed that Everingham would defy his mother sufficiently to be considered a suspect," Farwell said.

"As am I," the Duchess agreed, "but the driver's description of the crest certainly points toward him."

"What about Robert Dervigne?" Cousin Louisa said. There was a dead silence for a few seconds.

"No! By gad!" Papa exploded. "If he's harmed her..."

"She would not! Oh, George, tell me that she would not go with him!" his wife cried.

Phaedra said nothing, but she grew very pale and was forced to sink into a chair.

Mr. Farwell broke into the babble to say, "Dervigne is not the guilty party." At their disbelieving stares, he continued, "Man's a rake and a seducer of innocents, but he ain't stupid enough to get himself in a situation where he'd have to marry the girl. Which this would be. No, he's not the one—this time."

"Are you sure?"

"He was walking past White's as I emerged, just minutes ago." Again he waited until he had everyone's attention. "Unless there's a dark horse in the running, it's Everingham."

"Must we simply sit here and wait until they return? Oh, George, I cannot stand it," Mama cried.

"Neither shall you have to, my love. I will immediately drive out along the Great North Road and see what I can learn. We've still a few hours of light. Edgemont," he called. To the others he said, "I'll bring her home to be wed. My daughter's not going to be jumping an anvil. Not if I have a say."

"Yes, my lord," the butler said as he opened the parlor door.

"Have the horses put to at once. I depart immediately."

"Wait, my lord," Reggie said. "I have a racing curricle, and could make better time than you in your coach."

"If you do not fall asleep," Phaedra said softly.

"I shall not, Miss Phaedra, you may be assured. I never sleep while driving."

"I appreciate the offer young man, but she is my daughter. Would you take me on your curricle?" Papa said.

"Of course, my lord. I will pick you up here within the half-hour." He bowed to the ladies and left them.

Lord Gifford called Edgemont back to rescind his order for the coach and went upstairs to change into buckskins for the trip. The Duchess resumed her recitation, relating some really shocking *on dits*. Even Mama was interested in the tales, despite her distress.

Phaedra was initially embarrassed, for some of what the duchess related was quite warm, but as the recitation continued, she found she was rather enjoying the stories. They were neither vindictive nor slanderous, and were often quite humorous. She had had no idea that so much went on behind the respectable scenes of Society.

How unfair! Everything Chloe did was mild and innocent in comparison.

When Papa re-entered, he kissed Mama gently but thoroughly. "I'm off, Isabella. Try not to worry."

Phaedra ran ahead to the front door. Outside Mr. Farwell, in sensible buckskins and a riding jacket, was holding the reins of a pair of powerful, restive blacks. Phaedra went to the side of his curricle and held up her hand. As he took it, she said, "Mr. Farwell, I must apologize for my unkind remark. I sincerely appreciate what you are doing for my family. I wish you godspeed."

He leaned over and kissed her hand, causing her to snatch it from him. "I do this for you, Phaedra, not for your family nor for your sister's reputation. See you remember that." Before she could answer, she was shouldered aside by her father, who mounted quickly.

"Spring 'em, Farwell," he said, and the curricle raced away.

Phaedra's hand burned as she returned to the parlor. As she entered, a thought struck her and she laughed, somewhat hysterically. "She could not think of Everingham kissing her, because he looks like a sheep And now she will marry him. Oh, Mama, this is too much!"

CHAPTER ELEVEN

Lord Everingham's shiny black coach was well sprung and the squabs were of blue velvet. Chloe had never ridden in a more comfortable or more elegant equipage. She was sure she would not become sick in such a luxurious vehicle. In fact, she was determined not to, for she did not wish to give Lord Everingham a disgust of her. Gentlemen had little patience with ladies who did not travel well. Pleading the ravages of a night without sleep, she begged her suitor's indulgence and curled herself into a corner of the comfortable seat.

She slept until the first change of horses. While waiting for a new team to be brought to them, the coachman suggested that breakfast was in order.

"I think not," Lord Everingham told him. "Ask the landlord for some bread and cheese and a jug of ale. I want us to be farther from London before we make an extended stop."

Chloe could tell the coachman was not well pleased at being deprived of a hearty breakfast. For herself, she was content to nibble at a piece of dry bread, knowing that anything more substantial would not set well in a moving coach. Her queasy stomach was better after her sleep, but she still did not feel entirely well.

The journey resumed. Soon they were dozing in opposite corners of the coach. For some reason, now that they were alone, she could find very little to say to Jeremy. He seemed similarly lacking in conversation. The long and tiring night had put dark circles under his eyes and deepened the creases beside his mouth. Oddly enough, he looked less sheeplike this morning.

Shortly after one in the afternoon, the coach drew into yet another inn yard. The coachman opened the door. "My lord, it will be a while before they can ready a fresh team for us. There will be time luncheon. Shall I ask the innkeeper to prepare a parlor for you?"

Everingham yawned. "Yes. I confess I am feeling sharp set. Miss Hazelbourne, would you care to alight?"

Chloe, feeling the need to refresh herself, agreed. She was met by the innkeeper's wife who pointed her to the ladies' necessary. When she emerged, she was directed to the private parlor taken by Lord Everingham.

He was standing at the window, a tankard in his hand. For the first time, she saw him as the man she might spend the rest of her life with. *I must begin as I am to go on.*

But a small niggle of doubt ate at her. Was she certain she really wanted to be Lady Everingham for the next thirty or forty years?

"Jeremy, I am so tired of traveling. How much farther must we go today?"

"As far as possible, my love. We are sure to be pursued."

"I do not think so. I left no note, so no one will know where I have gone."

"But surely someone will seek you?"

"Probably, but how will they know where to search? Can we not stay here until tomorrow? Please?" She put on her most beguiling expression. She knew that if she ate luncheon, she would become sick if forced back into a moving carriage. And she was very hungry.

"No, my precious, we must continue. I would like to be well north of Hertfordshire before we halt for the night."

"Oh, very well, but I do so hate the idea of traveling farther today."

Luncheon was brought in just then, and they applied themselves to it. Unfortunately for Chloe, the meat pie was dominated by greasy mutton. Overcome with hunger, she ate a few bites. Surely so little would not affect her digestion.

But it did. They were scarce on the road for a quarter hour when her stomach began protesting. She relaxed into the squabs, hoping that she would be able to control her nausea. Lord Everingham, awake now, began to tell Chloe about his estate in Warwickshire. She managed to maintain her composure for nearly an hour, due mostly to the fact that the road remained relatively smooth. But inevitably the coach reached a bumpy, uneven stretch of roadway. Her rebellious stomach immediately made itself felt. She moaned.

Everingham was instantly solicitous. "Are you ill, my dear?" He attempted to put his arm about her shoulder.

"Oh, no," she protested, pulling away. "I am merely somewhat uncomfortable from the motion of the coach. I will be better soon."

He again attempted to comfort her, and this time he succeeded in encircling her shoulders. She sagged against him for a moment, and then pushed away. He tried to hold her. Just then her control over her stomach broke and she disgraced herself.

"My garments! Oh, it's vile! I am covered with it!" he cried. He pounded on the roof as the smelly remnants of Chloe's lunch dripped from his clothing and onto the seat. "Smith! Smith, I say! Stop the coach!"

When Smith opened the door, Everingham jumped out. "Help me get these wet garments off, Smith. Oh, this is horrible."

Meanwhile Chloe's sickness had worn itself out and she lay moaning in the corner of the coach. She made a halfhearted attempt to clean her own soiled garments with her dainty handkerchief. Fortunately only a portion of her skirt was damp and she soon had it wiped clean, although the dampness had soaked through, all the way to her skin. She shivered as a solitary tear trickled down her cheek. Always before when she had become sick from traveling, her parents or sister had held her head until she was recovered, and then had tenderly cared for her and offered abundant sympathy. Now she was left untended, and by one who had sworn his lasting devotion.

Smith climbed into the coach, holding a stained piece of sacking. He started mopping up the mess with it, completely ignoring her.

Outraged, Chloe said, "Give me that rag so I may dry my gown."

He looked at her, and then down at the mess on the floor. "I be sorry, miss, but I'm to clean the coach."

She stared at him in disbelief. "But I am cold and damp."

"Soon's I get master taken care of, I'll find you something to dry yourself with," he promised, as he continued to swab. "There, that'll do it. Can't do nothin' about the smell, but his honor won't be getting his feet dirty, anyhow."

As he was climbing down, he said, "I'll bring your bandbox in a bit, miss."

Chloe sat in the corner and fumed. She no longer felt the cold, for fury was warming her from within. The longer she sat, listening to Everingham's complaints as he changed his clothing, the more angry she became. When he opened the door, she attacked. "You are no gentleman! I could have died in here and all you cared about was your clothing."

"And you are no lady!" he retorted. "No woman of quality would have so forgot herself to have done this to me."

"I could not help myself. But to offer no assistance when I was sick. Oh,

Jeremy, you said you loved me," she wailed.

"My mother would have never allowed herself to become sick upon a gentleman's garments."

"Your mother is no doubt far too high in the instep to suffer from ordinary human frailties."

"At least she would have been more considerate. I have no valet to tend my soiled garments. Likely they are ruined."

"I have no maid, either, but I am not whining about the lack. You said you would care for me. What a thoughtless husband you will be."

"Now my lord, miss, let's have no more argufying," Smith told them as he handed Chloe's bandbox inside. "I've cleaned the worst, my lord. You just climb back in there and we'll see if there's not an inn nearby where you can clean up."

"I am not getting back into that noisome thing until it has been washed out," Everingham said. "I shall ride forward with you." He stalked out of Chloe's view.

Smith made to close the door again.

"Wait," she cried. "I do not wish to ride inside either. It smells so horrible, and the squabs are damp."

"I'm afeared you must, miss. There's scarce room on the seat for his lordship and me, and you couldn't hang on the footman's perch. It can't be far to the next inn; you can clean up there."

"I will not! You cannot force me to ride in this filthy, smelly coach."

The door in the roof opened and Everingham peered in. "Well, then, Chloe, you will have to walk, because it is my coach, and I will not ride inside nor on the footman's perch, and Smith must drive."

"Oh, you!" Chloe spat.

The trapdoor slammed shut. Smith quietly closed the door and left her alone.

I hate him. I hate them both, but most especially Jeremy.

Fortunately the next inn was reached in little over a quarter of an hour. It was not one of the better hostelries, but there were two bedchambers free, as well as a private parlor where they could dine. Insult was added to injury when the landlady informed Chloe that she would not be able to bathe immediately. There was only one tub available, and his lordship had commanded that it be brought to him first.

She stormed, she wept, she pled, but Everingham's chivalry stopped short of his relinquishing the inn's only bathtub.

She sat in her room, clad in her damp and smelly dress, for the better part of an hour before the tub was brought to her and cans of hot water were carried in. The water was dumped into the tub and a towel was tossed upon the bed. There was no maid to assist her, so she was forced to tussle with buttons and laces. Even worse, she had no soap, for she had not brought any and all the inn had to offer was harsh and scratchy.

She emerged from the bath, smelling better and feeling a little cleaner, but in no good humor. When she pulled her primrose challis morning dress from her portmanteau, she found it dreadfully wrinkled.

She put it on anyway.

Cleanly clothed at last, she attacked her hair, tangled from the night before and damp from her bath. It stubbornly refused to behave. She finally pulled it back and tied it with a ribbon at the nape of her neck. A quick glance at the cloudy mirror told her she looked less than her best. *I do not care. This is no longer an exciting adventure. I hate him. I wouldn't marry him if he were the last man on earth.*

With that resolve firmly in mind, she strode from the room and downstairs to the private parlor. She intended to demand that he first find her a maid, and second, return her to her family.

He was sitting at the table sipping brandy. "It is about time. I have been awaiting you this age."

When he made no motion to offer her refreshment, she planted her fists upon her hips. "I suppose I must order my own tea?"

"If you want some." He contemplated the golden liquid in his glass. "I have been thinking, Miss Hazelbourne, and have come to the conclusion that we will not suit."

"Ha! As if I would even consider you as a husband."

"I cannot understand what possessed me to yield to your importunities. I must have been drunk to consider an elopement."

"You were as eager as I. You said that you wanted to marry me and take care of me. If this is how you do so, I pity any woman foolish enough to become your wife."

"I did take care of you. I provided a handsome coach and ample funds. You cannot expect me to be a nurse or doctor as well."

"A husband should care for his wife in sickness," she said. "It so states in the marriage vows."

"You are not my wife, so I have not promised you anything of the sort."

"You should begin as you would go on."

"There are servants for that sort of thing. Mother would never have subjected me to such indignities." He refilled his empty glass.

"My mother would have held my head while I was being sick and then washed my face afterward."

"Perhaps you should return to her then."

"I would, if I could. Oh, Jeremy, you neglected me so dreadfully. How could you be so unkind?"

"I, unkind? I did not soil your clothing and practically ruin your coach," he replied, clearly unmoved.

"I could not help myself. I get so sick when I travel."

"Well, then, why did you suggest we elope? You must have known it is at least three days' travel to Scotland, if the roads are dry."

"I did not think of that when I made my plans. I only wanted to escape."

"And I was a convenient tool. What a selfish girl you are." His eyes no longer shone with devotion, but instead showed disgust.

"I did not mean to be. I truly wanted to elope with you." She began to weep again. "Oh, Jeremy, please do not be unkind. I am sorry I ruined your clothing. And I do appreciate your rescuing me." She lowered her chin and looked at him from under her thick lashes, a tactic that always worked with her father. "Jeremy, please forgive me."

His anger was not proof against her pleading eyes and quivering chin. He patted her hand and told her to stop crying. "Let me pour you some brandy. You will feel much more the thing, and I could use another glass myself. Dinner should be served soon."

Chloe sipped her brandy. She had never tasted it before, and was not sure she liked its burning sensation on her tongue. The glow emanating from her midriff after the third sip was pleasant, however. Their dinner soon arrived and they set to willingly. The meal was not as elaborate as they would have received in a better inn, but it was well enough cooked and plentiful.

While they ate, Chloe considered what she might do to free herself from the tangle in which she had become enmeshed. She had no intention of marrying Jeremy. How was she to get herself back to London without causing talk? Would he be willing to share his coach for the return journey? She doubted it, now that he knew of her tendency to motion sickness.

For the first time, she realized she might well and truly have compromised herself. Her papa might demand that Jeremy make an honest woman of her.

Oh, no, I could not abide that. Papa will understand. He must!

The covers had been removed and she and Jeremy were sitting in an uncomfortable silence when she became aware that the private parlor next door was also inhabited. From the half-heard comments and loud laughter, she decided it was occupied by a group of gentlemen making merry. When the waiter came in to remove the covers, Lord Everingham asked him why the inn was so full.

"It's that mill, my lord. Lawks, you was lucky to get here early. We're plumb full, for all we're twelve miles from Turvey."

"Good God!" Everingham exclaimed. "I forgot."

"What did you forget?"

"The mill. I was going to go to it myself. Now we are in the soup. We must get you to your bedchamber immediately, before someone sees you." He looked fearfully about the room as if expecting his mother's spies to be lurking in each corner.

"Why?"

"If there is a crowd of gentlemen from London in this very inn, someone may recognize us. You would be ruined."

He rose to pace the length of the chamber. "You must go to your bedchamber immediately, and remain there until everyone has left the inn tomorrow morning."

"I will not. It small and cold, and the chimney smokes. I wish to remain here. Why can you not go to *your* chamber?"

Everingham pulled himself to his full height, but somehow failed to look either imposing or commanding. "Go at once, Chloe."

"You may not give me orders. We are not married, nor will we be. I will not be dictated to. I shall remain here as long as you do."

"You are a spoiled brat, Miss Hazelbourne!"

"And you are a mama's boy with no hint of a spine."

"Well, you have the temper of a shrew and I am sick of it."

"As I am of your cowardice. I will stay in this room and I will not go to bed. If you try to force me to do so, I shall scream."

"Scream away, my dear," he said. "It will not be my reputation destroyed."

"It will too, for you will be as ruined as your wife."

"My mother would never forgive me if I made you my wife."

She was suddenly afraid. "She might not, but I will be your wife, if I am compromised." The possibility seemed somewhat more desirable than it had a few minutes ago.

"My mother told me you were a scheming female. Would that I had listened to her."

"Your mother!" Chloe shrieked. "Your mother may rot for all I care. I thought you were a man. You are nothing but a little boy still tied to his mother's apron strings!"

"I am a gentleman and a peer of the realm," he shouted back, "and I do not have to listen to vilification from a common chit."

"How do you propose to escape it, my lord?" she yelled. "You brought me here unaccompanied and I will tell everyone that you did so for immoral purposes. You will marry me, my lord, or I will destroy your reputation."

"And your own in the process. Cry quits, Miss Hazelbourne. My consequence is so much greater than yours that you will not be believed. Besides, my mother will come to my assistance, and her influence is considerable."

His mention of his mother was too much for Chloe. She seized the glass of brandy from the table and flung it, glass and all, at his face. His yowl of rage and pain, as the strong liquor stung his eyes and the heavy glass struck his forehead, followed her as she dashed into the corridor.

Chloe's headlong rush through the corridor was halted when a tall, dark man stepped from the door of the adjacent parlor.

"Oh, please sir, let me pass. I must escape," she cried.

"If you are being pursued, perhaps you could use some assistance," he replied.

Just then Everingham, still half blinded from the brandy, blundered after her.

"Ah, Everingham, I presume. Why are you pursuing this young lady?"

Everingham stopped short. "Wilderlake? Is that you, Wilderlake?" he said in a faint voice.

"Wilderlake?" Chloe whispered. "Oh, no!" She crowded past him and ran up the stairs.

CHAPTER TWELVE

Wilderlake and his companions had watched their favorite go down to defeat. The Plymouth Pug had proved no match for his bigger, faster opponent. After paying off their bets, they repaired to the inn where they had earlier reserved a private parlor. Despite their disappointment at the fight's outcome, they settled in for a convivial evening. Wine consumed with dinner and port afterward increased their jollity, so that all four were in high spirits when a woman's angry voice came from the parlor next to theirs.

At first he ignored the altercation, but as it continued, Wilderlake became concerned. He could not hear the words, but he could tell that the woman from whom they issued was in great distress. He decided to fetch the innkeeper, to suggest that he investigate. As he stepped into the corridor, a young woman in garments that spoke of her gentility flew from the next room and ran full into him. She immediately pulled back and asked to be let by, never once showing her face. As he moved aside, he saw a young man rush from the room in pursuit. His face and hair were wet. Wilderlake recognized him in the light shining through the open doorway.

"Ah, Everingham, I presume. Why are you pursuing this lady?" He was intrigued to discover the unimpressive young lord in such an inn with a woman. His impression of Everingham was poor, for the fellow seemed overly attached to his mother. Along with many bachelors of the *ton*, Wilderlake thought him a fussy, effeminate fellow.

The young woman, who had paused after passing Wilderlake, shrieked and ran up the stairs. Everingham attempted to follow her, but Wilderlake barred his way.

"I do not believe the young lady cares for your company" he said.

"Stand aside, Wilderlake," Everingham said, trying to dodge him. "This is none of your concern."

"No, it is not, yet she has the look of quality. I wish to know why she was so bent upon escaping you."

"I will kill her!" Everingham cried.

"I could not permit that," Wilderlake told him. "Come, Everingham, do calm yourself."

One of the others snickered "She probably attempted to seduce him and he is insulted."

"Or she turned him down, and he is enraged," another suggested.

"Here, Everingham, come into your parlor and tell me what this is about. You three, return to your port." He pushed the younger man through the open door and closed it on him. Turning to his friends, he said, "Everingham has probably embroiled himself in something that he has not the wit to handle. Let me see what I can discover."

"Good God, Herne," one of his friends said, "are you mad? The girl is obviously no better than she should be, else she would not be here with that young fool. Instead of helping him, we should be knocking on her door. Perhaps she could ease our loneliness this evening, and we could have a bit of sport."

"You always was a puritan," another added.

The third started toward the stairs. "I'll go and see what's amiss with the girl. She looked a choice bit, even in this dim light."

Wilderlake stopped the bantering and his friend's progress down the corridor with a stern, "That's enough. Get you back into our parlor. I can handle this without help from you three idiots. If the girl is truly a maiden in distress we must come to her aid."

"Aw, Herne, you just want her for yourself," the one who had attempted pursuit complained.

Wilderlake shoved his friends back, saying, "You're drunk. All three of you. Go back to your wine. I won't be long." He closed them into their parlor and returned to Everingham, whom he found sitting at a table with his hands covering his face.

"Now then, what is all this? Is the girl a lightskirt? Or is she the lady she appeared?"

"I do not associate with lightskirts!"

"Of course you do not. I daresay your mother would not allow it."

"My mother has nothing to say—" Everingham sat erect in the chair and let his head fall back. A deep sigh shook his slight frame. "I wish I had never embarked on this insane adventure. She is a terrible girl. Look at me, Wilderlake. My garments are ruined. The second time today! She threw brandy in my face. Nearly blinded me." His voice held a hint of tears.

"Perhaps you had better tell me the whole tale from the beginning." Wilderlake poured a glass of brandy. "Here, drink this, and then tell me all about it."

Lord Everingham did so, with many false starts and parenthetical animadversions on the girl's character and temper and manners. When he described her sickness in the coach, Wilderlake was hard put to refrain from a snicker. As the tragicomic tale wound to its close, he still did not know the identity of the young woman who had led Everingham astray. Although all but overcome with curiosity, he bit back his questions.

"When I told her I did not wish to elope with her after all, she threatened to tell everyone I had abducted her," Everingham said, still sounding terribly put upon. "I assured her that my mother would assist me in shifting all the blame to her, should she do so. And then, Wilderlake, she threw brandy into my eyes!"

Wilderlake kept a close rein on his amusement. "What do you intend to do now? Will you return her to her family?"

"I shall visit a friend in the neighborhood, as I had planned to do before...before she led me astray. Alone. I do not care what becomes of Miss Hazelbourne."

"Miss Hazelbourne?" Wilderlake half rose and loomed over Everingham. "Do you mean to tell me the young lady you eloped with is Miss Hazelbourne?"

"Why yes, did I not say so? She convinced me that her parents and her sister were in league against her to prevent her achieving a success of her Season. Having had a taste of her tongue, I believe them well justified."

Before he could speak another word, Wilderlake seized his shirt in both hands and shook him like a wayward pup. "You brought that innocent girl out here, mistreated her, shouted at her, threatened her, and now you intend to abandon her. You cad! I should call you out."

Everingham fought to free himself. "You may try, but my mother does not approve of dueling. I would not accept your challenge."

One last shake and he threw Everingham aside with such force that he skidded across to floor to come up against the wall with a solid thud. "Get out of my sight, you puling halfwit, before I do violence to you." He advanced toward the cowering man with outstretched hands.

Everingham scrambled to his feet and slammed out the door.

Wilderlake took a deep breath and slowly unclenched his fists. He could see no way to get Miss Hazelbourne back to London tonight. Besides, his friends had already seen her. Even though they had not learned her name, they would recognize her later. Even if he was able to convince them to keep silent, eventually one would be sure to let something slip. Colly, especially, had a tongue that wagged at both ends. Once in his cups, he would be unable to keep such a delicious *on dit* to himself. Soon the whole of Society would know how Miss Hazelbourne had been found alone with Everingham at an inn, a full day's travel from London.

Wilderlake had himself suffered from Society's gossip as a young man. His father's profligate ways had been the talk of the *ton*, making him the target of sidewise looks and whispered comments about fortune hunters whenever he happened to partner an heiress in a dance. He could not let Miss Hazelbourne suffer a similar fate.

He shook his head in consternation, for he was unsure of which Miss Hazelbourne was in need of his aid. He probably should find out, even if he had no clear idea of how to manage the task as yet. He rang for the waiter.

That individual was hesitant to direct Wilderlake to Miss Hazelbourne's bedchamber. The information cost him a crown and the indignity of being subjected to the servant's knowing winks and nods. He climbed the stairs and knocked upon her door.

"Go away. I never want to see you again," came a muffled voice from within.

"Miss Hazelbourne, it is I, Wilderlake. Please come to the door. I wish to help you."

Silence. He knocked again. Finally, he heard the key turn and the door was pulled open a crack.

He peered into the darkened room, but could see little beyond the shape of her face and the small hand clutching something at her throat. "Miss Hazelbourne, Everingham has declared he does not intend to return you to your family. I have come to offer my services in his stead."

"No."

"You will not accept my help? Come Miss Hazelbourne, you cannot stay here forever."

"I cannot return to my family." she sobbed. "They hate me. And I have ruined myself,"

He pushed open the door, forcing her to move backward. Now he could see that she was clad in a nightgown, with a ragged quilt wrapped over it. Her eyes were puffy from weeping and her hair was loose and straggly about her shoulders. She bore little resemblance to the confident and well dressed young woman who had soothed his brow after his accident.

Was this she? Or her sister? If only he could see the color of her eyes.

She retreated to the bed as he entered the room and closed the door behind himself. Leaning against it, he regarded the frightened girl cowering against the bed. "Miss Hazelbourne, I did not come here to offer you insult or harm. Please believe me."

She retreated farther, backing up onto the bed, and perching upon its edge. "He said...he promised...he called me..." she hiccupped as the tears streamed down her cheeks and she tried to find words. "Oh, Lord Wilderlake, I am ruined!" she finally wailed.

His heart torn by her distress, Wilderlake went to her. Sitting beside her, he took her hands gently in his. Her sobs slowly stopped and she wiped her eyes with a corner of the quilt. Lifting enormous, trusting blue eyes to his, she essayed a tremulous smile.

Which one has blue eyes. Damme. Why can't I remember?

"That is better. Now, we must discuss what we are to do with you."

"I cannot return to my family. Oh, what am I to do?"

"I am certain your family will welcome you back with great relief. They must be sick with worry for you. Unless they know where you are..."

"No, they do not. I stole out of the house during the night. I cannot go back. They will be so angry with me."

"I rather think that they would be so glad to know that you are safe that they will not even reprimand you, should you return unharmed."

"But I am not unharmed," she wailed.

"Not? Did he..." So great a rage consumed him that he could not continue.

"Oh, no, Lord Everingham did not touch me. But my reputation! He said that his mother would tell everyone that I had lured him here. And she would. She is a wicked, vengeful woman." The sobs broke out anew.

He pulled her into his arms. As she wept against his chest, he became aware of a great feeling of tenderness. No matter the cost to himself, she must be protected from the results of her injudicious actions. The solution, when it came to him, struck him as so perfect, so right, that he wondered why he had not seen it immediately.

"For Lady Everingham to blacken your reputation would be impossible, if you were my wife."

"You wife! But you would not... You could not wish to marry me!"

"If that is what it will take to ensure that your good name is unblemished, I will do so. Will you do me that very great honor, Miss Hazelbourne?"

"I cannot. I cannot take advantage of your chivalry."

He caught her chin on the edge of his hand and forced her to look into his eyes. "You were willing to take advantage of Everingham's foolishness to obtain him as your husband. You tricked him into this elopement, did you not?"

She blushed as she gave a tiny nod.

"Unlike him, I am fully aware of the implication of my proposal to you. I am no callow youth with an overbearing mother. You have not tricked me into anything. I had intended to seek a wife this Season, even though the restoration of my fortunes has still a long way to go.

"I found you attractive the first time I saw you." He ignored the small voice that asked him exactly when that was. Which Miss Hazelbourne did he hold in his arms?

"My mother will welcome you, for she has been after me to marry these past several years. Indeed, she even suggested that either you or your sister would make me an excellent wife, for she knew your parents many years ago, and admires them both greatly."

He waited for her to say something, and when she remained silent, he went on, "Come Miss Hazelbourne, make me the happiest of men." He waited again. "Or have you taken me into aversion?"

"No, my lord. I have liked you ever since I first saw you. But the duchess said your fortune was squandered. I had wanted to marry someone who would keep me in the first style of elegance."

The complete artlessness of her confession made him smile. "I cannot promise to do that, but my pockets are no longer completely to let. I think I could contrive to provide you with some of the luxuries," he told her with a wry smile. Sometime in the past while, he had come to believe she might suit him very well. "I, too, have been aware of a liking for you since our first meeting."

Wilderlake still did not know which of the sisters she was, but really didn't matter, for he had liked them both. If he was going to marry a total stranger, one sister would do as well as the other.

After what seemed an age, she said, "Well, then, my lord, it seems that I must accept your proposal with gratitude." Again the trusting look, as if he held the solutions to all of life's problems in his hands.

He vowed silently to merit such trust. "I will return you to your family on the morrow, Miss Hazelbourne. At that time I shall speak to your father, who should not object. As soon as possible I will obtain a special license, so we can be married by the day after tomorrow at the latest."

"I wanted to be married in St. George's," she said with a small pout. "I have heard that all the best weddings are held there."

"Unfortunately, that cannot be arranged. You will have to settle for a quiet wedding in the bosom of your family. Immediately afterward, we will go to Wilderlake Castle, so you will not be exposed to the rumors and snubs that might otherwise be your lot until Lady Everingham finds someone else to rip apart. Perhaps your family might care to join us in a few weeks."

"But the Season is not even half over!"

"There will be other Seasons, my dear." He became aware that he was still sitting on her bed, holding her in his arms. She felt entirely too good there. He stood and stepped away from the bed. "I think we can contrive to be reasonably happy. I am not averse to spending at least part of the Season in London. When we are at Wilderlake Castle, there will be much to occupy your time. It is badly in need of renovation. Within reason, you may have a free hand at redecorating."

Chloe sighed. This was not going as she had planned, but Lord Everingham's warning about his mother's power among the *ton* had hit home. She had gone too far this time, just as Phaedra had warned she would do. How convenient that Lord Wilderlake had been on hand to save her from her own folly.

He is a viscount. Not as good as an earl, but still... "Very well, my lord. I will be ready to depart at whatever hour in the morning you set. You will stand by me when we reach my parents' home, will you not?"

He reassured her that he would allow no one, not even her parents, to abuse his affianced wife. "For, my dear, once you accepted my proposal, you became my responsibility."

She sighed with relief. "Oh, my lord, are you certain that you wish to marry me? I am given to willfulness and tantrums and I do not always like to do as Society expects of me."

"Then you must endeavor to conquer such impulses, Miss Hazelbourne. Look where they have led you."

"I have done nothing else for the past hour, my lord," she said, wishing his arms were still strongly about her. "Tonight I was forced to admit that Mama and my sister were correct in accusing me of having become terribly spoiled and arrogant this past while. Today, finding myself penniless and abandoned so far from London, I suddenly became aware that I had lost all sense of restraint over my actions. I have resolved to act with more temperance and thoughtfulness in the future."

Wilderlake smiled warmly, but did not step forward to take her into his arms as she had hoped he would do. Instead he took her cold hand and bowed over it. "Get you into bed now, and sleep well. It has been a trying day for you. I will have someone attend you in the morning. Good night."

"Good night, my lord." Chloe waited until he left the room before she flung herself onto the bed to indulge in a new flurry of weeping. She wept for all her dreams, now lost, and for the future that she faced as the wife an impoverished viscount in a draughty castle in Cumbria.

WILDERLAKE DID NOT WEEP, BUT HE SAT LONG IN THE PARLOR AFTER SEEING HIS friends to bed. He had refused to give them details of the situation, but had informed them that the girl was indeed a lady and they were to keep quiet about what they had seen and heard. He would take the young lady back to London the next day, leaving them to make the return journey without him.

What would his mother think when she learned she was to have a daughter-in-law? He had not lied when he told Miss Hazelbourne that his mother liked her, but he had to acknowledge to himself that she had said that she liked Miss Phaedra Hazelbourne much better than her flighty sister.

He had to admit to a slight disappointment that the girl in the bedroom upstairs was most likely the flighty sister. Chloe.

"Chloe," he said, testing the word on his tongue. "Chloe." He cast his mind back to his university days, but all he could recall was a tenuous reference to summertime. Yes, the name fit her, for her smile was as bright and sunny as a summer's day, her tears as quick and warm as rain in July.

He hoped that his mother would accept her and learn to love his wife. *And will I learn to love her?* He had no thought of a marriage in name only. The young woman upstairs would be the mother of his children.

A sudden warmth filled him at the thought of the begetting of those children. *Yes, I can definitely see her as my wife. But love? I honestly do not know.* He had little time for such sentimentality, for the task before him was still Augean, though not insurmountable as it had seemed upon his father's death.

His own mother had admitted not loving his father, but she had been a good wife to him, in spite of his mistreatment of her. At least *his* wife would not suffer as his mother had, contriving to keep the bailiffs away, to keep food on the table, to hang onto the unentailed lands of the estate until her son reached his majority.

CHAPTER THIRTEEN

As the rain-washed day slowly dripped into evening, Phaedra found her thoughts drawn ever again to her sister's predicament. While she had never understood Chloe's desperate need to marry soon and well, she had sympathized with her determination to shape the future to her own satisfaction.

Theirs had never been the ordinary upbringing, for Mama was a great believer in education for girls, and Papa was determined his daughters would be trained in estate management and financial affairs. Both parents had encouraged their children to independent thought and open mindedness.

At the same time they had stressed the importance of society, for, as Mama had more than once quoted, "No man is an island..."

Phaedra had eagerly embraced the opportunity for education, and had read widely and voraciously, concentrating mostly on the natural sciences. Chloe, less able to be inactive for long periods, had spent many hours playing the piano and the harp, until she was an accomplished musician. Both girls had involved themselves with village and parish activities, although once discovered by the local swains, Chloe's interest in all but parties and routs and other frivolous pursuits had gradually excluded other social pastimes.

Lately Phaedra had wished she had spent less of her time on her education and more on visiting and mingling with the local gentry. Learning how to piffle might have prepared her far better for coping with the *haut ton* than a knowledge of Latin, Greek and botanical nomenclature.

"Mama was so determined that we marry well," she mused aloud as she stared out into the darkening street. "Perhaps she should have encouraged me more to practice inane social chatter and less to improve my mind."

Cousin Louisa was silent for so long that Phaedra wondered if she would answer. At last she said, "There is much to be said for the ability to prattle, but it is a talent that loses its charm under the burdens of everyday life."

"Chloe prattles quite well, yet I am certain she will be able to cope with whatever she must face. She really isn't the flibbertigibbet she seems." Even as she defended her sister, Phaedra wondered if Chloe really would be able to cope. She had changed so much in the past few years. *Sometimes I feel as if she's a different person, not my sister at all.*

"She is much like your father. I remember when he was courting your mother..." Cousin Louisa let her mending fall into her lap as she stared into the fire. When she spoke again, her tone was pensive, as if she were dredging up long forgotten memories. "I was fifteen, too young to put my hair up, yet too old to stay in the schoolroom with the children. Your mother was not quite eighteen, and just as lovely then as she is now. The whole family expected her to make a fine match, for all our fathers had been gentry, rather than noble."

"I had forgotten your mothers lived together after they were widowed. Were you close, like sisters?"

"Not really, for Mother and I moved in with my aunt Mirabelle only a few months before Isabella made her come out." With a quick glance over her shoulder at the closed door behind her, she said, quietly, "Your parents' marriage was not considered a good match by either family."

Phaedra turned to stare at the older woman. "Not a good match. But they are so...so much in love. I would wager there is not a better marriage in the whole of England."

"Probably not." Cousin Louisa picked up the mending, and set it upon the drum table at her side. "Your mother's come out was a great success. She could have had her choice of husbands. Everyone was surprised when she chose your father." She smiled. "A wise choice, as it turned out, which surprised everyone on the family even more."

"You speak as if Papa was not particularly eligible."

"He was not. His name was on everyone's lips that Season, spoken with great disapproval. That was the year he gambled his entire remaining inheritance on a tin mine that everyone knew was played out."

"Papa?"

"Oh, yes. And this only a few months after he had sunk a small fortune into a canal scheme that seemed on the brink of ruin." She shook her head. "Everyone knew he was a poor risk, both financially and as a husband. Any woman foolish enough to marry George Hazelbourne, for all he was the grandson of a duke, would surely live a life of abject poverty, and probably even be forced to outrun the bailiffs."

"Oh, I cannot believe you. Papa is not wealthy, but we have never lacked for necessities, and even the occasional luxury."

"I know. The tin mine later reopened and he sold it at a modest profit. He recouped his investment several times over from the canal. And hasn't that been a thorn in the side of many of the Verbains?" Cousin Louisa smiled widely. "Isabella has been proved wiser than her family, for your father has provided well for his family. Your portions are ample, your brothers will each inherit properties that will, with careful management, give them a decent living. And your father still gambles on endeavors most of the world considers foolish and improvident."

Phaedra thought back over her growing-up years. While she had never been told that the family coffers were full or empty, she remembered times when frugality and thrift were the order of the day. Although those times had been perhaps more frequent than when Mama ordered half a dozen new gowns, or Papa added yet another expensive hunter to his string, she had never felt, well, *poor*.

"So Mama followed her heart. She doesn't seem to have regretted doing so."

"No, she has not ," Cousin Louisa agreed.

"Then why is it so important to her that Chloe and I marry well?"

Phaedra waited so long for an answer that she began to wonder if Cousin Louisa would not reply. At last she said, "I believe it is because she sometimes found life...uncertain. No mother wants that for her daughters, no matter how happy she herself has been. Isabella must want you to have financial stability as well as love." Her sigh was heartfelt. "Unfortunately, Phaedra, mo one can guarantee love, prosperity, happiness, or any other blessing for another, no matter how good the intentions."

"But—"

Her question was lost as the door opened and her mother entered.

"No," she said, when both Phaedra and Cousin Louisa turned enquiring eyes upon her. "There is no word." Her voice broke on the last word.

"Mama—"

"I am sorry, Phaedra," Mama said, after a moment when she visibly controlled her worry. "I should have known better than to put so much emphasis on your marrying well. I should have encouraged you to look for love, not material wealth."

Phaedra knelt before her and clasped both her hands. "You did, Mama. I always knew that I wanted what you and Papa have, even if it meant living in a hovel."

"Perhaps." The word emerged on a long sigh. "I only wish..." She was silent for many heartbeats, until Phaedra wondered if she had forgotten what she had meant to say.

"You heard what I said about the importance of love in a good marriage, but I fear all Chloe heard was how important wealth and rank were to her happiness."

Tears clogged Phaedra's throat as she nodded. "Yes, Mama, I believe that was all she heard." She could not restrain a heartfelt sigh. "Poor Chloe."

THE SPRING NIGHT OVERTOOK MR. FARWELL AND LORD GIFFORD BEFORE THEY were many miles from London, and with it came more rain. They took refuge in an inn, requesting the landlord to wake them before dawn so they might be back on the road at first light. Neither spoke of the fact that Chloe would be spending another night with a man not her husband.

Lord Gifford had hitherto shared Phaedra's impression of Farwell's foppishness. A day in his company had showed that the younger man was not at all what he appeared. He was both sensible and competent, for all his foppish appearance.

The sun had barely begun to penetrate the tattered clouds on the eastern horizon when the two men set out in pursuit once again. Their speed was less than Farwell's racing curricle was capable of, for the night's rain had turned the road surface into sticky mud through which the horses had to struggle. At their first change, inquiries of the hostler yielded the information that a young gentleman, answering to Everingham's description, had obtained a change of teams the previous day.

"Damn this mud," Lord Gifford exclaimed, as they once again slowed to inch their way through a rutted swale. "At this rate they'll be in Gretna before we can catch them."

"We're making good time," Farwell said. "It only seems slow because of your concern."

Lord Gifford shot him a scowl, but refrained from a reply. Farwell had been pushing the horses all the way, and he had no complaint. Only overwhelming worry about his daughter. Sweet, foolish Chloe. If only he'd been more stern with her. *If only...*

After another change at midmorning, they made better time. The roads were drying under the influence of bright sunlight and a balmy breeze. Farwell gave the job horses their heads on a long, straight stretch. Lord Gifford hung on for dear life, but Farwell seemed glued to his seat. They were bowling along at a good clip when he said, "My lord, I would like your permission to pay court to your daughter."

Lord Gifford gaped at the younger man. "Chloe?" he finally managed to gasp.

"No, sir. Your younger daughter, Phaedra. I have learned to respect her very much, and believe that she and I would suit very well."

Remembering Phaedra's characterization of him as a precious fop with not an ounce of sense or a brain in his head, all Lord Gifford could do was stammer, "You want to marry her?"

"I do, sir. I am aware, however, that she views me with less than complete approbation. Convincing her I am worthy of her will be a difficult task."

"Well nigh impossible," Lord Gifford blurted, before he could stop himself. "Phaedra sees life in a more serious light than the usual chit. Convincing her that you're a likely husband will be an uphill battle."

"One I am willing to fight. Have I your permission?"

Damme, I wish Isabella were here. She'd know what to do. But the fellow deserved an answer now. "For what it's worth, you do. That's not a promise she'll have you, mind."

"It is all I asked." Farwell dropped his hands, and the horses thundered down the road.

WILDERLAKE ALLOWED MISS HAZELBOURNE TO SLEEP UNTIL LATE, WANTING TO see his friends well away before she emerged from her bedchamber. He had also seen a sullen Everingham on his way. When he finally escorted her to his private parlor, she said nothing beyond a polite good morning. He seated himself across from her after the waiter had laid out their breakfast and departed.

"Are you regretting your decision to wed me?"

"No, my lord, I do not regret it. Indeed, I am very grateful that you have offered for me. It is more than I deserve, I think." She gave him the ghost of a smile. "It is only that my throat feels raw and my eyes are burning."

He examined her. Aside from a certain puffiness under her eyes, she looked far better than she had last night. "Are you ill?"

"Not at all. I have often felt this way before, when I indulged in an excess of weeping."

He watched her help herself to porridge and toast. When she reached for a slice of ham, he said, with some concern, "Do I understand that you suffer from motion sickness, Miss Hazelbourne?"

She pulled her hand back. Looking up at him from under long, curled lashes, she nodded.

"Then I should warn you to take only a little unsweetened tea and dry toast this morning. My mother, who also suffers from that affliction, finds that having little on her stomach relieves the symptoms somewhat. Since I have only a curricle at my disposal, the trip back to London will not be comfortable for you. But you will have only to tell me if you feel sick, and we will stop."

"Thank you, my lord," Chloe responded gratefully. No one had been so sympathetic before. She sipped her tea and nibbled at her toast. "Will we be able to reach London today?"

"I believe so, despite last night's rain. You may not be home in time for dinner, but you will sleep in your own bed tonight." Chloe knew she had blushed at his last words. Casting a quick glance his way, she saw bright spots of color in his cheeks as well.

They departed the inn about ten, having waited for the warm sun to work its drying magic on the mud. Chloe found that her stomach did not protest at the motion of the curricle nearly as much as it had in the coach the day before, despite the lesser springing. Wilderlake offered the possibility that the fresh air was contributing to her well-being. "Sitting in a closed carriage on bad roads would be enough to upset anyone's digestion, I believe. My mother always keeps a window open when she travels."

They made fairly good time in spite of frequent patches of sticky mud, with no stops due to Chloe's stomach. His occasional observations about the other travelers they passed were amusing. Chloe had thought him a serious young man, but now she was seeing his puckish sense of humor. She decided that he was simply a quiet man, not given to idle chatter. *Perhaps that is a good thing. If both partners in a marriage were inclined to chatter, they might drive one another to distraction.*

One change of horses had been accomplished and they were going slowly through thick mud at the bottom of a swale when another curricle, bearing two men, approached them. It pulled to the side of the road to await their traverse of the muddy patch. As they drew nearer, something about the passenger caught Chloe's eye.

"Papa!" she cried. "It is my papa. Stop my lord. Oh, do stop!"

"Chloe!" her papa roared. "Wilderlake! You router! I'll kill you!"

Chloe threw herself from the curricle before it had stopped moving and ran forward. "No, Papa! Listen to me!"

Her father swung her aside. "Take care of her Farwell," he said over his shoulder. He advanced on Wilderlake, who was climbing from his curricle.

"Mr. Farwell, stop him!" Chloe cried. "He must not harm Lord Wilderlake. He saved my life." She ran forward and caught at her father's arm just as he drew it back to strike Wilderlake. "Papa! Papa, please, listen to me," she pleaded, hanging on his arm so he could not hit the younger man. "He did nothing wrong. You must not strike him!"

Her papa shook her clutching hands off. He swung at Wilderlake, who did nothing to defend himself as her papa's one fist smashed against his jaw just before the other one plowed into his midriff. He fell to the ground and lay still.

"Get up from there, you libertine, and fight like a man!" Papa demanded.

Wilderlake wiped blood from his lower lip. "No, sir, I will not. Your daughter came to no harm at my hands, and neither will you. I could not strike my future father-in-law."

Chloe rushed to his side and knelt beside him. She caught up the hem of her dress and tried to wipe the blood from his chin. "Papa, how could you strike him? I told you he saved my life."

"Ruined you, is more like it. Get up, pet, and get into Farwell's curricle. I am taking you to your mother."

"No, Papa. I will stay with poor Lord Wilderlake." She pushed him back as he attempted to rise. "Lie still, my lord. You are still bleeding." She looked again at her father's companion. *What in the world? Mr. Farwell?*

Papa opened his mouth to roar once again, but Mr. Farwell intervened. "Perhaps, sir, you should listen to their story. I cannot believe that Wilderlake is guilty of stealing your daughter away in the night."

He yawned into his lacy handkerchief. "How did he save your life, Miss Hazelbourne?"

Chloe, still patting at Wilderlake's chin, stammered out a disjointed version of her departure from home and the flight from London. "And when we were at the inn, Papa, Jeremy said he had changed his mind and no longer wished to marry me. He threatened to tell all Society of our adventure." She omitted a description of her sickness and the condition of Lord Everingham's clothing afterward.

Lord Wilderlake caught the hand that held the now bloodstained hem. "What your daughter did not tell you, my lord, was that she was revenged on him in advance." He told the part of the tale that Chloe, in her embarrassment, had omitted. "I could see no other remedy for the situation, sir, but to offer for her, and I did so. I hope you will entertain my suit, Lord Gifford, for I have every intention of marrying your daughter."

He raised Chloe's hand, still holding the hem of her gown, to his lips. "It was I, sir, who was in your daughter's company at the inn last night, not Everingham, for he had abandoned her. Therefore, it is I who must make the honorable amends."

Papa still looked more confused than comprehending. "Damme," he said at last. "I believe you are exceeding the demands of honor, young man. But there's no two ways about it. Chloe must be married. But I'd never give her to Everingham, not after the way he treated her. Young ass. No, not you my lord. Here, let me help you up. Sorry I struck you, and all that. I was enraged."

"Understandably so, sir." Wilderlake stood, and helped Chloe to her feet. "Reggie, may I suggest that we turn your rig and get back on the road. Will you take Miss Hazelbourne up with you, so that her father and I might become better acquainted?"

"But I want to ride with you!"

He caught her hand and raised it to his lips, pressing a lingering kiss upon her knuckles. "My dear, your father and I have much to discuss. Let us have this time to do so. We must come to an agreement on how to go on when we get back to Town."

"But—"

"No, do not protest. I will be right behind you with your father, and by the time we reach London, all will be arranged for our wedding tomorrow. If you become overset, you may again suffer from the motion of the curricle. Reggie is a good driver, and I will warn him to go gently." He led her to the other curricle and lifted her into it.

Chloe, rendered speechless by his continued solicitude, obeyed. He smiled at her before turning to Mr. Farwell. "Drive carefully, my friend. You carry a precious cargo."

"I think you mean that, Herne," Mr. Farwell replied in a voice quite unlike his usual mocking tone. "Well, well."

"So you have achieved your goal, Miss Hazelbourne," Mr. Farwell said when he had got his team moving. "Your methods were somewhat, ah, unusual, were they not? Are you sure that this is fair to Wilderlake?"

"He asked me, Mr. Farwell. I did not propose to him," she replied in a tone that might have frozen boiling water.

"After he had been put into a position that his honor required it. You would have been better served if you had married Everingham."

"How dare you!"

"Oh, we fops dare quite a lot, you know. I have seen your temper tantrums and your treatment of your sister. I have no illusions about you, Miss Hazelbourne. You will lead Wilderlake a merry dance. I am not sure I like it, for he is my friend."

"You have nothing to say about it."

"More the pity. I would not wish him to marry a spoiled brat with no thought in her head for anyone's wishes but her own. He is a fine man, honorable and decent, and he deserves better than you."

"You are despicable. I will not listen to your insults." She turned her back on him as well as she was able on the jouncing seat of the curricle.

"My dear Miss Hazelbourne, you will listen to whatever I have to say, for you are a captive audience. If you wish to have a happy marriage, let me give you some advice."

She covered her ears. "Be quiet. I will not hear you."

He was silent for a moment, and then he spoke in a gentler voice. "Listen to me, Chloe Hazelbourne. I will tell you something that may save you coming to grief later."

She removed her hands from her ears, but continued to stare at the road ahead.

"Your sister told me that you are often willful, but not unkind nor uncaring until lately. Because she thinks well of you, I will give you the benefit of the doubt and believe you are not spoiled beyond redemption."

Chloe hunched her shoulder and tried to resist the strong temptation to listen to whatever he had to say about the man she would marry.

"Lord Wilderlake—Herne Bradburn—is a gentleman of high principles. He will never mistreat you, nor will he neglect your creature comforts. As long as you strive to be a conformable wife and do not disappoint him, he will treat you with the kindness and consideration you expect. But if you ever go beyond what his rather overdeveloped sense of propriety considers to be the bounds of good behavior, he will become icy cold and withdrawn. If he ever does withdraw from you, all will be lost. Herne has seen what extravagance, selfishness, and a care-for-naught attitude can do to the members of one's family. He will be completely unforgiving, should you show symptoms of any of these traits. He has spent the past ten years paying for his father's and grandfather's profligacy. He will not tolerate it in a wife."

Anger flared in her breast. *I am not profligate.* Yet she could not resist asking, "What do you mean, he has paid?"

"Have you never heard of Herne's father and grandfather?"

"No, I know nothing about his family."

Reggie told her how the third Viscount Wilderlake had gambled and caroused and dallied with ladies and women of the other sort until the *ton* had withdrawn from him in horror at his loose living, even in an age when such activities were more kindly looked upon. So great had been the third viscount's fortune that he had not been able to waste it all before he died.

The fourth viscount, Wilderlake's father, had married Herne's mother for her fortune. "Instead of taking her on a honeymoon, he took her to the remote castle in Cumbria and immured her there, remaining with her only long enough to father Herne."

Chloe forgot her pique in her fascination with Mr. Farwell's narrative.

"I believe Herne was scarcely a month of age when he returned to Town, thereafter ignoring his family. Had there not been a trust, settled on Herne by his mother's father, he would not have even been sent to school, so little care had his father of him.

"By the time Herne came down from university," Mr. Farwell continued, "his father had wasted his entire fortune and mortgaged the estate to the hilt. He died in a gutter in London, frozen to death after having apparently fallen there in a drunken stupor. Herne was left with a mortgaged estate and creditors snapping at his heels. He barely managed to convince the creditors not to foreclose. For ten years he has labored with only one goal in mind—to lift the mortgages and restore some of the family's former fortunes.

"He has, he tells me, some way to go before the estate is back in the condition that it was before his grandfather began wasting it. The whole experience has given him a detestation of selfishness and extravagance. He could forgive you anything but that, Miss Hazelbourne, so you would be well advised to tread very carefully."

Chloe said nothing for a while, thinking deeply. Finally she said. "I cannot forgive you for your earlier words, Mr. Farwell, but I do appreciate your advice. I do not wish to be unhappy. Lord Wilderlake has promised me that we shall spend part of each Season in London, so I will not be imprisoned in Castle Wilderlake like his mother was." She sighed, not yet entirely ready to relinquish her dreams, yet knowing they were lost to her forever. "But life will not be as I had dreamed.

"I slept little last night, and I thought much. I should have listened to Mama and Cousin Louisa more, and taken their advice. When Lord Everingham threatened to have his mother tell Society of my mistakes, I was convinced I had ruined my whole life.

"Lord Wilderlake is kind and thoughtful. I will try to be a good wife to him. I owe him so much. And I will be married, which is the important thing." She bounced a little on the seat. "Oh, Mr. Farwell, it will be so wonderful to be married, and not to have to wear only demure muslins and always be chaperoned and everything. I know I shall love it."

"Just remember what I have told you, Miss Hazelbourne. Herne will, I think, be a kind and indulgent husband, but you will have limits. He will not tolerate any improper behavior, nor will he accept horns."

"Oh, I would not do anything like that," she exclaimed, shocked. "How could any woman ever be unfaithful to her husband?"

"Some find it easy." There was none of the usual ennui in his tone.

"I never could. I may have chafed at the restrictions on unmarried girls, Mr. Farwell, but I am not immoral."

"Only selfish and willful."

"I suppose I am. And spoiled, too, my sister says. I've always hated to be told what I cannot do, and recently—since my Season was twice postponed—I have felt driven to go my own way, no matter the consequences."

"Herne will expect good behavior, but I doubt that he would ever reprimand you if you misbehave. His way is to withdraw and become cold."

"I could not bear that. Thank you Mr. Farwell. Perhaps you have just saved my marriage. I could not stand to be unhappy, you know."

"But you were willing to marry for a title and money, and without love."

"One does not need love to be happy," she said airily. "I have seen my Mama and Papa for long enough to know that a good marriage depends on more than two people being happy together. I thought I liked Lord Everingham. But I think I will be happier with Lord Wilderlake."

"I hope so."

THE CONVERSATION IN THE OTHER CURRICLE WAS MORE BUSINESSLIKE. WILDERLAKE informed Lord Gifford of his prospects and described the lengths to which he had gone to recoup the family fortunes. He confessed to being slightly short of funds at present, but said that his investments in woolen and cotton mills should start paying off in a year or two.

Lord Gifford expressed his satisfaction that Chloe would not be impoverished. He admitted to being extremely impressed with Wilderlake's business acumen. "By gad, sir. I may come to you the next time an investment opportunity presents itself." By the time the two curricles had reached London,

Wilderlake and Lord Gifford had gone far toward becoming friends as well as prospective relatives and had, in general, agreed upon the terms of the marriage settlement.

They pulled up in front of the house off Grosvenor Square just behind Reggie's curricle. Phaedra burst from the front door as Wilderlake pulled his horses to a stop. Chloe tumbled from Reggie' curricle and the sisters embraced, laughing and crying together. Lady Gifford stood in the doorway, her expression apprehensive.

"We're home, Isabella," Lord Gifford called out. "And all's well. Edgemont, send someone to walk these horses." He climbed down as a footman ran from the house. "Here, Wilderlake, let the lad take the reins, and come in. Meet the rest of the family. You too, Farwell."

Reggie refused the invitation. "No sir, I think I would be better gone. You will want to speak *en famille* tonight. I will call in the morning, if I may."

"Hold, Reggie," called Wilderlake. He strode to the other's curricle. "You must stand up with me tomorrow, or whenever we get the arrangements made. Oh, God, and I still have to tell my mother. Look here. Could you go and get her? I would appreciate it no end. I do not want to leave Miss Hazelbourne to face her mother and sister without my support."

"Of course, Herne. And I will endeavor to tell her nothing except that you have asked for her. I'll leave it to you to break the news that she is to have a daughter-in-law."

"Tell her whatever you must to bring her here, old man."

"She will come. Would you doubt my ability to charm a lady into accepting me as her escort?"

Wilderlake laughed. "Never. And my mother has a tendre for you, you know." He reached out his hand and clasped Reggie's, aware of how much he owed his old friend. "Thank you, Reggie. I... Thank you."

He stood there on the steps for a moment after Reggie departed. At last he squared his shoulders and went in to greet his soon-to-be relatives.

CHAPTER FOURTEEN

A MILD HYSTERIA TOOK HOLD OF ALL IN THE HAZELBOURNE HOUSEHOLD WHEN Chloe was returned to them. Phaedra was too overcome with relief at having her sister safe to do more than ask again and again, "Chloe, are you sure you are quite all right?"

Mama uttered not a word of blame or rebuke. Everyone ignored Lord Wilderlake while the embraces and reassurances went on.

Finally Papa, with his usual roar, quieted everyone. "That's enough! Let the girl sit down and tell you her tale. Edgemont! Fetch the brandy."

When everyone was finally sorted out and seated in the parlor. Chloe was commanded to tell her story with no roundaboutation. She burst into tears. "I cannot. I am so ashamed. Oh, Mama, I was so wicked."

"Hush, Chloe," her mother told her. "George, she is too overset to tell us. What we really want to know if how you found her."

"With Wilderlake—"

Before he could finish his sentence, Phaedra exclaimed, "Oh, Lord Wilderlake, I had not thought it of you. For shame."

Before Wilderlake could say a word, Papa found his voice again. "Hell and damnation! Will you listen and stop interrupting, Phaedra? Wilderlake did not steal her away. He rescued her. 'Twas that idiot Everingham who took her."

"Papa, he did not take me," Chloe protested. "I took him. I mean, he took me in his coach, but I persuaded him to do so."

"Don't defend him, pet. He should have known better."

"Oh, he was terrible, Phaedra. He threatened to tell everyone that I am immoral. And to have his mother gossip about me."

"What did you do to make him say so?" Phaedra said, knowing her sister's usual behavior in times of stress.

"Will you all be quiet!" Papa pounded on the table. "Wilderlake, perhaps you had better tell the tale. These women will be here all night with their hysterical nonsense."

In a few well chosen sentences, Wilderlake told of his rescue of Chloe and his intention to marry her. "As for Everingham, I saw him depart for a friend's home this morning. If Miss Hazelbourne wishes to tell you of her adventures with him, she may do so at a later time. Right now, I think it best that we speak of the wedding."

"We'll get a special license in the morning," Papa said. "Have it before luncheon. Best get it done quickly."

"But I have nothing to wear," Chloe wailed.

"She must have bride clothes," Mama agreed, "and the notice must be posted in the *Gazette*." Phaedra could see her mentally making a list of all that must be done before Chloe could be wed.

"Hang the *Gazette*. As for bride clothes, she's got a whole wardrobe of new gowns. Why should she need more?" Once again papa pounded his fist on the table beside his chair. "The wedding will be tomorrow!"

"Lady Gifford, I have to agree," Wilderlake said quietly. "I feel it would be best if the wedding were to be a quiet one and held as soon as possible"

"But you said she was unharmed," Mama protested.

Chloe sniffled, but said nothing. Phaedra, who was squeezing her hand tightly as a warning to keep silent, could just imagine how she must appear to Lord Wilderlake. Her sister had early on learned the knack of letting tears well in her eyes, without ever having them drip down her cheeks. It gave her a most pathetic and affecting air.

"And so she is. No one else will believe it, though. We must get this thing done quickly." Papa said, his tone leaving no room for argument.

"Lord Gifford has the right of it," Cousin Louisa said, laying a soothing hand upon Mama's. "We cannot depend that Lord Everingham will not relate yesterday's events."

Mama gave way, but Phaedra knew she was unhappy about having to do so. The conversation turned to a discussion of what arrangements had to be made before tomorrow.

"Women's business," Papa said, rising. "Come, Wilderlake. We'll go to my study, finalize the financial details."

Mama and Cousin Louisa soon moved to Mama's morning room to set about making arrangements for a wedding breakfast.

"Well, Chloe, you have certainly landed yourself in the suds," Phaedra said, when they were alone. "What ever possessed you to run away as you did?"

"Oh, Phaedra, I could not stand it! You were all so unkind and there were so many rules and I was not having any fun. I could not even waltz."

"You did waltz, though."

"So I did." She plainly had no regrets. "But I hated being locked in my room and knew that Mama would never let me out."

"Fudge! Mama would have only kept you there for a fortnight. If you had promised to behave, she would probably have let you out sooner."

"Well, I would not promise," Chloe retorted. "For, you see, I would not have been able to keep that promise. I so wanted to enjoy myself."

Phaedra shook her head. She could not understand her sister's logic. "Do you enjoy being rushed into a marriage with someone you hardly know then?"

"Of course. He is not unhandsome and has said that he will bring me to Town for the Season each year. And besides, he has a castle," Chloe said smugly. "Perhaps in time I can persuade him to take me traveling about the world, or at least to Paris. Oh, he is not what exactly what I had dreamed of, but he is handsome and kind, and I am sure that I will be able to manage him."

"I doubt that you will be able to get him to do anything he does not choose to do, Chloe. He has a stubborn set to his chin."

"Fear not, sister, I shall have him twisted about my little finger within a month." Her smile faded. "Oh, Phaedra, I have been horrid to you and Mama lately. Will you ever forgive me?"

Phaedra hugged her. "Of course I will. But Chloe, do try to behave yourself from now on. Wilderlake is such a nice gentleman."

A commotion in the foyer told them that Lady Wilderlake had arrived. Chloe blanched. "Oh, Phaedra, what if she dislikes me?"

"Lady Wilderlake loves her son very much. If you are a good wife to him, I believe you will go on nicely together." Phaedra gave Chloe's hand a reassuring squeeze.

"Oh, I intend to be a good wife. Just think, Phaedra, I will be a married woman by this time tomorrow. I will not be surrounded by all the strictures and rules that I have so chafed under since we came to London. But," she said, sobering, "we are not to stay in London. He wishes to take me to Castle Wilderlake immediately."

"That is wise in him. It will give the gossip time to die down."

"Oh, I know that. He has promised we will return next year."

"Unless you are with child by then."

"No! Oh, how terrible that would be. I will not allow it!"

"You cannot prevent it, Chloe. He will be your husband. But perhaps it will happen immediately, so that you would be recovered by next Season."

"Yes, that is what I will do." She was silent for several minutes. "Phaedra, will it hurt?"

"I do not think so. Mama seems to enjoy it."

"Yes, she does, does she not?" Chloe laughed. "Oh, Phaedra, how I shall enjoy being married." She rose. "I am going to my room now, for I am sure that I must look a perfect mess. Will you come and get me when Wilderlake has finished speaking with his mother?"

Phaedra agreed to do so, remaining on the sofa when her sister left the room. She was not completely happy about Chloe's marriage, but there was nothing she could do, except worry and fret. She prayed that Chloe would curb her willfulness with Wilderlake, for she had the feeling he would not tolerate a spoiled and selfish wife. He struck her as having a serious component to his character. Surely he would have little tolerance for childishness.

WILDERLAKE MET HIS MOTHER AT THE ENTRANCE TO THE HAZELBOURNE HOUSE. She evidenced surprise at his presence, for she had thought him to be out of town. He kissed her, told her to hold her questions, and led her to the library. When they were private, he said, "Sit down, Mother. I have a surprise for you."

She did so, many questions evidently quivering upon her lips. Wilderlake paced about the small room for several minutes, before he knelt on the floor at her feet and took her hands in his. "There is no good way to say this, Mother. I am to be married tomorrow. To Miss Hazelbourne. Miss Chloe Hazelbourne."

"Tomorrow? But how, Herne? You were never interested in Miss Hazelbourne."

"It is a long story Mother, but when you have heard it, you will understand."

She studied his face a long time, until finally she sat back in her chair. "I sense this is not going to be a tale to my liking."

"No, probably not. However, Mother, I am determined to marry the lady."

She nodded. "Tell me."

Wilderlake did so, glossing over Chloe's having been the instigator of the elopement. His mother smiled slightly when told of her motion sickness and its messy aftermath. When she heard that her son was completely innocent of all but rescuing the girl from her own folly, she began to weep. "Oh, my dear, must you marry her? You did not compromise her. She should suffer the results of her sins alone, not drag you into it."

"Colly and Tony and Peter saw her clearly at the inn. They did not know her, but they would recognize her. You know Colly. His tongue cannot be still when he is in his cups. I will not have her name bandied about the *ton*. Mother," he continued gently, "you have wished I would marry for some years. Can you not wish me happy now that I have decided to do so?"

"But I hardly know the girl. She is the flighty one, is she not? Oh, Herne, if you must marry one of the Hazelbourne girls, can it not be the other, Phaedra? She at least is sensible. They look so much alike that no one would know."

"We've agreed on the Settlements. I can hardly tell Lord Gifford now that I have changed my mind and want his younger daughter. Come, Mother, be realistic. I have offered for Chloe Hazelbourne and I shall marry her. She is not a bad girl, you know. Only undisciplined and, I think, a little selfish."

"More than a little, if what I have heard is true. It is said she tried to seduce Everingham at their first meeting."

"That gossip is the product of his mother's vicious tongue. Chloe is guilty of little more than thoughtlessness and youthful high spirits. She will outgrow those."

"Your father never did."

"No, he did not. But he had no good example to follow. Chloe has. Lady Gifford is one of the kindest, sweetest ladies I have ever met, and Miss Phaedra is all that is gracious. I cannot believe Chloe could be anything but well-mannered, coming from a family such as this. I am convinced her father has indulged her far too much, encouraging her misbehavior. Coupled with her eagerness to taste all that life has to offer, that indulgence led her into this imbroglio."

"Little tasting she will do at home," she commented wryly. "You are going to take her home, are you not Herne? You could not remain in Town after all that has happened."

"Yes, Mother, I am. But I must ask you a favor." He hesitated before continuing. "Will you remain in Town for a few weeks? I feel that we have a thorny period of adjustment before us. Perhaps we will do better to be alone."

"I most certainly will remain. How tedious to play gooseberry to a couple on their honeymoon." She looked at him. "I had wished better for you, my son, but I will never let Miss Hazelbourne know she was not my choice for you. You will have enough problems without your women being at outs."

"I knew I could depend on you." He kissed her hands, and then pulled her into a close embrace. "Mother, please do not be too unhappy over this. I have never met any woman for whom I had strong feelings, so Miss Hazelbourne will probably do me as well as any. I am content, now that I have had time to think it out."

"As long as you give me grandchildren before I am too old to enjoy them, I will not complain, Herne. Unless she makes you unhappy."

"She will not, Mother, I am sure."

"I pray so. Now, should we not join the family? They will think us rude."

"No, for they understood that I must break the news to you. Now that I have, and you have dried your tears, we should go to them. Smile, Mother, your son is about to marry."

She smiled, and they went to join the Hazelbournes.

THE NEXT MORNING PHAEDRA ASSISTED CHLOE IN CHOOSING WHAT TO PACK FOR her honeymoon and what to have shipped to Castle Wilderlake.

Despite her excitement over being married, Chloe was somewhat subdued, as was Phaedra. They had never before been separated. Phaedra paused before adding a fringed silk scarf to the honeymoon pile. "It will be as if part of me is missing, Chloe."

"I know, for I felt that way in the inn. I was lying in that smoky little room, thinking that I wanted you to come so we could talk it over, and you were not there."

"We will see each other next Season, but that is so far away. Oh, Chloe, I shall miss you so!"

"And I you. But Wilderlake said that you could come visit us. He did. I just remembered. He said that perhaps my family could come to Castle Wilderlake in a few weeks. You must, Phaedra!"

"I do not think it would be a good idea if we did so. You and Lord Wilderlake will need time together to adjust to one another. Perhaps at Christmas, but no sooner. No, Chloe," she said as her sister's face clouded, "I know I am right this time. You will need to get to know one another, without your families to depend upon. I am sure that is why his mother is remaining in Town."

"I suppose." Chloe sighed. "How cruel life is. I am marrying, which I have so badly wanted to do, but I must give up you and Mama and Papa and the boys. Why can we not have everything all at once?"

"Silly. It is your wanting everything all at once that got you into this pickle in the first place. Now, do you want these gowns to be packed to go with you, or should they be sent? You will have little need of five ball gowns on your way to Castle Wilderlake."

"Oh, send them. I will have my wedding gown—how strange to be wed in a ball gown—and the rose wool and that should be enough. We probably will not dress for dinner every night at the inns where we will stay."

The wedding service took place just before noon, with a festive breakfast following. Cousin Godfrey Stevens performed the service. He had agreed to do so with reservations, admitting he did not like the hurried nature of Chloe's nuptials.

Chloe made a lovely bride. She was clad in the pink gown she had worn on her first visit to Almack's. Its soft color called attention to the slight blush in her cheeks. Her head was crowned with white roses, matching those in her wedding bouquet. Phaedra wore palest yellow with a golden overskirt. She carried a posy of white roses with gold streamers.

The ceremony was over quickly. Wilderlake kissed his bride's lips for the first time. It was a gentle kiss, for which Chloe was grateful. She was suddenly shy with this man she barely knew. When they drew apart, Chloe turned to her father, kissed him, and then embraced her sister.

As the sisters hugged one another, she saw her mother and Wilderlake's, each standing alone, both with tears streaming down their cheeks. Chloe was overcome. She flew into her mother's arms. "Do not cry Mama, please. I am so happy and so should you be." She kissed her mother's cheek before turning to the other woman. Shyly she put her arms around her husband's mother. "Oh, ma'am, I shall make him happy, I promise. Please do not cry."

"Why do women always cry at weddings?" Papa held out a glass of champagne. "Here, my lady, drink up. This is a happy occasion. Chloe, get some champagne. Everybody, have some champagne," he roared.

Even the Duchess laughed. "Your husband must have been sampling the champagne, Isabella," she said. "Or is it just that he's relieved to have her off his hands?"

"A bit of both, I think," Mama replied. "George, do calm down and let us toast the newlyweds."

Papa led the company in a toast to Lord and Lady Wilderlake. Chloe beamed. It was the first time she had been called Lady Wilderlake. The Duchess held up her glass.

"Never could see the sense in the men getting to make all the toasts. Phaedra, here's to your wedding next."

Everyone laughed as Phaedra's face grew hot.

"Hear! Hear!" Mr. Farwell contributed. "Too bad it was not a double wedding."

Phaedra gaped at him. He returned it with a wink. Had he already drunk too much?

Chloe's laughter interrupted her musings. "But she has not received an offer. How could it have been a double wedding?"

"Never mind, gel," the Duchess said. "Your sister will be wed sooner than you think. Now where is that breakfast you promised me? I am sharp set,"

They all trooped into the dining room where a lavish spread had been set out. Everyone but the newlyweds filled their plates more than once. Phaedra noticed that both Chloe and Wilderlake picked at their food, moving it about on their plates but consuming little.

FINALLY THE LAST TOAST WAS DRUNK, TO WILDERLAKE'S GREAT RELIEF. ALTHOUGH he had only sipped at his glass with each salute, he was lightheaded and queasy.

Chloe and her mother went upstairs together. Miss Phaedra engaged Wilderlake's mother in conversation, and Lord Gifford teased Lady Mary Follansbee. The Duchess and the Reverend Mr. Stevens began a good-natured argument about the role of the clergy in politics. Wilderlake paced, until Reggie caught his arm and led him out of the room and to the library.

"Here, man, you look ill. Nervous?"

"Reggie, I am scared stiff. We are only going as far as Claridge's. What am I to do?"

"Only one thing to do on your wedding night. Bed the girl."

"But..." He felt himself flush. "Reggie, I don't know... I mean... Damme. How can I say it?"

"Herne, are you virgin?"

"Yes."

"Oh, my God! But you've been on the Town. How could you be?"

"I was determined not to follow in my father's footsteps, so I avoided the cyprians. And there was never an opportunity at home. I just never did," he admitted, feeling the fool.

Reggie laughed. "And now you two innocents will come together, neither of you knowing how to go on. This is rich. Well, Herne, it is too late for lessons. You will have to muddle through somehow. There, I hear them coming downstairs. Go to meet your fate. I wish you luck." He continued to chuckle as they went back into the corridor.

Wilderlake felt the little food he had consumed congeal in his belly.

Chloe halted halfway down the stairs, holding her wedding bouquet. She looked at her sister and Lady Mary. "May the best girl win," she called, and threw it. Lady Mary made no attempt to catch the flowers, and they nearly fell to the floor before Phaedra put out a hand to catch them.

"Folks would say you don't want a husband, gel, from that poor catch," the Duchess remarked, under cover of the laughter.

"I am not sure I do," Phaedra told her softly.

"Well, you'll get one, want him or no," Her Grace replied.

Phaedra did not reply, for her sister had come to the foot of the stairs and was saying farewell to her family. All too soon the newlyweds had departed in a hail of rice. The Duchess's party followed them in a few moments, and shortly thereafter Mr. Farwell took Wilderlake's mother away. The remaining Hazelbournes were left alone.

CHAPTER FIFTEEN

Lady Gifford collapsed into a chair. "I never want to go through another day like this again in my life." The family had returned to the parlor after seeing the wedding guests on their way. "More than once I felt myself on the verge of saying something unkind to someone."

"Like 'why do you not all go away and leave me alone,' perhaps, Mama," Phaedra teased.

"Exactly like that. I am so tired, and it was such an effort to smile and say the correct things."

"Then why do you not go and rest until dinner?" Cousin Louisa suggested.

"No, I cannot. There is one more task..." She closed her eyes for a moment. "Would you excuse us, Cousin Louisa? Phaedra, come into your papa's study, if you will."

Phaedra was mystified. What on earth had her mother to say to her that would not wait until later? "Mama, you should rest."

"No, Phaedra," Papa said. "Now. Want to get this over with."

She was alarmed as well as mystified at her father's words. What could be so serious that Mama's well-being did not take precedence? She followed her parents into the study, where Mama seated herself in a comfortable chair. Papa did not sit, but paced back and forth between the fireplace and the desk. Phaedra stood uncertainly near the door, waiting for the silence to be broken.

Finally her father cleared his throat. "Sit, girl, sit. You look like a frightened colt, standing there."

She perched on the edge of an armchair.

"Your mother wants me to say this, though I think she'd do better at it. But still and all, it's my duty. Well, then Phaedra. Ah...you see..."

"George, say it, straight out!" There was an unusual sharpness to Mama's voice.

"Very well. *Ahem.* Reginald Farwell has asked for your hand. Told him it was up to you, but gave him my permission to ask you." His words came out in a rush and he scowled as he spoke.

Phaedra gaped.

"Say something, girl. Don't just sit there with your eyes boggling out of your face."

"Hush, George. Give her time to take it in."

Her mind spun. She could not move. Finally her thoughts stopped tumbling over and over and sorted themselves into a fantastical sort of sense. *Reginald Farwell has asked for your hand. Reginald Farwell has asked for* your *hand. Reginald Farwell has* asked *for your hand. Reginald Farwell...*

No!

She burst into tears. Mama came to kneel on the floor beside the chair and embraced her.

"Hush, my dear, hush," her mother crooned. "If the notion makes you so unhappy, you need only refuse him. Hush, now. Calm yourself." She continued in this vein for some minutes until Phaedra gained a measure of control over her wayward emotions.

"George, please ask Edgemont to fetch some tea."

Papa snorted. "Tea! Nothing restorative about that. She needs stronger medicine."

Phaedra heard the sound of glass clinking on glass. In a moment, Mama held a fragile snifter to her lips.

"Sip this, my dear, slowly. It will make you feel better. No," she said as Phaedra tried to pull away from the strong fumes, "take it. Just a few sips. There. Now sit quietly until you feel more calm." She moved back onto the sofa and accepted a glass for herself.

Phaedra was aware of a warm sensation in her midriff within a few moments of drinking the brandy. She took several deep, shuddering breaths. Her thoughts were no longer going 'round in circles, but instead seemed to be mired in something sticky, for they would not move through her mind.

"Mama," she said in a croaky voice. She cleared her throat. "Mama, did

Papa really say that Reggie—that Mr. Farwell..."

"Yes, love, he wants to marry you. Is the thought so repugnant to you?"

"I was sure no one would ever offer for me. They were all hanging after Chloe. Are you sure he asked for me?"

"He did, by name," Papa said. "Happened on the way to find Chloe. Told me that he'd been thinkin' on it for a couple of weeks."

"There must be some mistake."

"No mistake. He wants you."

"Why are you so convinced it is a mistake?" Mama said. "Mr. Farwell always seemed to prefer your company to that of Chloe's,"

"We forever argue when we are together. Or he lectures me about my 'intellectual pretensions'. I was sure he held me in dislike."

"Likes you well enough to want to marry you," Papa said.

She knotted her hands in her skirt, twisted. When Mama reached to soothe, she let go, lest she damage the fragile muslin. "Mama, I cannot marry him. I do not love him. He is nothing but a fashionable fribble, a fop. How I could live as he does, going from one fete to another, spending most of the year at house or hunting parties or in London?" Again Mama caught her hand, to the benefit of her gown. "We would not suit, not at all. We have nothing in common. Nothing."

"He told your father that he had come to care for you, because of your kind heart and your sensible outlook." Mama tilted her head up with one finger under her chin. "Phaedra, are you sure? He seems a nice enough young man, and he says he cares for you."

She shook her head. The reason for Mr. Farwell's offer had just occurred to her, but she did not wish to speak of it to her parents. They were upset enough over Chloe's recent escapades. "Quite sure. I am sorry, Papa, for I know you wish me to marry, but I do not love him." She would never admit that her words had engendered a sinking sensation in her middle.

"Balderdash, girl. You would learn to."

"I doubt it. But even if I thought there was a possibility that I might, I would not wish to take the chance. I want a marriage like yours and Mama's, and will not settle for less, even if it means I shall never marry."

"Well if you won't have him, you won't, and that's that," Papa said, with regret thick in his tone. "Too bad. Got to like him while we were looking for Chloe. Competent young man, even if he dresses like a fop."

"You must be mistaken, Papa. Reginald Farwell is a useless, hedonistic, snobbish clothes horse. His only competence is in being a decorative addition to a ballroom or a drawing room." Phaedra could not understand how her father could have received such a misleading impression of Reg...of Mr. Farwell..

Mama spoke before Papa. "Enough, Phaedra. You are still overset. Go to your room now, and rest. We will inform Mr. Farwell tomorrow that you do not wish to consider his suit."

"Oh, would you, please, Mama? I do not even wish to see him. Not now." She yawned. "I think I will rest, for I did not sleep well last night. I am sorry to disappoint you, Papa. I truly do not wish to be a burden upon you." She left the room hurriedly, needing solitude to contemplate this latest information.

"WELL, WIFE?" LORD GIFFORD SAID, AFTER THEY WERE ALONE. "YOU WERE RIGHT. She doesn't want him."

Isabella shook her head at him, more a gesture of disappointment than disagreement. "I knew she would not have him, not at first. He has given her no time to learn to know him, and he has managed to offend her nearly every time they have spoken. I myself am not sure that I would wish her to marry someone like Mr. Farwell. Their interests are far too divergent. I wonder what he sees in her?"

"Told you. He likes her kind heart and her sensible outlook. At least that's what he told me."

"That is not enough to base a marriage upon." She raised a hand when he opened his mouth to argue the point. "No George, you know it is not. There must be joy in each other's company, not merely admiration of character. You know, I do not always admire your character, my dear, but you always bring me joy."

Lord Gifford finally ceased his pacing and sat beside her, putting his arm about her shoulder. "While I, my love, always admire yours, as well as having joy in your company." He nuzzled her neck. "Confound the girl! How many offers does she expect to receive, that she can refuse this one with hardly a thought?"

Isabella shivered, but pushed him gently away. She had to convince him that Phaedra knew her own mind. "She will probably receive several. Phaedra is a delightful person in her own right, particularly when she does not stand in Chloe's shadow."

"Offers from elderly widows, artists, penniless writers, more than likely," he snorted.

"Not if I have my way. I will not allow her to forego all of Society's entertainments, no matter how she pleads. We brought her to Town to be seen by eligible gentlemen, and I will continue to ensure that she is."

"Will she be tarred with the same brush as Chloe, do you think?"

"No, I do not. So far she has taken well. Not spectacularly, but there is certainly interest aplenty in her. Even that dreadful Lady Everingham has said she is nicely behaved."

"Well, I don't like it, but I'll leave you to settle her then. Still think Farwell's the man for her, though."

Satisfied she had won the concessions she needed for today, she laid her head on his shoulder. "George, I am truly in need of a nap."

"And do you wish company, my lady?"

"You know I do," she replied, as she pulled him to his feet. "Let us stop acting as parents and take joy in each other's company."

PHAEDRA, UPON REACHING HER BEDCHAMBER, FOUND HERSELF TOO OVERWROUGHT to sleep. She removed her dress and curled up in bed, but her eyes remained open and her body tense.

Mr. Farwell—Reginald Farwell, useless but decorative man about Town—had actually asked for her hand in marriage. Even if made for all the wrong reasons, she, Phaedra Estelle Hazelbourne, had received a *bona fide* offer.

Chloe had been wrong, after all. She was not to receive offers only from widowers wanting mothers for their children. A member of the *ton* had asked for her. Never mind that he was an absurd fop and cared nothing for intellectual pursuits, never mind that he did not love her, but only admired her kind heart and sensible outlook—he wanted to marry her. She would cherish his offer all her life, because he was at the forefront of Society, a fact that had initially made her question Society's collective wisdom.

Phaedra had always compared herself to Chloe. How could anyone notice her beside someone so bright, so personable, so...so lovable? Particularly, how could someone so much a part of Society as Reginald Farwell consider her, a plain gray dove rather than a bright peacock, as a wife?

She had secretly agreed with Chloe, that she would eventually marry someone older, more settled. Someone staid, for anyone exciting and interesting would not be interested in her. She had almost resigned herself to remaining unmarried, even to receiving no flattering offers.

But someone had offered for her. Not a sober, settled older man, but a Pink of the *Ton*, a graceful, handsome, polished man. That he dressed in outrageous fashion...that he fell asleep whenever the conversation bored him... did either matter? He had asked for her hand, and she would always treasure the gesture. Oh, she was grateful to Mr. Farwell, even knowing she could not be the sort of wife he wanted.

If only I could love him.

She tried to imagine him kissing her the way she had seen Papa kissing Mama on rare occasions when they thought themselves unobserved. Long ago she had decided that she wanted that kind of loving passion for herself, even though the very thought of having a man's hands on her body sent embarrassing waves of heat through her.

No, I simply cannot imagine doing that *with Reggie Farwell.*

Yet the very thought of his lips touching hers, warm and intimate, brought a strange, fluttery sensation to her middle.

Phaedra forced herself to stop indulging in silly, romantic fantasies. She told herself that Mr. Farwell's offer had nothing to do with her more sterling qualities. It stemmed from pity, pure and simple.

As a longtime member of the *haut ton*, Reggie Farwell was, probably more than most, conversant with gossip and rumor. Surely Lady Everingham's evil tongue had not confined itself to Chloe's reputation, but had attacked hers as well. Since she and her sister were so similar in appearance, they were often thought of as being just alike. Thus, if Chloe's reputation was in tatters, so must hers be. Society would not care that she was the sensible sister. She would be considered as shameless—no, have the word with no bark upon it—as wanton as her sister.

Those three friends of Wilderlake who had seen Chloe in the inn had assumed her to be a cyprian. They would not keep silent, she was certain. Chloe had vowed that the one called Colly had been quite aware of who she was, for she had danced with him at their come out.

So. Mr. Farwell had offered for her in order to save her reputation, knowing that no one else would care enough to do so. She did not understand why he, with whom she had ever disagreed, had done so, but she appreciated his kind gesture.

But marry him? She could not.

How could she ever love such a man, with his garish clothing and his mincing manners, and most of all, his sleepiness? And what did she know of him, after all? He had spoken of hobnobbing with Mr. Brummel, of attending house parties at various estates, and of hunting with the Quorn.

Her father must have been satisfied with his prospects, or he would not have considered Mr. Farwell's suit. Papa would never allow one of his daughters to marry where she would not be comfortably situated, though he would not demand a vast fortune. No matter. Mr. Farwell's life style could never be hers, and that was the end of it.

She forced her eyes closed and tried to sleep, but the same thoughts kept scurrying about in her head. *Reginald Farwell wants to marry me.*

She did not love him. She would not marry him.

Reginald Farwell wants me.

She finally drifted into sleep, but her dreams were uncomfortable. She awoke with a splitting headache when Cousin Louisa tapped on her door.

"Your mother thought you might wish to stay in your room tonight. She and your father are doing so." Cousin Louisa set the tray on a table near the window.

"Oh, thank you. I could not have faced Papa tonight. He is so disappointed in me. Did Mama tell you?"

"She told me this morning that your father had received an offer for you and that you would probably refuse. I take it you did?" Cousin Louisa held a dressing gown out for Phaedra to don.

"Yes. Did she tell you from whom?"

"She did not have to. I have been expecting Mr. Farwell to offer for you for some time."

"How did you know? I mean, he gave me no indication that his intentions were such. Cousin Louisa, the man hardly spoke to me but to criticize what he called my intellectual pretensions. We disagreed every time we met."

"That was why," came the answer. "When he woke enough to dispute with you, I was sure he was interested. My late husband knew Mr. Farwell when he was at Eton. He was vastly amused with the young man's predilection for napping whenever he wanted to avoid a situation." She smiled, as if she shared her husband's amusement. "I never saw Mr. Farwell show so much animation with other young ladies as he did when you and he were brangling, even though he flattered them effusively and was all that was polite."

"But he is such a useless, fashionable person. I know we should not suit, even if I were to learn to care for him!"

"Of course not, my dear. I was not trying to change your mind. I merely told you of my observations. Here. Come and eat. After a good, substantial supper, followed by a hot bath, you will rest very well. Tomorrow will be better."

She pushed Phaedra unresisting into the chair she had pulled to the table. Lifting the covers, she revealed a large platter of thick cream soup, a dish of spiced applesauce, and a buttered muffin. "I told Cook that you would not wish anything heavy. I will put the teapot on the hearth so it will not cool while you eat. Good night, my dear."

Phaedra ate with relish. After she had cleaned the tray of edibles, she poured herself a cup of tea and sat musing. Perhaps she was being unfair to refuse Mr. Farwell's offer out of hand. Would he consider waiting for an answer until they were better acquainted?

No. That would not do. She did not love him and they had nothing in common. But still... She toyed with the notion of asking him to wait for an answer.

When her bath arrived, she was no closer to a decision. The dilemma kept her from relaxing completely in the tub of warm water. The problem was, she finally admitted to herself, that despite all the very good reasons why she should do so, she did not really want to refuse her one and only offer out of hand.

Despite her confusion and indecision, Cousin Louisa's prescription for a good night's sleep must have worked. When she finally climbed into her warmed bed, she fell asleep immediately and slept the night through, with no bad dreams.

BY THE TIME LORD WILDERLAKE AND HIS NEW LADY WIFE REACHED CLARIDGE'S Hotel, Chloe was more than a little apprehensive. She realized she knew nothing about this man who she had married, except that he was handsome, thoughtful, quiet, and moderately wealthy. On the short trip to their night's lodgings, he had been polite, excessively so, she thought.

Perhaps he is as anxious as I. Oh, no, how could he be? He is a man.

She dutifully explored and admired the suite that her new husband had engaged for their wedding night, until she came to its single bedchamber. Her polite smile froze on her face as she stood in the doorway of the room in which she was to share a bed with this stranger. Suddenly his dark face and lowering brows seemed threatening, and she shrank away from him as he stood behind her looking into her nuptial chamber.

Wilderlake, too, was suddenly aware of the lack of a second bedchamber. He had not specified a larger suite. Now he wished he had. As he stood behind this stranger whom he now called wife and looked into the elegant bedchamber, with its silken white hangings and its immense bed, he became aware of Chloe's withdrawal. Feelings hurt, he said, "I have arranged for one of the hotel maids to assist you, my lady. I shall retire to the lobby until you are settled. Please send for me when you are ready to dine." He bowed to her and hurried to the door.

He found a chair in a corner of the lobby and threw himself into it. Calling a footman, he requested that a bottle of brandy be brought to him. *My God, what have I done? We are practically strangers, and she is afraid of me.*

Alternately regretting his chivalrous gesture and wondering how to go about bedding his wife, he sipped at the strong spirits until a footman informed him that his wife desired his escort to the dining room.

He could think of nothing more unnerving than to sit in a public room among strangers, while he dined for the first time with his wife. He arranged for dinner to be served to them in their suite. "Oysters," he said, remembering what he had heard about their effects upon manly prowess. "And champagne, let there be champagne." He quickly listed several other dishes that were to his taste, and added, "Bring sweets too. Something a lady would choose."

Satisfied with his own cleverness and fortified with bottled courage, he made his way carefully to the stairs. When he knocked on the door of their suite, Chloe opened it.

Wilderlake stalked into the room with careful dignity. He looked his new wife up and down, and then awkwardly enfolded her in his arms.

Chloe, smelling brandy on his breath, drew her head away. His arms tightened, pulling her against his hard body. "My wife," he muttered. "Got a right to kiss my wife." He found her mouth and pressed his lips against it.

Chloe had been kissed before. She considered herself quite sophisticated. But this was nothing like the gentle kisses she had hitherto experienced. His lips were open on hers and his tongue probed at her sealed lips.

"You reek of brandy." she cried, jerking her head to one side. "No! Let me go!"

Undaunted, he nibbled at her earlobe, sending little shivers along her spine. Confused, embarrassed at the strange, new feelings his touch engendered, she once again attempted escape. But her arms were pinioned between them and she was his captive.

He returned to her mouth and probed her lips with his tongue.

She sank her teeth into his lower lip.

"Ow!" he yelled, releasing her. Blood welled from his lip. He held his hand against the wound for a moment, before pulling it away to stare at the glistening stain on his fingers. "You little vixen."

He reached for her again, but was distracted by a knock on the door. When he opened it, three waiters entered, carrying large trays. They cleared the table of its knickknacks and unloaded their trays. Two champagne buckets, each holding an iced bottle, were placed beside the table. A waiter opened one and filled two tall stemmed glasses with the golden, bubbly libation.

"Will that be all, my lord?" the first waiter said.

Wilderlake, who was holding a handkerchief to his bleeding lip, nodded. Reaching into his pocket, he withdrew a guinea and tossed it to the leader. "Yes, that will be all. You may clear in the morning. We will not wish to be disturbed again this night."

As soon as the door had closed behind the waiters, Wilderlake said, "Be seated, my lady. Our dinner grows cold." He held her chair.

With a wary glance at him, Chloe sat. She reached for a serving spoon, saying shyly, "May I serve you, my lord?"

"First a toast." He handed her one champagne glass and raised the other. "To us, my dear. May we build a comfortable life together."

Chloe smiled as best she could. She wanted to tell him that her dreams of marriage were for more than comfort. At her come out ball, she had discovered a taste for champagne. Tonight it seemed even better. She drained her glass. "May I have more?"

He refilled both their glasses. When she offered him the plate of spiced beef, he waved it away and pulled the platter of shelled oysters to him. "I have little appetite. I shall just eat a few of these while you enjoy the rest." He ate the slimy shellfish slowly, dabbing occasionally at his still oozing lip. Each time he slipped one of the revolting things between his lips, Chloe had to contain a shudder.

She also had little appetite, but under his intense gaze, she could not admit it. She took a small helping of the beef, a few vegetables, some savories, and a lobster patty. While pushing the food about her plate, she said, "I wish you would eat something besides those awf...uh, oysters, my lord. Surely so many of them are not good for you."

"Yes, they are. Good for me. May I pour you more champagne?" He fumbled with the bottle. Nearly as much of the sparkling wine spilled to the table as entered her glass. Wilderlake refilled his glass as well.

Finding it impossible to swallow anything solid, Chloe drank off her champagne thirstily. When he saw her glass was empty, her husband opened the second bottle and refilled it again. Her spirits revived after the third glass, and she ate the lobster patty and nibbled at a piece of cake. By the time Chloe had finished her fourth glass of champagne, she was quite in charity with her husband, despite his silence. She looked at him and giggled.

"Wha's so funny?" he mumbled.

"You are, my lord. You sit there scowling while you should be celebrating.

Come, dance with me." She rose to her feet and began to waltz around the room, still holding her champagne glass. She curtseyed before him. "Come," she repeated, taking hold of his arm and attempting to pull him to his feet.

Wilderlake clutched his glass and stood, unsteadily.

"Waltz with me, waltz with me," Chloe caroled, as she drew him after her into the steps of the dance. He took three faltering step and stumbled onto the sofa. Eyes closed, he sprawled back, breathing heavily. His almost empty glass landed on the rug and rolled, leaving a sticky trail.

Chloe glared at him a moment before she began giggling. "Foxed," she said. "How very odd." She began again to waltz, circling around the room alone. Faster and faster she spun, humming to herself. Suddenly she became horribly dizzy, and grabbed at the nearest solid object, the frame of the bedchamber door. She clung with both hands until the room stopped spinning. She leaned against the doorframe and looked across at her husband. He had slid from the sofa to the floor, and was curled on the rug, snoring.

"Wake up," she said, but her voice was small and shaking. She wanted to go to him, but when she tried to stand alone, she swayed and nearly fell herself. Leaning back against the doorframe, she covered her face with her hands and sank to her knees.

I wanted to be married in a great church, with bridesmaids and a wedding breakfast for all the ton. I wanted to marry a man who would pamper me, who would tell me I am beautiful. A man who would swear his everlasting love.

Instead, her husband lay sprawled on the floor, dead drunk. She knew he had consumed too much champagne because he regretted marrying her.

What have I done?

Chloe's eyes burned but no tears would fall. After a while she slid the rest of the way to the floor and fell into a troubled sleep.

Sometime in the night she woke, shivering. The room was dark and the bed under her was rock hard. For a few moments she was confused, until she remembered her wedding day. She pulled herself to her feet and fumbled her way along the nearest wall until she came to a bed. On the bedside table, she found a candle and a lucifer. She used the first candle to find and light others. Once she could see her surroundings, she sought her bridegroom.

In the other room, he lay on the floor, snoring stertorously. What sort of man would drink himself into insensibility on his wedding night?

One who married for pity, not for love.

Their wedding dinner still littered the table. As she drew near, she smelled the oysters he had not consumed. They were never her favorite viand, and tonight she detested even the thought of the slimy things. She upended a plate over them and piled the rest of the dishes and plates together. The waiters must have taken the tray with them, for it was nowhere to be seen. "Bother," she muttered.

She pulled the corners of the tablecloth up, laid them over the table and shoved the whole thing toward the door. It moved easily. With only a little effort, she had it standing in the corridor outside their suite. Once she had pushed the door closed, she breathed a sigh of relief. At least the air was no longer redolent with the smell of oyster.

Again she went to the bedroom, this time removing the satin quilt from the bed. She tucked it around her husband's supine body. Once she had him covered, she eased herself under it and curled up beside him. Putting her arm around his waist, she snuggled against him and quickly fell asleep.

CHAPTER SIXTEEN

WILDERLAKE AWOKE WITH A POUNDING HEAD AND A COTTONY MOUTH. HE lay quietly, knowing it was early morning, for the windows were lit with a grey, cold light. The bed on which he lay was devilishly hard and a weight was pressing against his chest and shoulder.

He remained perfectly still for a few minutes, seeking some memory of the previous night. Obviously he had imbibed far more than he should have, something he had never done before. Why?

Slowly images of the past few days painted themselves on the canvas of his mind. A convivial evening in an inn, good wine, good company. A girl, pretty, distressed.

Oh, my God! Chloe. His wedding. The uneasy silence as they traveled to the hotel, alone at last. The fear in Chloe's face. Too much brandy. Too much champagne.

Dinner, which she had only picked at. The oysters he had eaten, each one sliding down his throat with a nauseating slickness. More brandy. Chloe caroling, "Waltz with me."

That memory, at least, made him smile. She was such a gay little thing. A good foil for his dark pessimism.

He cautiously looked for the source of the weight on his chest, barely moving his aching head. Chloe was sleeping beside him, with her head on his shoulder, her arm wrapped across his body.

Why are we on the floor?

He moved carefully, pulling his half-asleep right arm from between them and easing it around Chloe. She shifted slightly and made a small sound of contentment before relaxing again. With his left hand, he explored first his chest, then his legs. Yes, he was fully clothed. He wriggled his toes. Even to shoes. He tentatively touched his wife's arm. It was bare. He slid his hand up to her shoulder, finding there a puff of soft fabric.

His touch must have disturbed her, for Chloe tightened her hold on his chest and drew her knee up so that her leg rested on his. He became conscious of the first stirrings of desire. Turning his head, he found that he could reach her forehead with his lips. He kissed her gently and tightened his arm around her. Perhaps, if he turned just so, and lifted her chin with his other hand...

Yes. He found her lips and kissed them, softly at first, and then with increasing hunger. As his tongue thrust against her lips, he became aware that her arm was no longer resting quietly on his chest, but was creeping up to encircle his neck. Her mouth opened and she moaned against his.

Chloe's response drove away the last of Wilderlake's fears. He was clumsy in his haste, but so was she. They tugged and pulled at each other's clothing, tossing each item aside as it was removed. Finally seeking hands found nothing but warm skin and the urgency grew unbearable. All clumsiness, all uncertainty was gone.

While still capable of rational thought, Wilderlake breathed a mental sigh of relief. In this, at least, their marriage promised to be a success.

Later, as they lay entwined together, Chloe spoke her first words of the day. "No wonder Mama seems to enjoy that. I do too."

Wilderlake smiled, still caught up in the wonder of what they had shared. "To think I was nervous. Why it seems the most natural thing in the world."

"You, too, my lord?" She kissed his shoulder, which was all she could reach without moving. "I feel so deliciously comfortable that I do not even want to move enough to reach your lips."

"Then I will do the moving, my darling," he said, and did so. After a long, satisfying kiss, he had to ask her, "Did your mother tell you she enjoyed, ah, that?"

"No, but we could always tell. She and Papa used to disappear occasionally in the afternoons, and when they returned, they always seemed so contented. When I was about seventeen, I finally deduced why." She paused. "My lord, you must instruct me in what pleases you. This is all so new to me."

"My name is Herne, lovely Chloe. And if I am to instruct you, so shall you me. For it is equally new to me."

She sat up, the blankets falling from around her upper body. "Never say so!" she exclaimed, shocked. "Do you mean you never had your bits of muslin? Why, Mama said..."

"When I was young, I never had the funds," he interrupted, "and at home there was little opportunity. Or perhaps I never sought one."

"Oh, I am so glad, Herne," she said, snuggling back into his arms. He pulled the blankets back over her. "I was prepared to accept my husband's mistresses, for Mama warned us that most men have them. But Papa, never did, I think, and I confess that I do not like the idea."

"Nor do I. My father was enough of a rake for both of us. I think that I am more exclusive in my tastes."

"See that you stay that way, husband, or I shall show you just how great a temper I have," she warned him. She pulled away from him and stood up. "Now, I am hungry, and this floor is so hard."

He caught at her ankle as she started to walk toward the bedroom. She stopped and looked down at him, suddenly aware that she had not a stitch of clothing to cover her. She was momentarily embarrassed, but told herself that there should be no false modesty between husband and wife.

"Wait, Chloe, let me look at you." He suited deed to word. When heat bloomed in her cheeks, he chuckled. "Why, I believe you blush all over." He rolled out of their improvised bed and chased her into the bedroom.

A long time later Chloe had her breakfast.

PHAEDRA AWAKENED EARLY THE DAY AFTER HER SISTER'S WEDDING, KNOWING what she must do. At breakfast, she asked that she be allowed to tell Mr. Farwell of her decision.

"You need not, dear," Mama said. "Your father can relay your refusal, thus sparing you the distress of doing so."

"I am not going to refuse him, Mama," she answered, twisting a handkerchief between nervous hands.

Her father looked up from his newspaper, eyebrows raised.

"I am going to ask him for more time to think about his offer. I realized last night that I had never considered Mr. Farwell in the light of a suitor. It would be unfair to refuse him until I have time come to know him as a prospective husband rather than a potential brother-in-law."

"Now that's more like it, girl." Papa was obviously relieved. "Get to know the man a bit. Then you'll see there's more to him than meets the eye."

"I probably will still refuse his suit, Papa, so do not be too optimistic. I cannot believe that Mr. Farwell and I would ever deal well together."

"Give the man a chance, that's all I say," Papa said, as he rose from the table. "Now I must be off. Got to put the wedding announcement in the *Gazette*. Then I thought I'd drop in at the club." He kissed his wife and ruffled his daughter's hair. "I'll be home in time to take you to the theatre tonight."

"Oh, Mama, must we go?" Phaedra said. "I had hoped that we could live more quietly now that Chloe is married."

"If anything, I shall require you to accompany me to more affairs, rather than fewer now, Phaedra."

Phaedra caught her breath in surprise and disappointment. She had hoped...

"We must show Society that we are not downcast over Chloe's hurried marriage," Mama told her. "You must be seen frequently enough that all will realize that you are not the hoyden your sister was. I know I can depend on you to behave in a most proper manner for the remainder of the Season."

"I had hoped we would now return home, and forget the rest of the Season," she replied, frowning.

"Absolutely not, my dear. We will continue to be seen everywhere that is fashionable, until the *ton* is convinced your manners and morals are impeccable. Besides, how could you get to know Mr. Farwell at such a distance?"

"Yes, Mama." Phaedra sighed. "If we must, we must. So what is our schedule for today?"

"Today you are free to do as you wish, after you have spoken with Mr. Farwell, that is. Tomorrow, there is a tea at Lady Sefton's, and in the evening is the Duchess's musicale."

Phaedra had folded her napkin carefully while her mama was speaking. Now she rose and went to the window, which looked out upon the small garden at the back of the house. Her breath made a small smudge of steam upon the cold glass. "And the day after that, I will drive in the park with Lord X, attend the opera with Lady Y's party, and then drop in at the Earl of Z's ball, I suppose."

For a moment she let her hands clench into fists and her back teeth grind together. Then she turned, forcing herself to smile. "Very well, Mama, I will be cooperative. I warn you, though, I will not enjoy most of it."

"I think you will, despite yourself. Except for the musicales, perhaps, and I will not insist you attend any except the Duchess's. You may have two afternoons to yourself each week, after this one. Cousin Louisa and you can go about as you please each Tuesday and Friday."

"Thank you, Mama. You have always understood."

Lady Gifford went in search of Cousin Louisa, whom she found in the sewing room, mending sheets.

"What on earth, Louisa?"

"I felt the need to do something soothing. The past few days have been almost too exciting."

"Have they not?" Lady Gifford replied, as she too picked up a sheet to turn. She related Phaedra's hope for time to consider Mr. Farwell's proposal. "I have been thinking. If— No, when Phaedra marries, I shall be in need of female companionship. Would you consider coming to the Court with us? I cannot promise peace and contentment, for the boys keep us hopping, but I would very much like to have you there."

"I could come and visit you for a while, and we shall see. I admit I have been lonely myself, this past while. But before we make our plans, should we not see that Phaedra does indeed marry."

Lady Gifford laid down the sheet and smoothed it across her knees. "Do you think she will have him, Louisa?"

"I cannot guess. Phaedra keeps her own council. I confess myself surprised that she will ask him to wait. Perhaps she is not so averse to his suit as she says."

"We can but hope. I like that young man, Louisa, despite his outrageous costumes and his sleepiness. I am not certain in my own mind he is the right husband for her, although I do believe his offer will make a difference in Phaedra's life, whether she marries him or not."

Cousin Louisa patted her hand. "At this point, we can only wait and see."

The pile of mended sheets grew as they sewed in silence, content in quiet domesticity, after the excitement of the past few days.

Phaedra greeted her suitor with damp palms and a shaking voice. After the usual polite exchanges, she said, "Mr. Farwell, I must thank you for your offer..." She could go no further. She simply could not imagine kissing him, let alone sharing his bed for the rest of her life.

At her words, his lips tightened, then relaxed, so quickly she was unsure she had really seen the subtle change. He stepped to the fireplace and stared down into it for a moment, before he turned and laid his arm along the mantel. His stance showed him at ease and prepared to wait as long as was necessary for her to find her voice again.

"Oh, why did you have to do it?" she cried angrily. "Now I cannot be comfortable with you, and I was, before."

This time the tightening of his lips was unmistakable. After a brief silence he said, in an uncharacteristically serious tone, "Will you sit, Miss Phaedra, while you rail at me? I confess that I do not wish to receive your refusal while standing."

She sat on the sofa, expecting that he would take the chair whence he could look into her face. Instead he seated himself beside her.

She clasped her hands tightly in her lap and stared at them, waiting for him to speak.

After a moment, his hand covered hers. His skin was warm, firm, his touch somehow comforting.

How strange. His hand does not look like I would have expected the hand of a fop to appear. It is strong, not delicate and useless.

She stole a peek at him. His expression was guarded, and his gaze was fixed steadily on her face.

Phaedra took a deep breath, seeking courage. "I am not refusing you, Mr. Farwell. Not yet. But I cannot accept you, either."

"So I am to hang about on tenterhooks until you make up your mind?" His lips twisted in a grimace.

Pain? Or anger?

"My dear Miss Phaedra, I want to marry you now, as soon as the banns can be called. I do not wish to wait for months while you dither about."

"Why?"

"Why? Why do I not want to wait? You silly chit, because I am not a patient man." He pulled a lacy handkerchief from his sleeve and wafted it at her. "We fops do not like delayed pleasures, don't you know."

Where was the sleepiness, the ennui? Phaedra frowned. "Why do you want to marry me?" She peered at him, wishing she could see beyond the abrupt opacity of his grey eyes.

"Why? You ask why? Great God, what a foolish question." Again the lacy handkerchief waved between them. "Because it is time I took a wife. Because you are suitable. Because I want to set up my nursery. Why does any man wish to marry?" His voice had increased in volume as he spoke, until his last words were close to a shout.

Still wondering who this strange, new person was, this impatient, forceful man who wore the façade of Reginald Farwell, she shook her head. "None of your reasons is sufficient," she told him. "Perhaps I should not ask you to wait on my decision."

He sat back, but left his hand over hers. "What do you consider to be a sufficient reason?"

"Love. I will not marry where there is not love. I have seen what my parents have and I want it too."

"Well, then, I love you. NOW will you marry me?"

"I think you said you love me because I wanted you to, not because you do. We have known each other barely a month and we have fought continually. I wonder if we should suit at all. I had hoped you would offer for Chloe. She and you seem so like."

When he opened his mouth, she held up a hand. "No, let me finish. We have never agreed upon a single topic, not once. To me this says we are entirely unsuited, but you obviously have a different understanding of our relationship. Until I am convinced one way or the other, I cannot give you the answer you desire, or any answer at all." She turned her hand under his, so that their palms touched. "Please, give me time."

"I would not have had your sister as a gift. Had I wanted a social butterfly for a wife, I could have had one long since." His hand tightened on hers, squeezing until she winced. "Blast you, Phaedra, must you be so stubborn?"

"I have no choice. Will you wait one month?"

"If I must, but I will not like it." He released her hand and relaxed against the back of the sofa. "Since you are determined to know me better, you may begin the inquisition."

"The inquisition? What do you mean?"

"The questions. To get to know me. I am waiting. Go ahead."

Phaedra found herself without speech. *Questions? I am supposed to ask him questions so I can learn more about him? Has he no understanding of how a man and woman become acquainted?*

After a moment in which thoughts spun madly inside her head, she said, "I will not ask you impertinent questions as a way of getting to know you better. We must spend time in each other's company, learn each other's habits and likes and dislikes. We will that way learn much more than mere words could impart." She lifted her gaze to his face, seeking his understanding.

His eyes were closed.

"Reginald Farwell! How dare you go to sleep when I am speaking to you?" Filled with hot anger, Phaedra picked up a pillow from a nearby chair and began to beat him with it. "Wake up, you idiot! Listen to me! Wake up!"

More swiftly than she had ever seen him move, he wrested the pillow from her and grabbed her wrists in one hand. Before she could think of struggling, he had them behind her, manacled together with long, strong fingers.

His other arm went around her, and he pulled her hard against him. "If you will prose on with nonsense, I will fall asleep. Now, what was it you would like to know? My teeth are good. I am told that I snore, but I have never heard myself do so, and it is therefore probably a lie. I do not keep a mistress and I gamble only in moderation. I am twenty-nine years of age. I was schooled at Eton, but did not go on to university. I have a small estate and a modest income, enough to house you and clothe you comfortably. Is there anything else you wish to know?"

She could not answer, for immediately upon uttering his last question, he had captured her lips with his. He held her so tightly she could only struggle weakly.

In the next instant, she lost interest in breaking free. A warm glow kindled in her toes and swept through her. She struggled no longer, but was content to be held. This close, she was aware of his subtle scent, a faint spicy odor suggestive of cloves and cinnamon.

When he pulled away, she felt a strong urge to catch hold of his ears and pull his mouth back to hers. Instead she leaned her head against his chest and waited for him to speak.

A minute passed. Then two. She could stand it no more. Phaedra looked up into his face, seeing not the bland expression he usually wore, but something hot and insistent. Her breath caught.

"Will you marry me, Phaedra?" he said, his voice soft but somehow not entirely gentle. "Now? As soon as possible?"

"Not yet," she replied in a whisper, hating her words, but knowing she was making the right decision.

His arms dropped releasing her. He stepped back and bowed. "Very well, ma'am. I will endeavor to play the ardent swain for one month. But at the end of that month, I expect an answer. And it had better be yes." He walked out of the room without a backward glance.

Phaedra stared after him, mouth agape. Somehow the fop had been transformed into an assertive, very masculine gentleman, despite the frivolous clothing. After a few minutes' stunned immobility, she backed up and sat on the sofa. When her mother entered an hour later, her chin was still in her hands, her elbows still on her knees, a thoughtful expression still on her face.

REGGIE, STRIDING TOWARD GROSVENOR SQUARE AFTER LEAVING THE HAZELBOURNE house, silently castigated himself for his poor handling of Phaedra. He had expected her to be surprised at his offer, had assumed that her first impulse would be to refuse it. But he had been determined to convince her to change her mind. Reggie knew he could be very persuasive. Never had any woman stood against his will for long.

Not that there had been all that many, for he had been a figure of fun since he first outgrew his school fellows when he was scarcely twelve. The façade he had constructed for himself had served him well, but it had kept the world at a distance. Especially the feminine portion of the world.

Instead of amusing Phaedra, his apparent sleepiness had angered her. Unlike most women he dealt with, she had been neither amused nor intrigued. At least she had not twigged that his principle reason for offering for her at this time was to protect her from Society's gossip. His original plan had been to defer his offer until he could woo her properly, but Chloe's foolishness had put an end to his plan.

He prayed she would never suspect. Nothing would influence her refusal so much as to think herself the object of his pity. He began to devise a new strategy as he strode along. By the time he had reached the Duchess' imposing mansion, he was whistling.

Lady Mary greeted him as he entered the drawing room. "Well?" she prompted.

He shook his head.

"Pay me," she demanded. He pulled a roll of bills from his purse and peeled off one hundred pounds.

"I knew she would not have you." She smiled widely as she tucked the bills into her reticule. "Have you any hope?"

"She wants a month to get to know me. Worse yet, she says she will not marry without love."

"I told you that."

"You did, indeed. And I refused to believe you." He followed her into the small parlor at the top of the stairs. Throwing himself into an armchair, he contemplated the pointed toes of his high-heeled shoes. "She seemed to show a preference for me, as much as she did for any man."

"You great looby. Of course she prefers you. She's half in love with you already, but does not know it yet," the Duchess said from the doorway. "I've seen how her eyes follow you."

"What are you going to do now, Reggie?" Lady Mary said.

"Oh, I'll do the usual thing. Take her driving in the park. Send her flowers at every opportunity. Squire her around. What else can I do?"

"You treat her like any ordinary gel and you'll lose her for sure," the Duchess warned. "Phaedra's got an odd kick to her gallop. You'll need different tactics with her."

Lady Mary reached up to pat his cheek. "Why will you not show her the real Reggie Farwell? She still thinks of you as a fop, as does everyone."

"Mary, I have worn the fop persona for so long that I do not think I can doff it. Not in Town, at least."

"Can you try? No one will laugh at you any more. You are no longer the Storky Farwell of your schooldays, you know. You are really very handsome, at least when you wear something other than those awful waistcoats." Lady Mary looked him up and down, wincing when her gaze passed over the primrose and royal blue brocade of his waistcoat. "Reggie, come out of hiding. Let Phaedra see the man behind the peacock. Please."

He clenched a fist, pounded on his bent knee. When he opened his mouth to reply, the words caught in his throat. A deep breath, a cough, and he was able to whisper, "I am afraid to. I want her so terribly." He buried his face in his hands and muttered through them, "She might not have me if she saw the man behind this ridiculous façade. At least this way I have a chance, for she knows the fop."

"Do you expect to carry out this inane masquerade all your life, Reggie? She will learn what you really are soon enough. How can you hide your writing and your agricultural experiments from your wife?"

The Duchess laid a hand on his shoulder. "Mary's right, Reggie. Show her what you really are. If you feel you cannot do it in Town, we'll go the country for a while." Her hand tightened and she gave him a small shake.

"You and the Hazelbournes will come to us for a fortnight. We'll leave next week." Having decided everyone's schedule, the Duchess called for her butler so she could issue instructions.

"What about your Season, Mary? Do you wish to leave Town in the middle of it?"

"Pooh. There will be others. I am in no more hurry to marry than you were at my age, Reggie." She looked away from him and said, with a casual air, "Do you suppose Mr. Martin might like to join us? His presence would make the group more balanced."

"Great God! Have you developed a tendre for that romantic puppy?"

"No, not at all. I do like him, for he is a kindly person. He and Phaedra are friends, but we could never go beyond friendship. I am being selfish, for I would feel left out, with you and Phaedra playing your romantic games, if I had no one with whom to flirt. And I feel sorry for him, for no one ever seems to take him seriously. He will be absolutely devastated when he discovers that Chloe has married someone else, you know."

"Then suggest it to Her Grace. But be sure you do not toy with his affections, Mary."

"I would not do anything so unkind. If it will reassure you, I will be very frank with him as to why he is being invited."

"You do that. I'd like to see the good fellow's face when he is told he is being invited on a house party so that the Duchess' granddaughter can have someone to flirt with."

Reggie felt shame that he was amused, for at least no one had ever invited him to a house party to provide the hostess with a cicisbeo.

Had they?

CHAPTER SEVENTEEN

TRUE TO HIS WORD, REGINALD FARWELL PLAYED THE PART OF ARDENT SUITOR for the next few days. He came to take Phaedra driving in Hyde Park the very afternoon of their discussion. His equipage, a dashing phaeton with yellow spokes and red hubs, red trim on a forest green body, and yellow harness, was a surprise. She had never seen him in the park except as a pedestrian or a passenger.

His groom was also a surprise. Instead of livery, he wore a turban of spotless white. His dark brown trousers and jacket resembled a military uniform, with brass buttons and leather belting, and his bare feet were shod with sandals. She looked curiously at the groom as Mr. Farwell handed her to her seat. The swarthy groom man returned the look with an interested directness not usual in servants.

Once the horses were in motion, Phaedra said, "What an unusual fellow your groom is. A native of India, is he not?"

"Yes. Haresh came with me when I returned from there." He guided his team into a side path. "May I say, Miss Phaedra, that you are looking uncommonly lovely. That rich brown pelisse and russet gown suit you very well. And your bonnet is charming."

She thanked him courteously. "I did not know you had been in India. When were you there?"

"Years ago, when I was just up from school. Do you attend Lady Dillingsworth's musicale tomorrow evening? I would count myself privileged to escort you there."

"Oh, I suppose so, if you wish." She had not planned to attend the musicale, but if he would be there... "Why did you go to India?"

"I wanted to see more of the world, I suppose." He shrugged, his shoulder moving against hers.

She wanted to scoot away from the contact, for it had a somewhat disturbing effect upon her thought processes.

"Miss Phaedra, the Duchess will be sending your family an invitation for a house party at Verbain. I hope you will come, for the company will be sadly flat without you."

"If my parents accept, I will be there, I imagine. Tell me about India. How long were you there?"

"Just over five years. It is hot, disease ridden, and the women are not nearly so lovely as you. Has anyone ever told you, my dear, that your eyes are the most beautiful in the world?"

"Will you stop this! I did not come with you to endure the sort of nonsensical flattery with which you shower every female. If you cannot converse seriously, you may take me home."

"You know I never converse seriously. It sends me to sleep."

"Twaddle. You could not possibly sleep when driving. Please, tell me about India. I have never met anyone before who has been there. All I know of the country is what I have read in books. Are the flowers beautiful? Do tigers really prowl the streets?"

Giving up his intention of wooing her with flattery, Reggie described the parts of India he had seen, making it sound as if he had been touring the country. She could not possibly be interested in his real adventures, for they had not been pleasant. On the spot, he invented an anecdote about a man-eating tiger who only caught boy children below the age of seven, and those only on Sundays. He concluded with, "So they finally caught him, by gathering all the little boys of the village in front of the local mission church and luring the tiger thence, to be caught in a gigantic net. The natives were told that God had helped in his capture, and so the good parson had several new converts that week."

Phaedra giggled. "I do not know how much of that tale is true and how much of it you invented, but I enjoyed it. Did you make your fortune in India?"

"No, I inherited it from an aunt. Fortunately she was somewhat miserly, else I should have inherited a good bit less."

"Did she leave you property also?"

"A small estate north of Oxford. My agent manages it for me." Feeling backed into a corner by the trend of the conversation, he extracted his handkerchief from his sleeve and waved it. "Can you imagine me with my feet in the furrows and hay in my hair?"

"No, but I would like to. How much better a life it would be for you than this useless gallivanting about Town, wasting your youth at parties and balls."

"But such a bore, my dear, such a bore." He forced a yawn. "Society is ever so much more diverting."

They returned to the main road, which was crowded with other carriages and many riders. Further conversation was made difficult by the constant necessity of responding to greetings from acquaintances.

Phaedra was enjoying herself, despite her frustration with Mr. Farwell's insistence on keeping their conversation superficial. The oily Mr. Dervigne appeared and rode alongside the phaeton for several minutes. He was clearly curious about Chloe's sudden marriage. When Phaedra made it apparent she was going to tell him nothing, he smiled at her and said, "May one assume you will continue to grace Society, my dear. I would delight in becoming better acquainted with you." His smile widened and became, in Phaedra's opinion, positively lascivious as his gaze swept over her body. "Much better acquainted."

"Move aside, Dervigne. My horses are restive." Mr. Farwell made no obvious move, but his team surged forward. Dervigne had to jerk his horse aside to keep it from being struck by the back corner of the phaeton.

The team settled back into their slow walk within a few yards. Again Mr. Farwell seemed to do nothing to control them.

"Thank you for getting rid of him. I cannot like the man. He makes me uncomfortable," Phaedra said, with heartfelt gratitude.

"He is a rake of the worst sort. Preys on young girls in their first Season who are flattered by attention paid them by an older man. He has ruined at least three, that I know of. Stay as far away from him as you can, Miss Phaedra."

"Trust me, I shall." She turned to stare at him, suddenly curious. "Do you mean he has really ruined them, or just caused unpleasant gossip"

"What a shocking question for an innocent young woman to ask. What must I think of you?"

She scowled until he replied.

"One died in childbirth and disgrace; two others were married very suddenly to suitors previously thought unacceptable." His mouth suddenly closed into a hard line. "There is Lady Everingham," he said, his words audible only to her. "Put your chin up, and smile your prettiest at me."

She gave him a dazzling smile and laid her hand affectionately on his arm as they passed the Everingham carriage. Conscious of the poisonous stare of its occupant, she chattered brightly until they were well past the Everingham carriage.

Her words did not match her carefree expression. "Can nothing be done about people like Mr. Dervigne? How can he continue to be acceptable to Society? Oh, dear, she hates me, I can see it in her face. What an evil woman." Her smile faded as they drew away from the Everingham carriage and she sighed in relief. "I hate to act someone I am not. How happy I will be to l return to the country where I may be myself."

"You may always be yourself with me. In fact, you may always be yourself in London, once the gossip over Chloe has died away. Your behavior is beyond reproach."

"Oh, but I am afraid that my unruly tongue will lead me into disgrace. I become so tired with always keeping it in control."

"Once we are married, Phaedra, you may say whatever you like. A married woman may be much more frank than her unwed sisters."

She let the artificial gaiety drain from her voice. "I have not yet said that I will marry you, Mr. Farwell." Suddenly she was very tired. "I think you had better take me home."

Reggie mentally kicked himself. What was it about Phaedra that made him forget his public persona so frequently?

The drive home passed in silence. Phaedra seemed depressed. He berated himself, because for a while they had been in perfect accord—until his mention of marriage had driven her to withdraw into herself.

When he escorted her to her door, she said, "Thank you for a lovely afternoon, Mr. Farwell. I enjoyed it very much." The tone of her voice belied her words. He bowed over her hand, keeping his lips a scant quarter-inch from her leather-covered fingertips.

I wish I could kiss her hand. Her mouth.

Great God, I want to kiss her.

EDGEMONT HANDED PHAEDRA A NOTE AS SHE ENTERED. "FROM YOUR SISTER, MISS Phaedra. She wrote to your parents, as well."

She tore it open and read it, standing in the foyer. "Oh, Edgemont, she sounds very happy," she said, knowing the butler had been almost as concerned as she that Chloe's marriage was not a mistake.

"Very good, Miss. May I take the liberty of saying that I was quite impressed with his lordship. He seems a proper gentleman."

"Not like the madcap Hazelbournes, you mean," she teased.

"I am quite satisfied to serve your family, Miss Phaedra. What I inferred was that I think he will do very well for Miss Chloe, I mean to say, her ladyship."

"Yes, he'll keep her in line, I'll wager. I am so glad to hear that she is happy. I was worried, you know."

"Of course you were, Miss Phaedra," he said in his most butlerish tones. But he winked as he so often had when she and Chloe were children.

She laughed and returned the wink, and then ran up the stairs to change her dress. The faint depression that had taken possession of her after the encounter with Lady Everingham was gone.

The next day Phaedra, her mother, and Cousin Louisa went to a tea party at Marie Sefton's. The announcement of Chloe's marriage had appeared in that morning's *Gazette*, so they were expecting to be questioned about the suddenness of it. And so they were. Lady Gifford had decreed they would say that Wilderlake had been unexpectedly called back to his estates. Not wanting to depart without Chloe, he had begged that their nuptials be moved forward. His mother had agreed to support the story.

They had reckoned without Lady Everingham and her cronies.

Lady Sefton's first words to Lady Gifford were, "My dear, I was so surprised to read of your daughter's marriage. Why I had heard that she and Everingham were practically betrothed."

"Nonsense, Maria, you should not listen to gossip," Lady Gifford replied. "She and Wilderlake fell in love at first sight and wished to marry immediately. So impetuous, you know, as all young lovers are. We told them that they must wait until they knew each other better before formalizing their relationship."

"What made you change your minds? Surely not her behavior at the Duchess' ball, Isabella?"

Lady Gifford smiled serenely as she told of the emergency situation at Wilderlake's estate. "He feared that, because of the distance, he might not get the situation resolved until it was too late to return to Town this Season. So he convinced my husband and me to give our consent to an immediate marriage. We could not, you know, leave London at this time, because of Phaedra."

"I had heard that the gel was seriously ill," a nearby woman said, her tone positively dripping unction. "Surely, Lady Gifford, you did not let her be married from her sickbed."

"Of course not. Her illness was not serious, and she was quite recovered from it."

"Enough to take a little jaunt into Hertfordshire, dear Lady Gifford?"

came a syrupy voice from across the room. Lady Gifford ignored the question, but her back stiffened and her face reddened.

Phaedra started to turn to see who had made the remark, but Cousin Louisa prevented her from doing so. Just then, Lady Mary came up and drew Phaedra away, saying, "I am so glad to see you today, Phaedra. Grandmama has said your parents have accepted her invitation to a house party at Verbain. What fun we will have."

Phaedra ground her teeth, but she managed to smile back at Lady Mary. "Yes, I am sure we will, Lady Mary. I am quite looking forward to it." She smiled at the quiet girl who waited in the corner. "How do you do, Miss Graham."

"Oh, Miss Hazelbourne, how brave you are," Miss Graham ventured, in a near whisper. "I would not have come here for anything, had I been you."

"Sarah, come here," Mrs. Graham called from across the room.

"Not just now, please, Mama. Miss Hazelbourne just arrived and I wish to visit with her for a few moments," the girl replied, not moving from where she sat. Both Phaedra and Lady Mary stared at her in amazement. She blushed furiously.

"Good in you, Sarah," Lady Mary said. "For we know your mother would not wish you to associate with Miss Hazelbourne, after the gossip that has been raging in this room today."

Still blushing, Sarah Graham said, still almost whispering, "I know she does not. She told me this morning that we would no longer acknowledge the Hazelbournes. But I could not obey her. Miss Phaedra was kind to me before anyone. I could not desert her when she is in need of friends." It was quite the longest speech either of the other two had ever heard from the shy girl and their amazement grew.

"Sarah, there are depths to you that I never suspected," Phaedra told her. "I am honored to have you for a friend. But friends are not so formal with one another. My name is Phaedra."

"And mine is Mary," the tiny redhead added.

"Oh, I could not..." Sarah said, awed at such familiarity.

"Of course you could," Lady Mary assured her with a kind smile. "I cannot allow such formality from my friends. It is most uncomfortable."

The three girls chatted quite happily for quite some time. Sarah, ignoring her mother's frequent beckonings, was found to be quite a delightful person, well read and interesting. When her mother finally insisted that it was time for them to depart, she did so reluctantly, but with an invitation to call upon Lady Mary after her return from Verbain. She said, quite decisively, "I appreciate the invitation, Mary, but I do not think I will accept. I would not expose your grandmother to Mama. We will see each other at parties, where Mama will not be able to hang upon the Duchess' skirts. Goodbye, Phaedra. Please, do not let the gossip depress you. Yes, Mama, I am coming."

"Well!" exclaimed Lady Mary as the girl and her mother left the room. "I never thought that she would speak up like that."

"Nor did I. What a nice girl. I quite like her. But what a terrible mother," Phaedra said.

"Is she not?" Mary giggled. "I do hope that Sarah will not receive too harsh a scold. Now, Phaedra, what is this I hear about your refusing Reggie's offer?"

"Oh, dear. He should not have told you. And I did not exactly refuse him."

"Reggie and I tell each other practically everything. I knew a fortnight ago that he intended to offer for you. Come, Phaedra, do you hold him in such distaste?"

"No, I do not. I am just not sure we would suit. Oh, Mary, I am in such a quandary. I do like him, but I cannot feel I know him. Have you—" He closed her mouth, not wanting to reveal her uncertainties. "You and he have been friends for many years. Can you tell me of his childhood? His interests?"

Lady Mary shook her head. "Reggie is a very private person. I must let him tell you of himself."

"But Mary, how can I make such a momentous decision when I have no knowledge of the man. I greatly fear his values are widely divergent from mine."

"Are they? I think you would be surprised. Perhaps you will learn better while you are at Verbain."

"But I am not sure..."

"Well, I am sure. We all will have a perfectly marvelous time. Oh, dear, it looks as if Grandmama is ready to leave. Please excuse me, Phaedra. Will I see you this evening at the Dillingsworth musicale?"

"We will be there. Mama says that we will refuse practically no invitations until we leave for Verbain." Surely not admitting she was attending because Mr. Farwell would be there was only a small fib.

Deserted by her friends, Phaedra conversed with some of the other young ladies at the tea party. Most were kind to her, but a few ventured unpleasant remarks about Chloe's sudden marriage. Phaedra was able to return unexceptionable replies to most of these, but her patience was strained almost to the breaking point. When Miss Evelyn Stockton asked her if she was not ashamed of her sister's quite improper behavior, she lost all control of her temper and her tongue.

"My sister has done nothing for which any of her family is ashamed, Miss Stockton. It is only the evil gossips, of which Society has far too many, that have besmirched her good name. If the so-called ladies of the *ton* would spend less time watching the behavior of innocent girls and more in mending their own questionable behavior, the world would be a much better place. What have you done recently to improve the world in which you live, Miss Stockton? Or is all your time spent in shopping, partying, and gossiping?"

Miss Stockton drew back in alarm from Phaedra's flashing eyes and caustic voice. "I can see that you are no better mannered than your sister, Miss Hazelbourne. How rude you are!"

Ignoring the hand Cousin Louisa had laid on her arm, Phaedra continued, "It is you who are rude. Spreading rumors about my sister, whom you hardly know, and making remarks calculated to discomfort me. Your manners are in need of mending, not mine! Good day, Miss Stockton. I hope I will not meet you again." She turned on her heel and stalked away, Cousin Louisa in her wake, to where her mother sat against the opposite wall, speaking with Lady Jersey.

"Mama, forgive me, but I wish to return home. There are persons here with whom I do not care to associate further. Lady Jersey, I do not include you, unless you choose to be among those who would insult my sister." She ignored the shocked expression on her mother's face and walked from the room.

Lady Gifford half rose from her chair, but sat again when Cousin Louisa told her, "Stay here, Isabella, and enjoy yourself. I will see her home."

Lady Jersey let out a peal of laughter. "Lud, Isabella, I never thought she had a temper. That one always impressed me as being too quiet, too serious. Good girl, standing up for her sister like that. I saw her talking to that mealy-mouthed Stockton girl. She probably gave the chit a good tongue-lashing.

"Here, Isabella, cheer up. Your daughter's done nothing to harm herself. Those who matter will admire her for her defense of her sister, you know, just as I admire you for holding your head up and coming here today.

"Oh, yes, I've heard what Lady Everingham has said, and I'll wager there is some basis in it, but no daughter of yours would ever do anything more than mildly improper, and you've got her married off now, so you can stop worrying about her. Now all you have to concern yourself with is whether the first little one comes along too soon.

"No, now don't you frown at me. I did not say that Chloe was ruined when she married Wilderlake, but you must admit that it would be better for all concerned if they waited a few months before she started breeding. But there, no expecting any man to hold himself back, just to still the gossip, so all we can do is hope.

"By next Season this will all be forgotten anyway. I still call myself your friend, Isabella, and you just remind yourself of that whenever the gossip gets too thick. I am not without influence, you know. I'll do what I can to still the talk about your other girl. Oh, dear, Maria is beckoning to me. I must go see what she wants.

"Now, Isabella, you just worry about finding a husband suitable for Phaedra. She will need someone quite out of the ordinary. Yes, Maria, I am coming. So good chatting with you, Isabella." She left a breathless but relieved Lady Gifford behind her.

Phaedra left the tea party and went home, fully expecting to receive a thorough scold from her mama later. She was mildly surprised when Cousin Louisa said nothing about her outburst, but only related *on dits* she had heard that afternoon.

When Mama came home later, she merely cautioned Phaedra to choose her words carefully, "For it would not do for you to say anything really insulting to anyone. I do not expect you to refrain from defending your sister, as long as you do so in a ladylike manner, you know."

Phaedra was quite relieved to know that her mother was not unduly upset by her loss of temper. She vowed to keep a better rein on it in the future.

The rest of the week passed all too slowly. Everywhere they went, Phaedra was forced to bite back angry words more than once. No one ever said anything overtly derogatory about Chloe to her face, however, so she managed to hold her temper.

Lady Everingham glared at each of their two encounters. She had not discontinued her criticisms of the Hazelbournes. Phaedra was therefore pleasantly surprised to find that few members of Society paid heed to Lady Everingham's words. In fact, most seemed arrayed on the side of the Hazelbournes.

The most distressing part of the next few days was being forced to be polite to Mr. Dervigne. That gentleman sought her out at every opportunity. He continued to voice flattering phrases, and frequently invited her to drive with him.

She never quite gave him the set down that she wished to, however, because Lady Mary had warned her that he was capable of exacting revenge when snubbed as he deserved. "In Grandmama's words, he can damn with faint praise. Without saying anything precisely true, he is adept at spreading the worst sort of gossip and innuendo." After that Phaedra was grateful for Mr. Farwell's almost constant presence. When he was with her, Mr. Dervigne kept his distance.

Mr. Farwell, in fact, was proving to be quite a useful person to have about. He knew, and was known by, nearly everyone in Society, it seemed. At Lady Jersey's ball, he had introduced her to a number of young gentlemen, all of whom had asked her to dance, so that she had not sat out even once. He was ever at her side when neither was engaged to dance with someone else. His presence ensured that she was rarely exposed to unkind remarks or cuts direct.

He took her driving in the park nearly every afternoon. On Sunday he accompanied the family to church. The following Tuesday, her free day, he invited her to visit Astley's Amphitheatre. The proposed outing held far more charm than Mrs. Stewart's weekly literary salon, although she had to admit that if this week had been the meeting of the Association for the Preservation of British Compositae, she might have wavered.

He kept both her and Cousin Louisa in stitches that afternoon, making often quite acerbic comparisons between the antics of the clowns and those of certain members of the *ton*. His foppish dress and behavior still bothered her, but once in a while, she caught a quick, elusive glimpse of another, more serious man beneath the outward dandy. Intrigued, she decided she was quite content to have him constantly in attendance.

The night before the house party was to depart for Verbain, she and her mama again accompanied Lady Mary and the Duchess to the weekly ball at Almack's. For the first time, Phaedra found herself looking forward to it. She wore a new gown of silk, a deep, rich bronze-green in shade, her mother having decided that the restriction to pastel muslins could be relaxed.

Phaedra had again lost the battle to have the neckline modestly high, and the curve of her breasts showed above the unadorned silk. The skirt, with its demi-train, was fuller than she was used to. When she twirled, it billowed out to show a paler olive-green slip, embroidered with emerald green leaves for about six inches above the hem. Her grandmother's pearls encircled her throat, and dainty pearl eardrops, leant by her mama, matched them.

Mr. Farwell had again sent her ivory roses. She broke one from her posy to tuck into her curls among the bronze-green ribbons that held them high on her head. Gazing at herself in the pier glass in her mama's dressing room, she decided she looked quite well indeed.

Mr. Farwell was waiting in the foyer with her father as she and her mother came down the stairs. She stopped halfway down, frozen in surprise. Gone was the fop in primrose inexpressibles and colorful, almost garish, waistcoat. An elegant gentleman in black evening clothes was in his place. She could not take her eyes from him as she descended. His snowy cravat was tied in a tasteful and restrained knot, his shirt points rose to a modest height, his clocked hose showed strong, shapely calves.

She caught her breath and looked quickly away when she realized she was staring at his thighs, clearly defined by his clinging satin breeches. Why had she never before noticed how golden his hair was, how gray his eyes? How strange she had never she really seen the determination bespoken by his square, firm jaw.

She managed to greet him politely, but found that she could not talk so easily to this elegantly dressed stranger as she had to the fop. She allowed him to place her cloak over her shoulders, shivering as his fingertips lingered a moment on her bare shoulder.

When she took his arm to enter the ballroom at Almack's, Phaedra finally found her voice. "How elegant you look tonight, Mr. Farwell and how restrained your garments. Are you sure you are not ill?"

"My dear, I am dressed this way in an attempt to win your favor. You have so many times deplored my foppish styles that I was forced to purchase these to please you."

"You did not! Oh, you should not have. Not for me."

"Only for you, my love," he said softly. "Now, may I have your dance card before all your other admirers steal away my waltzes. There, I have put my name down for all of them."

"But you cannot! There are three; I can only dance with you twice."

"Then we will sit out the third. But I do not want you to waltz with anyone else." His eyes held hers, compellingly, until she agreed.

Phaedra's card was soon filled. She danced that night as she never had before. Her sense that she was in her best looks gave her confidence. She never felt at a loss for words, never felt clumsy or awkward.

The second time she waltzed with Mr. Farwell, he pulled her closer than propriety allowed and whispered, close to her ear, "You are the loveliest woman here. Your eyes sparkle and your smile invites everyone to share your joy."

Unable to respond, she could only look up at him. His smile was tender, his eyes warm.

Mr. Dervigne attempted to engage her for a dance shortly after supper, but she was relieved to be able to refuse him. As she did so, Mr. Farwell materialized at her side.

"Evening, Dervigne," he said, shortly.

"Your servant, Farwell. Miss Phaedra, surely there is someone who will yield me just one dance. I cannot believe that you truly wish to dance with all these callow youths."

"Indeed I do, Mr. Dervigne. Much more than I wish to dance with you. Mr. Farwell, I am thirsty. Could you escort me to the refreshment table, please?" She turned her back on the older man. *Such a detestable creature.*

When Phaedra had danced away with her next partner, Reggie strolled toward the far side of the room. He was in no mood to dance with anyone else. Phaedra had ruined his taste for sweet innocence and wicked sophistication alike. He had just slipped into a curtained alcove on the opposite wall when Robert Dervigne joined him.

"Your attentions to Miss Phaedra Hazelbourne are becoming particular, Farwell. Are we to assume you and she are...involved?" His tone spoke volumes about what the involvement entailed.

Reggie looked down at the older man. He let his lip curl. "I do not like your tone, Dervigne. You malign the lady."

"Oh, come now. All society knows of her sister's escapades. Can we not expect the same lack of discretion from her?"

Reggie felt his carefully maintained air of ennui slipping, and realized he cared not a whit. "I would watch my words if I were you Dervigne. A loose tongue can be dangerous."

A harsh bark of laughter burst from Dervigne's mouth. "You threaten me, Farwell? A useless fop like you? Don't be ridiculous."

A red haze clouded Reggie's vision. Without hesitation, he doubled his fist and buried it in Dervigne's middle. His other fist caught the man on the chin and sent him sprawling against the alcove wall. "Although you are no gentleman, Dervigne, I promise you that the next time you venture to speak ill of Miss Phaedra or of her sister, I will challenge you. Is that clear?"

Dervigne opened his mouth. Closed it. His eyes narrowed. "So the fop is not all he seems." He sighed lustily. "Very well. Henceforth I will avoid any discussion of the Hazelbourne sisters." He shook his head but made no other move. "Go away, Farwell. I refuse to add to my humiliation by attempting to stand with you here."

Reggie went. *Good God. I must be going out of my mind. I need fresh air before I do something foolish.*

LATE IN THE EVENING, PHAEDRA SEATED HERSELF BESIDE HER MOTHER.

"Do you not dance the waltz, dear?"

"No, Mama, for I have already danced twice with Mr. Farwell."

"I doubt it will harm you to do so a third time. Everyone is aware that his attentions to you have been most particular. But I will leave it to you." Phaedra did not see her give a quick nod to the gentleman as he approached. He held out his hand to the girl.

"Come, dance with me. I do not want to sit this one out."

She hesitated. "But what will people think?" She wanted to dance with him. Her mother said it would be all right. But still...

"They will think that I am the most fortunate man in this room, to be dancing with the most beautiful woman here. Come, Phaedra."

His smile overwhelmed her better judgment, and she went into his arms.

CHAPTER EIGHTEEN

THE JOURNEY TO THE ESTATE OF THE DUKE AND DUCHESS OF VERBAIN ALLOWED Phaedra plenty of time to think about her feelings for Mr. Farwell. She rode with her mother and Cousin Louisa in the family coach, the Duchess and Lady Mary having gone ahead on the previous day. Mr. Farwell and Mr. Martin rode alongside with her papa. She frequently had a glimpse of one or the other of them through the coach window. Somehow she had expected a fop to be a poor rider, but Mr. Farwell sat a horse as if he had been born astride. His garments were every bit as colorful as any she had seen him wear, so she never mistook him for one of the other men. The bright lime green of his elegantly tailored coat shone in the sunlight like some outré lantern.

After dancing until the ball at Almack's had ended the night before, Phaedra slept through the first change of horses, in spite of wanting to see the new country through which they passed. They were pulling into a posting house for the second change before she woke fully.

Once Mama and Cousin Louisa had alighted, Phaedra gathered her skirts and prepared to follow. Before she could hop down, as was her habit, Mr. Farwell appeared in the coach's doorway. Holding out his hand, he offered his assistance.

She took the waiting hand, once again noticing how strong it was, for all the skin was white and smooth. To cover the tiny thrill his touch engendered, she said, "I must say, Mr. Farwell, having an attentive suitor is quite exciting. I have never felt so cosseted." She smiled up into his face, and was momentarily nonplussed to see in his usually unrevealing eyes a gleam of...of *what?* It put her in mind of coals left smoldering in a fireplace. The gleam was gone in an instant, replaced by sleepy ennui.

"Become used to it," he replied, taking her arm. "I have every intention of becoming indispensable to you."

"Well, I do not understand why you are showing this partiality to me, but I shall not complain. It is making the journey ever so much more comfortable than I am used to. Papa always took great care of Mama, when we went to the Assemblies at Huntington, you know, and Chloe required Jem's assistance because she always became so ill from the journey. I was left to manage for myself.

"Oh, do not think I was neglected in any way. I much prefer to be independent. I am not so delicate that I cannot alight from a coach without a gentleman's assistance. All the same, it is a pleasant novelty to be treated as if I were a fragile blossom."

He touched her cheek lightly with a gloved fingertip. "A particularly lovely blossom."

A shiver found its way up her spine.

Their light luncheon was soon consumed. Afterward Phaedra and her mama, desirous of exercise before once again immuring themselves in the coach, walked down a short path to a nearby stream. Phaedra gazed at the moving water, deep in thought. "Mama," she said finally, "Do you receive the impression that Mr. Farwell is really two different people?" She watched a leaf as it floated past, twirling and dipping in the chuckling stream.

"Why, what do you mean, dear?"

"When I first met him, I dismissed him as a fop. His dress bordered on the preposterous, his conversation was full of meaningless flattery. He never said anything of great significance, until one day he scolded me for what he called my snobbery. But then he promptly went to sleep, so I assumed he was teasing." She leaned over the stream, examining the plants growing along its banks. "In the past few days, he has changed, somehow become more serious."

"Mr. Farwell has always seemed a most congenial and intelligent gentleman to me," Mama replied. "I wonder if you have not let his style of clothing influence you too much, so that you failed to perceive the person within. He and I have had several interesting conversations while you were dancing."

"Perhaps." Phaedra knelt at the water's edge, reaching for some floating plants in a tiny pool formed by piled rocks. It looked like a duckweed, but somehow different. She wished she had a bottle so she could collect some. Dipping her fingers in the water again, she washed away the few leaves that had clung. "Mama, there is another thing I wish to ask you about," she said, without looking away from the water.

"What is it, dear?"

Although she knew what she wanted to ask, the words came with difficulty. "Several of the young ladies I become acquainted with, those who are in their second or third Seasons, told me that Mr. Farwell has the reputation of being an excellent escort and very good company, but he has never been known to pay attention to any female in particular. Selina Carruthers said she developed quite a tendre for him in her first Season and made sure he knew of it. He discouraged her firmly but kindly. According to Sarah, he has never been known to go beyond what is proper with any lady and that there was never any gossip about his having a mistress or pursuing the opera dancers, although her older brother had once seen him at Harriet Wilson's establishment, where he was apparently well known."

"Good heavens, Phaedra. Is that what young ladies discuss these days? How shocking." Her mother chuckled. "Nothing has changed since I was a girl." She sobered. "I do hope that you did not ask Miss Carruthers about Mr. Farwell's amours."

"Of course not, Mama. She volunteered the information. You know how she does run on. I did not discourage her revelations, though," she admitted. "Mama, how could I marry a man who has patronized that...that house of ill repute?"

"If we women refused to marry any man who had indulged himself thus before marriage, England would be populated with old maids. Most gentlemen visit Mrs. Wilson's establishment, or others that are not nearly so well kept, before they marry."

"Do you mean...did...Papa?"

"That is none of your concern. Your papa is an exemplary gentleman, but he is a man. As is Mr. Farwell—both exemplary and a man."

Miserable, Phaedra returned her gaze to the stream, as if she might find answers writ in the moving water.

"I could not bear it if my husband were to be intimate with another woman."

"Then it is up to you to see that he does not. A woman who does not endeavor to please her husband only gets what she has merited when her husband is physically unfaithful to her."

"And that is why I must be sure to love the man I marry, Mama. I could not bear to be so intimate with a man for whom I merely felt respect and admiration." She sat back on the grassy bank with no thought to her gown. "Oh, Mama, I must be sure! You were sure you loved Papa when you married him, were you not?"

"I was, but most women are not so fortunate. Most of the girls I knew during my Season married for money or position or because their parents wished it and chose their husbands."

Mama pulled her into a soft embrace. "Phaedra, I am not trying to push you into marriage with Mr. Farwell, no matter how it must seem so to you. I do wish you to marry well, and your opportunities of meeting worthy young men will be so much less if you return home unwed, so I encourage you to give his proposal serious consideration. Give him a chance while we are at Verbain. If you are still certain that you and he would not suit when our visit is over, you must tell him so in no uncertain terms. Then you will be free to enjoy the remainder of your Season heart whole and fancy free."

"I will try, Mama," she promised, with a heartfelt sigh, "but it seems like such a short time to decide the course of one's entire life." She stood up and attempted to brush the mud from her skirt where she had knelt upon it. "I almost wish that he had never offered for me. It has become so complicated, trying to decide how I really feel about him, and now he seems like a different person than the one I thought I knew. If he had not changed so, my decision would have been easier, for I could not have married him as he was when I met him."

"It is your doubts that cause me to urge you to give yourself more time in which to decide," Mama said. "Were you certain you could not marry him, I should cease to do so. I only want you to be happy, my dear, and would be the first to object to any man with whom I felt you would not be." She hugged Phaedra briefly. "Let us go back. Your father will be most out of sorts, so long have we been gone."

Papa demanded to know what had kept them away so long and promised that they would not arrive at Verbain until well after dark, due to their disappearance. He continued to grumble as the ladies entered the coach and did not subside until his wife leaned out the window. She laughingly told him that he was now delaying them and if he would cease his grumblings, they could get on their way.

Behind his back, Mr. Farwell winked at Phaedra.

Winked? Mr. Farwell? Never.

As the coach pulled onto the road, Phaedra cast a last, longing glance at the pretty streambank where, under other circumstances, she could have spent a happy hour or two, collecting plant specimens. Spring was well along, and she had done no collecting at all, there being no place in London where wildflowers grew. The vegetation in Town was either weedy or cultivated. Although she had seen some very interesting weeds, she had not had the opportunity to collect any of them.

She smiled to herself. What would the *ton* have thought, to see a respectable young woman pulling up weeds with great care and stowing them in her collecting bag? What would Mr. Farwell think if she asked him to assist her?

Why not? Tomorrow I will. If he truly wishes to marry me, he will respect my avocation.

She leaned forward to catch sight of him through the coach window. He was nowhere to be seen, to her considerable disappointment.

By the time they reached Verbain, the passengers in the Hazelbourne coach were travel-weary and stiff. Phaedra hardly noticed the magnificence of the Duke's principal seat. All she wanted was to get to her bedchamber and remove her wrinkled garments, wash her face, and move about a bit. Lady Mary escorted her up the soaring flight of stairs and along a seemingly endless corridor, explaining that the house party was to be lodged in the west wing, while the family inhabited the east.

"Grandpapa is not well, you know, and so we thought you would be more comfortable here, where you would not feel you had to be quiet, so as not to disturb him. Here." She opened a door. "These are your rooms."

Phaedra saw a cheery sitting room, the walls hung with yellow-flowered paper, a wide window that let in the rays of the setting sun, bowls of daffodils on every level surface, and a fireplace burning brightly. She followed Lady Mary to another door and saw beyond it a large bedroom with leaf green hangings and draperies, a forest green rug, and painted pale yellow walls.

"Do you like it?" Lady Mary said, after she'd stood a long moment in stunned silence. "It is quite my favorite of all the guest apartments. I thought you would be comfortable here, for it reminds me of a forest glade."

"Oh, it is so grand. I shall become spoiled staying in so lovely a room." She hugged Lady Mary.

"Mrs. Arbuckle is just across the hall and your parents are next door." Lady Mary indicated. "Reggie and Mr. Martin are at the other end of the hall. Now, I shall send Ellen to you, to help you unpack and change. She is so excited, to be asked to be your maid while you are here. Her dream is to become a fine lady's maid, or even a dresser. She is only sixteen, but she has already proven to have a talent for hairdressing. I think you will like her."

"You do not have to provide me with a maid. Mama's dresser can assist me," Phaedra protested.

"But I wanted to. I also wanted to give Ellen a chance to prove herself. My maid, Annie, is so jealous of her prerogatives that I have not dared let Ellen wait upon me."

"Very well, but having my own maid will only increase the danger of my becoming spoiled, you know. I shall be quite insufferable by the time we return to London." Phaedra pulled the bonnet from her head and tossed it upon the bed.

Just then a pale, rather homely girl in a maid's uniform entered somewhat precipitously. Her breath was coming in short gasps. "Lady Mary, am I late? Oh, I am." She curtsied. "I'm that sorry, mum. I was in the kitchen when Mrs. Swinton told me the company was here. I ran all the way, really I did." She turned a blushing face to Phaedra and smiled tremulously.

"It does not matter, Ellen. This is Miss Phaedra Hazelbourne, whom you will serve while she is our guest. Phaedra, I will see you later. Can you find your way or shall I send a footman in half an hour?"

"Send him, please. I was not paying attention when you pointed out the drawing room. It would not do for me to get lost on my way to dinner."

"No, for we would then have to send out a search party, and you might starve before we found you. This is a monstrous big house." Laughing, Lady Mary let herself out the door.

Ellen curtsied again as Phaedra turned to her. "Oh, mum, I really am sorry I was late. Would you want to bathe before supper? I can have a tub up in a twinkling."

"No, I think I will settle for just a wash. Half an hour is scarcely time for the tub. Perhaps just before I retire." Ellen helped her to remove her pelisse. As the maid was hanging it in the wardrobe, there was a knock on the door.

The girl dropped the pelisse and scurried to open it. "It's your baggage, mum. Oh!" she cried as she stepped aside to allow the footman to carry Phaedra's trunk and portmanteau inside. "Your pelisse! I'm sorry, mum." She hurried to pick up the garment and this time saw it safely hung in the wardrobe. "Shall I unpack, Mum? Which gown was you wanting to wear?"

Phaedra took pity on her. "Calm yourself, Ellen. We have plenty of time for me to dress, for I shall wear the yellow gown. It does not wrinkle easily, so we should be able to just shake it out before I put it on. Yes", she said when the maid located the dress, "that is the one. See how the wrinkles fall out of it? Now, if there is some hot water, I shall take the worst of the road dust off myself." She looked around.

Ellen's expression showed horror when she founds no water in the pitcher on the commode. She begged Phaedra's pardon and ran out the door. In just a few minutes, she re-entered, carrying a pitcher of hot water and leaving a trail of droplets in her wake. Again she abased herself, and again Phaedra told her to be calm.

The nervous little maid proved to be all that had been promised as she assisted to dress and arrange Phaedra's hair. Apparently apprehension and excitement had combined to make her seem scatterbrained.

"I was that surprised, yesterday, when her ladyship called me in to tell me I was to wait on you while you was here," she confided as she held a mirror up. "Oh, Miss Phaedra, I shall do my best to please you. You just be sure and tell me if I don't."

"I shall, Ellen, but do not worry. I am really very easy to please," Phaedra replied, liking this plain but bubbly girl. "And you have done my hair most attractively. Thank you."

"Oh, thank you, mum. I'll unpack your things while you're gone, and you be sure and send for me when you come to bed, won't you?" Phaedra started to say that she could put herself to bed without help, but not wanting to hurt the obviously eager-to-please maid, she agreed.

Mr. Farwell met her at the door to the drawing room. He bowed over the hand she held to him, but instead of releasing it, he lifted it to his lips. Turning it over, he pressed a kiss on her palm.

Heat exploded up her arm. Startled, she pulled her hand away. "Don't do that!" She forgot her resolve to keep her temper with him, no matter what he did. "Must you act the suitor with me? Can we not just go on as we have?"

"I have only a fortnight to show you my sterling qualities, Phaedra. If I am to be on my good behavior all the time, I shall be thoroughly distraught by the time we return to Town. Surely you can allow me an occasional lapse of decorum."

"I would have thought your lapses would have been more on the order of losing your patience with me or giving me a scold," she countered. "Or going to sleep while I am speaking to you."

"No, all those are my normal behavior. It is other behavior you tempt me into, my love," he said, as he led her across the room to where her mama and papa sat with the Duchess.

Phaedra thought it best to ignore the intimate appellation. "Your Grace, thank you so much for inviting me here. I had never dreamed that such a magnificent mansion could be comfortable as well as beautiful."

"No need to be uncomfortable, just because you live in a pile like this. I won't have cold bedrooms or draughts about my feet. You are welcome, gel. Now, take that lanky fellow away and entertain him. I want to visit with your parents."

Phaedra was thrown into Mr. Farwell's company the entire evening. He took her in to dinner and was seated on her right. After the men had drunk their port and rejoined the ladies, Lady Mary and Mr. Martin joined Mama and the Duchess in a game of whist, while Papa buried his nose in a book, saying he'd been wanting to read it for an age. Even Cousin Louisa deserted her, saying that she had the headache from the rocking of the coach and wished to retire early.

So Phaedra had to entertain her suitor alone until the tea cart was brought in. She seated herself on a sofa near the fireplace. He promptly sat beside her, his knees nearly touching hers.

Remembering her mother's advice on how to converse with a gentleman, she first asked him about his interests.

"I pay visits to my friends, drive in the park, and visit my tailor and my bootmaker. Occasionally I visit Tat's with friends, but not often." His ubiquitous lace-edged handkerchief came into play. "The odor of horse is quite unbearable."

"Tell me of your estate. You said it is near Oxford. What crops do you grow?"

"Oh, dear me, I have no idea. Green ones, I suppose."

Gritting her teeth, she said, "Yes, I imagine so. Most plants are green. Do you have an agent who manages it for you?"

"Of course. Do you think it will rain tomorrow? I thought I saw clouds gathering as I came down for dinner."

"I saw no sign of clouds. What does it matter, anyway? If we waited for clear weather, we would never go outdoors. This *is* England, you know." What an exasperating man. Just when she had decided there was some substance to him, he blighted her hopes. He was, without a doubt, a silly fop, without a thought in his head for aught but frivolities.

"It is now your turn to suggest a subject of conversation, Mr. Farwell. I have quite exhausted all of mine."

He rose and paced to the fireplace and back, moving with a restless energy that was completely foreign to her previous impression of him. When he reseated himself, it was in a chair at right angles to the sofa. "Are you familiar with Sir Francis Beaufort's research on wind, Phaedra?"

Astounded, she let her jaw drop open.

He smiled at her, a twinkle in his gray eyes, and slowly wafted the handkerchief back and forth before him.

Finally she recovered enough from her astonishment to say, "I have only read a little on the subject and understood less. I do remember reading that he developed some sort of scale whereby wind speed can be accurately measured.

Do tell me more."

What followed was the most amazing experience of her life. Reginald Farwell, the fop, expounded knowledgeably and at some length on scientific research concerning weather prediction. She found the information he imparted to be fascinating, and asked a number of questions. The subject kept them occupied until they were interrupted by Lady Mary who offered them tea.

Later Phaedra thought back over the evening. Who was the real Reginald Farwell? The man who had so learnedly spoken to her of weather research? Or the London fop?

CHAPTER NINETEEN

The clouds Mr. Farwell had seen the evening before did indeed bring rain during the night. The inhabitants of Verbain woke to grey skies and a drizzle that promised to continue indefinitely. Despite the depressing weather, Phaedra went down to breakfast feeling that the day promised to be a very good one. A footman guided her to a bright, cheerful room with white wainscoting below wallpaper of green and gold stripes. Numerous green plants were on stands against two of its walls. The third wall was almost entirely of windows, and the many panes, in their white painted frames, looked out upon a colorful vista. Phaedra had to look a second time to see that the wall of windows showed not the outdoors, but a painted background of a sunny garden. Lady Mary, who was seated behind a silver coffee urn, an emptied plate before her, laughed at her expression of surprise.

"Do you like it? I so hate to awake to rain or grey skies, and so I persuaded Grandmama to let me decorate this room. The craftsmen who did the work thought I was out of my senses, but they followed my instructions."

"I love it. An eternal springtime."

Lady Mary looked beyond Phaedra, greeting Mr. Farwell and Lord Gifford as they entered, bringing the scent of rain with them. Both men were dressed for riding and their hair was damp.

"Good morning, my love." Papa bent to kiss Mama's cheek. "Too bad it's so wet. I know how you detest riding in the rain. There's a little chestnut that I'd like to see you try. Phaedra, did you bring your riding clothes?"

"Of course I did, Papa. Have you ever known me to go anywhere without them?"

"Good. You can come out with us after breakfast. Never let a little rain stop you from riding, have you?" He took his plate to the sideboard, where he proceeded to fill it with an assortment of meats and hot breads. "Farwell has promised to show me around the estate. Young Martin has already gone out, and we're to meet him later."

"Thank you, Papa, but I do not think I will ride this morning. I want to improvise some presses and prepare for an expedition to the home wood this afternoon." She followed her father to the sideboard. "Mary told me last night that there are usually quite a number of plants in flower at this time of year. Mr. Farwell, would you care to accompany me?"

He paused, a server in his hand. "If I have the strength, after leading your father about the fields this morning, Phaedra, I would enjoy exploring the woods with you. But what are presses?"

When he smiled at her, Phaedra experienced a glow of inner warmth. "Real presses are bundles of paper and thin boards, held tightly together with straps, into which I place plants to flatten and dry them. The drying preserves the plants so they may be examined later," she explained. "Mama did not allow me to bring mine to Town, so I will contrive substitutes from newspapers and heavy books. Mary has offered a warm closet off the kitchens for my use, and I intend to fill it with plant specimens." She said the last with a hint of challenge to all and sundry.

Her mama, whom she had expected to object to her planned activities, merely said, "I hope that you will not become too wet while you are collecting your plants, my dear."

"I will not collect if they are wet, Mama, but I do intend to see where they might be, so I may return later to collect them." She glanced at his highly polished boots. "Mr. Farwell, those boots will be ruined if you come with me. Perhaps you can borrow some stout shoes. The paths in the wood are bound to be muddy."

"I shall be appropriately dressed, I assure you," he answered, smiling.

Phaedra finished her breakfast and departed the breakfast room. After the door closed behind her, Reggie said to Lady Gifford, "Where is your companion this morning, ma'am? Does she still have the headache?"

"She never did, and you know it, sir. We were doing all we could to ensure that Phaedra had to converse with you last evening." Lady Gifford eyed him, quizzically. "Did you not appreciate our efforts?"

"I most assuredly did; but I do not need your efforts in my behalf, my lady. If Phaedra does not herself choose to be with me, your machinations will do nothing to advance my suit."

"Shall we not conspire against my daughter, then?"

"No, please do not. I believe I can keep her attention upon myself as much as is necessary. If I cannot, perhaps I would not be the husband for her after all." He gazed through the false windows, his cup held against his chin. Last night he had retreated into his Town persona without thinking, and had seen Phaedra's disgust writ plain on her face. Today he was determined to be himself, no matter how strange it felt after so many years of living a lie.

"Phaedra must wish to be me of her own accord. If she does not care enough to give me a chance, I must assume she feels not the slightest attraction for me." He held up a hand when Lady Mary would have argued. "No, Mary, do not offer me false coin. Phaedra must find me interesting enough to be with, or there is no hope."

"I believe she is quite interested, Mr. Farwell," Lady Gifford assured him.

"Perhaps. I can only hope. I certainly intend to do my utmost encourage any attraction to grow into love. But I must do it myself, don't you see?" *Yes, and you may be the greatest fool in England, to refuse their help. What if she does turn you down?*

He shook his head, unwilling to contemplate such an occurrence.

"Aye, Isabella, let the man do it his way. Got a cool head on his shoulders, he does," Lord Gifford said. Reggie set his cup down and rose. He bowed to the ladies and promised to meet the other gentlemen at the stables in a half-hour.

"Do you really think he will be able to convince Phaedra to love him, George?" Isabella said, when he was safely gone. "If I know her, she will avoid being alone with him whenever she can. She is interested, but extremely uncertain of her own emotions."

"Taking him out into the woods this afternoon isn't she? Stop fretting, my love," he said, patting her hand. "Leave Farwell to his schemes. He's the man for our girl and he knows just how to bring her around. Talked about it on the way here. I'll wager that he'll have a yes from her before the week is out."

"What will you wager, my lord?"

"A new bonnet for you against a game of chess?"

She smiled fondly at her husband. "Done. And much as I would delight in a new bonnet, I hope I will lose." Since their daughters had become young ladies, she and her husband had formed the habit of engaging them in conversation of an evening at home, to give them practice for their Season. This had left them with fewer opportunities to indulge in the board game which both of them enjoyed. Some months had passed since she and her husband had fought a game to the last pawn. "Do you know, George, I think I am as eager to have Phaedra married so that we can return to country life as I am for her own sake."

"I admit I'll be glad when we can go home. I believe I've lost more hair since we went to London than I had in the past year."

"And I have gained more white ones," she said, rising from the table and leaning to kiss him. "The Duchess has asked me to come to her after breakfast, so that we may plan some activities for the young people. I think she wants to give a small ball while we are here. Enjoy your ride, my love."

WHILE THE GENTLEMEN EXPLORED VERBAIN'S EXTENSIVE ACRES AND THE OLDER ladies planned all sorts of entertainments, Phaedra happily arranged her closet and prepared her improvised plant presses. She was pleased to find the closet quite warm, backing as it did upon the kitchen chimney. Her plant specimens would dry quickly and not mold.

As she worked, she found herself, as usual these days, thinking of Reginald Farwell. Why had he asked her to marry him? He was accepted everywhere, was an intimate of the famous Beau Brummel, was a favorite of the Season's hopeful mamas. To be noticed by Mr. Farwell, she had discovered, was to become an instant favorite among the young men who populated balls and soirees and hops. Both she and Chloe had benefited by his notice, and for that she was grateful. She had enjoyed her Season far more for being moderately popular.

"Why me?" It was a question she had asked herself too often. She smoothed several more sheets of newspaper and added them to the pile. Perhaps she should ask herself why she had asked for time to consider his offer. She certainly had no intention of accepting. How could she ever live the life he led, a constant round of parties and balls, a frivolous life with no time for serious pursuits?

And yet...

He had studied the results of weather experiments well enough to explain them.

He cuts such a ridiculous figure. His waistcoats...his collars. I am surprised he hasn't scars on his face from their sharp points.

But...

This morning he had entered the breakfast room clad in sensible garments, beautifully tailored for his unusual height. His boots had shone, but she had noticed an old scratch on one, evidence of hard use.

He was a denizen of the ballroom and the salon, both places she delighted in visiting on a rare occasion. She could not imagine spending the rest of her life flitting from one to the next.

Still...

He was showing Papa and Mr. Martin around Verbain, so he must have considerable familiarity with it. In the rain. Without bemoaning the damage to his clothing or his boots, as most town tulips would.

Baffled, curious, and uncertain, she decided she must spend as much as possible of her time in his company while here at Verbain.

How else can I learn who he really is?

Phaedra was ready to go into the home wood, seeking flowers that grew beneath the thick canopy of beeches and oaks, but Mr. Farwell was nowhere to be found. She waited for nearly a half hour, before deciding he had fallen asleep somewhere. "If Mr. Farwell asks where I am," she told Lady Mary, "please remind him that we had an appointment at two."

"I'm sure there is a good reason for his tardiness."

"Oh, so am I. 'Twould be a shame if he missed his afternoon nap." Without waiting for a reply, she picked up her trowel and a hessian bag for carrying her specimens and went on her way.

Why am I surprised? Never say the elegant Mr. Farwell would be found grubbing in the dirt in a dark wood. Why he might get his precious, primrose trousers stained.

She was nearing the woods when she heard her name called. Turning, she saw him striding toward her. For just a moment, she considered ignoring him and going her own way, but good manners got the best of her. She waited.

"I apologize for my tardiness, Miss Phaedra. I was visiting His Grace and he tricked me into a game of chess. I would be there yet if I hadn't let him win."

"Let him win, Mr. Farwell? I have heard that His Grace is a superb chess player. Papa learned from him, and my papa rarely loses to anyone." She smiled her understanding of his need to preen.

His lips parted to show his teeth, but there was no smile in his eyes. "Of course. How could I have expected you to believe me a worthy opponent at chess. Never mind. I am at your disposal for the rest of the day. May I carry something?"

"Thank you, but no. I am entirely capable of carrying my own equipment." She turned again toward the woods, leaving him to trail behind.

Phaedra had to admit she was both surprised and pleased to see him dressed in an old and frayed tweed jacket and stained buckskins, with heavy woolen stockings inside wooden clogs such as were worn by the poorest peasants. She herself had found the wooden shoes to be most practical for use in wet weather, for the mud did not stick to them as it did to leather shoes or boots. As the afternoon wore on and her serviceable boots picked up an ever heavier load of sticky mud, she wished she had her own, but they, like her presses, had been left at Gifford Court.

She happily added several mosses, a small buttercup, and a particularly fine specimen of *Chrysosplenum alternifolium*, a species she had only collected once before, to her bag. He followed her in silence for the most part, only occasionally asking the name of a plant. After an hour or so, her skirts were wet, her boots heavy with mud, and her fingers numb from digging in the cold soil. She straightened and attempted to brush plant fragments and streaks of soil from her skirt.

"It seems to me that you would be far better off in trousers," he observed. "Skirts have always seemed to me particularly impractical garments"

"I rarely wear skirts when I am collecting at home," she confessed, surprised at his comment. She would never have expected him to approve of trousers on any female, no matter what the circumstances. "They are so unmanageable when I am forever kneeling or crawling in the shrubbery. Trousers are much more practical, though Mama refuses to allow me to wear them into the house and I must change in the dairy barn."

"Why are you in skirts today?"

She grimaced. "Mama would not let me bring my trousers to London with me. She said that she feared that I would not be able to resist wearing them. Chloe supported her, too, for she was certain I would steal out in them to look at plants and be seen by someone, to my complete ruin."

"I would like to see you in trousers, Phaedra. You would be quite fetching, I imagine."

"I am quite disreputable looking, sir, and you will not see me in trousers. They are outgrown ones of my brothers' and they fit like a second skin."

"Then I would definitely like to see you in trousers." He grinned widely at her blush when she caught his meaning. "Come," he continued, and held out his hand. "It is getting too dark and damp to find flowers. Let us walk down to the lake. It is particularly attractive in the rain. Or are you too cold? It is fully a mile to the vantage point."

She took his hand and let him pull her to his feet. Although he did not release it when she was standing beside him, she did not attempt to disengage it. His clasp seemed...comforting.

"Tell me," she said, when they had walked a little while in companionable silence, "how you became interested in the Beaufort experiments? It does not fit my perceptions of you at all."

"Oh, I am interested in many things. I attended a meeting of the Royal Society a few months ago and heard a talk about his work. Later I studied some of his papers."

"At a meeting of the Royal Society? How did you come to attend?"

"I am a member," he replied, simply.

"But do you not have to be invited to join? And is not the invitation based on original scientific discoveries?" She was amazed, and intensely curious. She knew little of the Royal Society, but was aware that it was a most select group. She had sent plant specimens to one member, a gentleman who was compiling a flora of England. Phaedra had trouble believing that this fop could claim to be a member of that august group.

"Doubtless, it was a mistake," he said with a wry smile. "But I have done some experiments on breeding better varieties of fruit, you see, and they elected me to membership on that basis."

"What fruits?"

"Oh, there were some rather interesting peaches and apricots that I encountered in Arabia on my way back from India. I brought the dried flowers home and was able to apply their pollen to the flowers on trees in my own succession houses. The resulting fruit is more cold hardy and larger than the varieties that commonly grow here. A poor effort, but mine own."

"Why that is perfectly marvelous, Mr. Farwell. I did not know you were interested in botany. Tell me more, please."

"It is not botany that interests me, but food plants. I have seen the efforts of horse and cattle breeders to improve their breeds and often wondered why the same principles should not be applied to plants. But I am a mere amateur and only dabble at it. His Grace reported my results to the Royal Society, and I am sure he overstated their importance."

Phaedra stopped in the middle of the path and looked up into his face. Since he had retained his hold on her hand, he, too, was forced to halt. "Reginald Farwell, Mary told me you were not at all what you seemed. I have noticed some inconsistencies in your behavior myself. What other surprises are there in store for me?"

"I will let you discover them for yourself, love. Look, we are only a few steps from the vista I wished to show you. Let us go on."

He started down the path and she kept pace with him. As they emerged from the trees, a large lake came into view. In its center was an island where stood a miniature castle, complete with turrets and battlements. Even through the light rain, she could see that the small building was exquisite.

"Oh, how lovely. But why a castle on an island? And so tiny. What is it for?"

"The present Duke's mother wished a castle and he, not willing to destroy the beauty of his home, built it here. It is not a real castle, of course, but a hollow shell. Inside is a single room, with tables and chairs and even a fireplace. You can see, if you look closely, that the doors are much out of proportion to the rest. They are cleverly painted to look as if their tops are part of the walls. Although it is rarely used now, it is maintained for its beauty. When the weather clears, Mary intends us to have a picnic there."

"Can it be seen from the house?"

"Only from Their Graces' apartments. The trees block the view from the other rooms. I understand that several venerable beeches were cut so that the lady could view her castle from her bedroom."

"I do not blame her for wishing to. Thank you for showing it to me." The rain had become heavier during their walk, and Phaedra suddenly realized that she was both wet and chilled. "Perhaps you will bring me here again on a warmer day. Right now, lovely as is the view, I must beg you to show me the way back to the house. I am becoming quite cold."

He put an arm around her waist. "Before we return, Phaedra, I must ask you a favor." His gray eyes seemed to glow as he gazed down at her.

"A favor?"

"Yes, a very large, very important favor. Will you?"

Curiously enough, she wanted to say yes, no matter the question. Clinging desperately to the last of her common sense, Phaedra said, "I cannot promise until I know what it is you wish."

"Will you say my name?" His forefinger slipped under her chin and lifted it. "Please."

She licked lips suddenly dry. "Mr. Far—"

He shook his head. "Reggie. Say it."

Phaedra jerked her chin aside. "Oh, very well. Reggie. There. Are you happy?"

"Not until you promise never again to call me 'Mr. Farwell' in that uppity tone. I vow, it hurts my ears like someone scraping fingernails across glass."

A giggle threatened, but she caught it before it could emerge. "I will try, as long as Mama does not forbid it."

"She will not." He took her hand again and turned her back toward the path. They had walked a little ways when he said, "Do you detest me so much, Phaedra?"

"I have never detested you. I will admit you did not at first seem to be the sort of man I admire. Once I came to know you better, I began to count you among my friends."

He pulled her to face him, so close she could feel his warmth. Before she could step back, he had his arms around her and was pulling her even closer.

"Mr. Farw—, Reggie, this is not proper. Oh, please, release me." She tried to push him away, without success.

"Look at me, Phaedra," he commanded.

She hesitated, and lifted her chin. Her breath caught, so intense was the fire in his eyes.

"My love, I keep telling myself to be patient, to go cautiously with you. But I cannot. Phaedra, I love you and I want you."

Aware of a strange feeling in her midriff, Phaedra stood very still as she attempted to sort her feelings. She was giddy and warm, despite the inclement weather. Her thoughts seemed unable to settle, but kept spinning in her mind. The one that spun to the top most often was *He is going to kiss me.*

Right behind it was *I want him to kiss me.*

Reggie's left hand lifted to stroke her cheek before moving to the back of her neck. His fingers speared into her neatly coiled hair. One by one he removed the pins holding it. Before she could protest—if she had wanted to do so—her hair went spilling down her back.

"Lovely." His hoarse whisper seemed forced from his mouth. Again his fingers sifted through her hair, and this time they caught and held. He tipped her head up and held it immovable. And then he bent to touch his lips to hers, softly at first, and then with more pressure.

As his mouth moved softly against hers, she relaxed against him and opened her lips. His tongue against her own caused the giddiness to flare into a blaze that threatened to consume the last dregs of her doubts. She lifted her arms to encircle his neck.

The kiss was endless. Phaedra lost all sensation save those of his hard body against hers and his tongue seeking all the secrets of her mouth. When he finally lifted his head, she went on tiptoe, wanting to protest the deprivation. Her lips were hot and swollen. Her body tingled. Her eyelids were so heavy that only with great effort could she raise them to look into his face.

"Say yes, Phaedra," he said, husky-voiced. "Say you will marry me."

Yes. The word hovered on the tip of her tongue. Quivered there, ready to fall off. Until common sense once again reasserted itself. "I cannot, Reggie. Not until I have had time to think about the feelings I have just experienced. I cannot be sure they constitute love," she said, with enormous regret.

His arms loosened and he stepped back, smiling. "From your response, my darling Phaedra, I imagine your feelings would more properly be called desire. It is a good beginning to love, you know."

"I do know it, Reggie. Desire is not enough, though, to base a marriage upon," she said, each word painful to speak.

"No, it is not. How wise you are. And how foolish I am. If you are not sure yet of your own feelings, it is unfair in me to force you to a decision."

With the taste of him still on her lips and her hands remembering the feel of him, Phaedra could not resist saying, "You will, I hope, keep reminding me of what desire feels like, will you not, Reggie?" She had to smile at the astonishment in his face. "I should not like to forget, and who knows? Constant reminders might speed my decision."

She dodged away as he reached for her again. "Oh, no sir! Not that constant. But at least once a day, I should think. I have a very short memory, you see."

"Baggage! Perhaps I should withdraw my offer. You are, madam, quite without morals, I see." His smile belied his words, and he again tried to catch her in his arms. She skipped out of his reach and started walking up the path.

"No, but I am cold. Come Reggie, take me back to the house and find me a fireplace." She held out her hand to him and he took it and tucked it under his arm. As they walked up the path, she said, "When am I to receive the next installment in the story of the real Reggie Farwell? I can hardly wait."

"When you receive your next reminder in the delights of desire, love, and not until. I should not wish to hand you too many surprises in one day. Will you ride with me in the morning?"

"I should love to, but Mary is to take me to the village school. I would not wish to disappoint her. I think it is wonderful that she and the Duchess care so much about educating the children of the estate."

"Another time, then." He sounded...disappointed?

Surely not.

The rest of the short walk back to the house passed in conversation about the school the present Duchess had founded to educate the children of the estate's tenants. Originally confined to male students, it had been recently expanded to include girls.

"Mary has quite a social conscience," Reggie said. "She insists upon teaching at the school whenever she is in residence. The Duchess resisted allowing girls to be taught the same curriculum as the boys, but Mary insisted. She said that the girls' minds were as worthy of improvement as any boy's and that if she could not teach them the same subjects, she would not teach at all.

"Some of the mothers objected, for they wished their daughters to be trained exclusively in the housewifely arts, but she convinced them otherwise. Her latest campaign is to convince the parents to allow the children to stay in school longer. Most of them quit when they are ten or eleven and old enough to be of significant help at home."

"That is too bad. Can the parents not see how much better off they would be with a better education?" Phaedra said. "I am glad to know, Reggie, that you do not believe the lower classes are unworthy of education. Papa has always made sure his dependents have a chance to learn to read and write. Should the opportunity arise, I intend to do the same."

"I hereby offer it to you, Phaedra. Come to Oakhurst and educate my tenants."

Again she was forced to dredge up her rapidly weakening common sense. "One proposal a day is all that you are allowed. Ask me again tomorrow."

CHAPTER TWENTY

THE RAIN CONTINUED. PHAEDRA VISITED THE VILLAGE SCHOOL IN THE MORNING of the second day and was duly impressed. Someday she hoped to have the opportunity to follow Lady Mary's example. That afternoon she had just settled in the library with a novel she had been longing to read when Reggie entered.

"Do you play billiards?" he said, without pausing to greet her.

"Why...why, no, I do not." She stuck one finger between pages to mark her place. "I am not even sure what the game entails."

"I'll teach you. Come."

She followed him to the ground floor and along a corridor to a large room at the back of the house. In its center stood an enormous table, a wide lip forming its edge, its heavy legs ornately carved. The strangest thing about it was the woven leather bags hanging below the lip, at each corner table and in the middle of each long side.

Reggie motioned her inside and pushed the door almost shut. She raised her eyebrow and he smiled. "It's not quite closed. Your reputation is safe."

"Barely. I gather that is a billiard table?"

"It is. And this—" He picked a long, tapered stick out of a rack against the wall. "This is a cue." He demonstrated its use by tapping one of the colored balls scattered on the green felt tabletop. The ball rolled a few inches, and stopped.

"How interesting," Phaedra said, letting her tone show her real opinion.

Reggie chuckled. "The game is a bit more exciting than that. The object is to send the balls into the pockets." He went on to demonstrate, showing no little skill. Almost every ball he struck dropped into a pocket, sometimes after careening across the table and back several times.

"Would you like to learn?" he said as he sank the last ball.

"Yes, although I doubt that I would ever attain your skill."

"I am an excellent instructor." He handed her another cue and showed her how to hold it.

The next two hours tried her patience, her strength, and her resolve. Phaedra discovered that using a cue required strong fingers, that leaning over the table to stroke the ball required long legs and a limber back. She also discovered that pretending she could not understand Reggie's instructions meant he would wrap his long arms around her, lay his warm, hard hands over hers, and show her with a delicious intimacy exactly how she was supposed to move.

The first time she knocked a ball into a pocket, she squealed with glee.

"Keep going," he told her. "See how many you can sink before you miss."

The next ball must have hit a bump in the felt, for it ran straight for a few inches, and then it careened off to the right. "Pooh! I can see that I need much more practice."

He took his turn then, and sank one ball after another until the table was clear.

"You are showing off," she accused.

"But of course. Isn't that what a gentleman must do, when in the company of a lovely lady whom he wishes to impress?"

She deliberately fluttered her eyelashes. "Are you flirting with me, Mr. Farwell?"

"No more than you, Miss Phaedra." Catching her hand, he lifted it to his mouth. Instead of kissing the air a small space above her knuckles, he turned the hand and pressed his mouth to the soft skin just below her palm. His lips opened and his tongue laved the skin, hot and wet.

Phaedra drew in a long, slow breath, feeling the thrill of his touch clear to her toes. "Ohhh."

"You taste so sweet, like some exotic fruit." His words were rough, as if dragged across a harsh surface. He turned his head, looking directly into her eyes. "Marry me, Phaedra. Soon."

Unable to speak, she shook her head.

Slumberous eyelids hid his thoughts as his head dipped again. This time his kiss filled her palm, sending alternating waves of heat and cold up her arm. She fought to prevent her fingers pressing against his face, clenched her other fist to keep from sliding her fingers through his thick, wavy hair. When he straightened and set her hand free, she felt as if he had stolen something precious from her.

"I think, my dear. That we had better join the others. The atmosphere in this room has become somewhat...dangerous."

In full agreement, Phaedra let him usher her from the room. She walked beside him along the corridor and up the stairs. Even with some distance between them, she imagined she could feel the heat of his skin, smell the faint spiciness she now associated with him.

The experience again left her shaken and thoughtful. Unable to separate her emotions from her intellect, she found herself wondering if, after all, mutual desire might not be sufficient grounds upon which to build a marriage.

In her more rational moments, she knew it was not. She must be satisfied in her own mind that there was more than their physical yearnings for one another to carry them through a life together. She had to admit that his company was always pleasing, even when they argued. Even worse was the admission that she felt incomplete when he was not with her.

The next day Reggie again sought her out in the library. Although she had advanced only to the second chapter of the book she had so desired to read, she willingly set it aside when he entered, looking as if he had just come from outdoors.

"Good afternoon. Have you been riding?"

"Not today. I walked over to the village with Mary this morning, and met a fellow I knew in India. We became lost in reminiscence and the time slipped away from us." He handed her a slim book bound in red leather. "As I was coming home, I remembered this and wondered if you might like to read it."

Curious, Phaedra opened the book. "*Through the Eyes of a Stranger*? What is it about?"

"I would rather you discovered for yourself. I must go."

Before she could object, he had departed. She stated after him, wondering what had caused his shortness. *Men! Mama warned me that sometimes they pass all understanding.* Curious, she turned to the first page of text.

More than two hours later she closed the book, having read straight through without a pause. It was an entertaining account of the author's visits to several less populated parts of India, with amusing anecdotes and colorful descriptions of places visited. The information imparted to her a vivid picture of the way people in the far off land lived from day to day. She had frequently found herself chuckling over the humorously told tale of the author's misadventures in a strange land populated by people who spoke unfamiliar tongues. Somehow he had managed to make himself understood well enough to discover how they lived their daily lives. Or had he made it all up? No, she could not believe that, for there was a ring of truth in the well-written prose.

She turned to set the book on the table beside her chair and saw Reggie seated across the room. He seemed to be watching her closely.

"What a delightful book," she told him. "I thoroughly enjoyed how amusingly the author relates his adventures. Do you suppose that he really did go on the tiger hunt and manage to fall onto the beast's back as it was caught in the net?"

"I guarantee you he did, and has scars to prove it. Even enmeshed in the net, the cat was able to give him a good scratch on the leg. Had the village headman not risked his life to run forward and sink his spear into the tiger's side, the author would probably have been mauled to death. The net, you see, only slowed the tiger; it did not stop him. It took many men with spears nearly half an hour to kill the beast, finally. In the meantime, the author was bleeding on the ground, quite disappointed to be excluded from the party."

"You must be teasing me, Reggie. I cannot believe that they would so neglect him. Or that he could tell of it so hilariously, after being in danger of his life."

"I give you my word. The tiger was a man-eater, and it was more important that he be eliminated than that one insignificant foreign devil's life be saved. Besides, it was only a little scratch and he was able to staunch the bleeding by wrapping it tightly with his neck cloth. Afterwards they were kind enough to carry him back to the village, along with the dead tiger, rather than leaving him to die in the jungle."

"How do you know all these things? Are you acquainted with the author?" Realization struck her then. "Oh, Reggie, did you write this?"

"I cannot tell a lie" His mouth twisted into a rueful smile. "I was short of funds when I returned from India and it was some time before I could draw on my late aunt's estate. The income from this book kept body and soul together for several months."

He rose and came to stand behind her. After a slight hesitation, he laid his hand on her shoulder. "Now you have all my secrets. I dabble in agriculture and I write amusing little travelogues. Will you forgive me?"

She reached to cover his hand with hers. "Forgive you?" she said softly.

"There is nothing to forgive, unless it is your modesty in not telling the world of what you do. Why do you keep all this so secret?"

"For fear of ridicule, my love."

"No one would ridicule you, Reggie."

"Perhaps not now. But when I was at Eton, I was known as 'Storky'. I was quite a figure of fun, for I had attained my full growth very early. At the age of twelve, I towered over all my contemporaries, yet was so thin that one of the older fellows claimed that if I turned sidewise, I would not cast a shadow.

"No one took such a ludicrous fellow seriously. I adopted a manner of cool distance and cultivated a superior, somewhat sarcastic manner of speech. Sleepiness was apparently a result of my rapid growth, for it began about the same time. By the time I had reached my present height—before I was fifteen—I had learned to depend upon my unexpected naps to save me from ridicule or malicious pranks. Thereafter I pretended to nap frequently, until it became part of my persona."

She drew him down to sit beside her. "How cruel children can be. But why did you not change, when you were grown? Why did you let everyone think you were a useless fribble?"

"My father died when I was scarce sixteen. He had squandered his small fortune and had sold the manor that had been in the family for three generations. I was left destitute. My aunt had always paid my school fees, unbeknownst to me. When I discovered the depth of my obligation to her, I was consumed with guilt. The stepfather of one of my classmates was a nabob, and I went to him and applied for a position with his shipping firm. He sent me to India on a fact-finding mission, certain that a lad such as I would never be suspected of spying on his employees."

A good choice, she decided, examining his face, still youthful and somewhat boyish. "How old were you then?"

"Not yet seventeen." He looked beyond her, as if seeing far away places. "I played my part well, deliberately making myself a figure of ridicule, although often I hated doing so. Occasionally, when on holiday, I attempted to be myself, but found it uncomfortable. My few acquaintances accused me of acting high and mighty."

"But when you came home—"

"Old habits die hard. By then the habit of flippancy was well ingrained. Only my aunt and the Duchess ever knew that the real Reggie was hiding inside, afraid to expose himself to the world. Later, when we became friends, Mary saw through my façade too.

"Herne Bradburn and I were close when we were at Eton together. He never ragged me, and often took my part against the others. When we met again, a few months ago, we resumed our friendship as if we had never been apart."

"You poor man. How difficult it must have been, to play so repugnant a role for so long." Without thinking, she stroked his hair, letting her fingers trail through the silky waves. "Why did you not let me see the real Reggie when we first met? You must have known how I disliked the fop."

"I was afraid. Even though Mary said you would like me better for being myself, I was afraid you would laugh at me."

He knelt on the floor in front of her and took her hands in his. "I could not have borne that."

"My dear sir, surely you knew I would prefer you as you are now?" Phaedra smiled into his troubled eyes. "The fop was amusing, but I could not see past his so elegant, so foolish clothing and manners. I came very near to having my father refuse your offer immediately, you know, for I knew I could not marry you as you were."

"And can you as I am now?" His hands tightened on hers until she cried out.

She bit her lip.

His expression tightened, the faint lines bracketing his mouth deepening. "Can you, Phaedra?"

"I...I think so," she said, "but I am still not sure. Oh, my dear, can you not wait a little longer for my answer? I am grown quite fond of you in the past few days, but I am still uncertain whether it is love." Seeing the agony on his face, she reached out and touched his lips. "Perhaps you had better not remind me today of how I desire you, Reggie. It is not fair of me to allow you to hope, and it does quite shake my resolve to be sure of my own feelings."

"Damn your resolve," he growled, lunging upwards and grabbing her about the waist. He pulled her onto his lap and wrapped his arms about her.

Although taken by surprise, Phaedra reacted as she would have if wrestling with a younger brother who outweighed her. She went limp.

Her strategy very nearly worked. His arms relaxed somewhat and she was almost able to slide free.

"Oh, no, my dear, You won't get away so easily." He pulled her close against him.

His arms were unbreakable bonds, his thighs hard and strong under her.

"Let me go!" Was that weak, uncertain voice hers? She tried to free her arms from his embrace, even as he bent his head close and breathed against her ear.

"Be still, love." He nuzzled her neck.

The next instant she felt a cold touch, as if he had...licked? "Reggie... Reggieee?" Her will weakened, as his tongue and teeth explored the curve where her neck and shoulder met. Hot breath, cold moisture, tiny not-quite-hurting nips of his teeth, all worked against her intention to remain strong, resistant to his pleadings.

"Turn toward me, Phaedra. I want to kiss you."

"Nooo." Yet her head rotated on her neck, as if it was a thing apart from her. She looked into...drowned in...his gray eyes.

He bent his head even closer. "Yesss." The barest sound, a whisper touch of breath against her mouth. "Kiss me, Phaedra."

All inclination to resist him fled and she relaxed in his embrace. The next instant his mouth covered hers, hot, insistent, demanding.

After an endless interval, he lifted his head long enough to whisper, "I love you, Phaedra. Can you doubt it?" Giving her no opportunity to reply, he kissed her again and again, her eyelids, her cheeks, her chin. His tongue swept along the line of her jaw to her ear. His teeth closed on her earlobe, sending such heat through her body that she wondered if she would not melt.

When she felt him pulling at the neck of her gown, she had no wish to resist. Instead she strained her body against his. Reggie loosened the strings at the neck and pulled the bodice even lower, pressing hot kisses on the upper swell of her breasts. When she felt the feather touch of his tongue on her nipple, she shuddered and arched herself against him.

The sound of the door opening registered dimly on her consciousness.

"Phaedra!"

"Reggie!"

Reggie loomed over her, blocking her view of her mother and the Duchess. And theirs of her. She attempted to pull up the neck of her gown with nerveless fingers.

"Well, Phaedra," Mama said in a voice portending disaster, "I am happy to see you have accepted Mr. Farwell's offer at last. We were quite wondering how long it would take you. Do tidy yourself. Mr. Martin is not far behind us and it would not do for him to see you in your dishabille."

Abashed, embarrassed, and perhaps just a bit jubilant, Reggie straightened his neck cloth. When Lady Gifford came to smooth her daughter's hair, he stepped aside, but did not go far. If there was going to be a scene, protecting her was his first responsibility.

Phaedra stared at her mother, tears welling in her eyes. He had the impression that her first choice would be to run screaming from the room, to hide forever in her bedchamber. Seeing her poised to leap to her feet, he sat upon the sofa's arm and put a restraining arm about her shoulders.

"There, you look more presentable," Lady Gifford said, giving Phaedra's hair a last pat. "Now behave yourself until we can be alone, for I have something to say about your unwise behavior. Reggie, you will behave yourself as well. Even if you are betrothed, there are certain rules of conduct that must be met." She glanced down at her daughter. "You may, if you fear she will become hysterical, hold her hand."

Reggie removed his arm from Phaedra's shoulders and took her hand. She did not respond to his quick squeeze.

When he met her eyes and smiled, she remained sober. His heart sank.

As if nothing untoward had occurred, the ladies requested his advice concerning the ball. They inquired which of his acquaintances in Bath and London should receive invitations. He did his best to give coherent answers, but his primary attention was upon Phaedra. She was being uncharacteristically silent and passive.

Shortly thereafter Lady Mary and Mr. Martin entered, having returned from a gallop. The conversation became general and no one but Reggie seemed to notice that Phaedra took no part in it. The discussion had endured nearly an hour before she extricated her hand from his and excused herself. By that time the small ball had grown to a grand affair, with a guest list numbering more than two hundred. A date was set for two nights before the Hazelbournes' return to London. The long disused ballroom was to be opened and refurbished. An orchestra would be brought down from London.

Wishing he could escape and follow Phaedra, Reggie ventured the opinion that perhaps their plans were becoming overly grandiose, both Lady Gifford and the duchess turned on him.

"Don't be foolish," the Duchess told him. "It will be just the thing to silence any lingering gossip. There will be nothing havy-cavy about Phaedra's betrothal. Not if I have my say."

"How else should we celebrate your engagement?" Lady Gifford demanded.

He cast a pleading glance at Mary, who smiled evilly. "Give it up, Reggie. With your reputation and all the talk about Chloe's clandestine wedding, you have no choice but to make a splash with yours."

He buried his face in his hands, certain he had sealed his fate by his lack of self-control. Phaedra would never consent to be his wife if forced to be part of a gaudy spectacle.

UPON ESCAPING THE LIBRARY, PHAEDRA RAN TO HER BEDCHAMBER AND CAST herself upon her bed to weep.

Her mother had congratulated her on finally accepting Reggie, but she had done nothing of the sort. She had merely been kissing him. Well, perhaps it had been more than a perfectly chaste kiss.

A few kisses do not constitute a betrothal, do they?

Her skin still burned in memory of Reggie's lips on her shoulders, her neck, her breasts. She *had* allowed him to go far beyond what was proper, even for an engaged couple—which they were not.

And will never be. He will not wish to marry a...there must be a word for the sort of woman who allows such liberties. A wanton? A tart? Oh, no!

Confused and miserable, she burrowed into her pillow. Her sobs were so violent that she did not hear the door open nor her mother walk to her bedside. Only when a cool hand was laid on her brow did she become aware that she was no longer alone.

"Well, Phaedra?" Lady Gifford said. "What have you to say for yourself?"

"Oh, Mama, I have ruined myself," she sobbed. "I had not accepted him, and now he will not have me, so depraved have I shown myself."

"Nonsense! He would have you no matter what. But you had not accepted him? How can you say so?" Mama's expression was a mixture of condemnation and consternation. "Surely you knew better than to allow any such liberties if you do not intend to marry him. Phaedra, I trusted you."

"It is all so terrible, Mama. I told Reggie I would probably accept him, but wished more time in which to decide. Then he kissed me and I forgot everything but that." She burst into fresh sobs.

"Stop it, Phaedra! Right now. You may have wished more time, but your behavior gave him his answer. Unless you truly despise Mr. Farwell, I am very much afraid that you must marry him." She paused before adding, "Or never see him again."

"Oh, I could not bear that!" Phaedra cried, as she pushed herself upright. "I could not bear to be parted from him, even though I am not sure I love him."

"Your feelings for him bear a great resemblance to love, my dear. That's all right, then," she said, patting Phaedra's shoulder. "Do try to sleep a while. Your eyes are quite red and swollen. It would not do for you to appear until you are looking more the thing." She pulled Phaedra's slippers from her feet and spread a light blanket over her. "I will have Ellen wake you in time to dress before you meet with Mr. Farwell, for you must formally accept him, you know. I will send him to you in the blue salon shortly before dinner. Sleep well, my dear."

Surprisingly, Phaedra fell into a deep slumber almost immediately. When Ellen woke her, she felt wonderful. Her confusion had been replaced by a calm certainty. She knew the right choice to make and she would make it without a qualm.

Only a slight redness about her eyes remained of her emotional storm. A few minutes under a cold compress erased even that. She was soon dressed in the ice yellow gown she had first worn to Almack's, and went to meet Reggie with only a small twinge of doubt.

Reggie was waiting in the blue salon, immersed in pessimistic thoughts, when the door opened.

"Reggie?" came a hesitant voice from beyond it.

"Here," he answered, dreading the coming interview. He was certain it would be full of tears and recriminations.

"Yes."

"I said I am here, Phaedra. Do come in."

"I cannot until you reply." She was standing out of sight, no matter how he craned his neck to peer through the door.

"I did reply. I told you I was in here."

"That is the wrong reply."

"Well then, what the devil is the right one? Will you come in here where I can see you?"

"I did not ask a question, I gave an answer. The answer is Yes." Was that a giggle? *Impossible.*

He stood abruptly and started to the door.

"If you come out here, I will run away. You must reply."

Feeling as if he had somehow fallen into bedlam, he said, in his most foppish tone, "What, ma'am, was the question?"

"The same one you asked earlier."

"Damn it, woman, will you have done?" He threw himself back into his chair. "I am in no mood to play silly games. Tell me what you wish me to say, and I will say it."

Again the giggle.

As if the sun had suddenly burst from behind a black cloud, Reggie knew what words she wanted. "I love you, Phaedra. Will you be my wife?"

She came running in the door and threw herself into his arms. The face she lifted to his was rosy, but there was no mistaking the love glowing from her eyes.

"I knew you would understand, Reggie, if you would only try. Yes, I do love you, and yes I will marry you. When can we do it?"

"Soon, my love. Very soon," he said softly, as he leaned down to kiss her lips.

Many kisses later, Lady Gifford knocked on the door and reminded them that the dinner bell had run long since.

To his great surprise, no one at the table commented on Phaedra's pink cheeks and swollen lips.

THE DUCHESS'S BALL WAS SAID TO BE A RESOUNDING SUCCESS, BUT AFTERWARD Phaedra had no memory of it, except for the moment when she and Reggie stood before everyone and their betrothal was announced. Her life became a whirl of activity when they returned to Town—parties, balls, soirees, musicales, and any number of other social events. She and Reggie were invited everywhere, and Mama insisted that they accept every invitation humanly possible.

They had little time together, even chaperoned. Now that they were formally betrothed, Phaedra had almost no opportunity to be reminded of her desire for Reggie. He went to Oakhurst to arrange for the house to be prepared for her. She was thrown into choosing her bride clothes, with fittings and shopping expeditions every day, until her head swam.

Papa decided he and Reggie should meet with their solicitors to do the thing in style. Mama required that Phaedra's presentation to the Queen go ahead as planned. The wedding was set for late May.

A week before her wedding day, Phaedra received an almost incoherent letter from Chloe. Written in her sister's usual lackadaisical style, the missive was filled with congratulations. Chloe vowed that she was every day more in love with her new husband, to Phaedra's great relief. There was no news of an imminent heir, which brought both a smile and a sigh from Mama. The invitation for everyone to spend Christmas at Wilderlake was repeated, and extended to include Lady Mary and Mr. Martin, who had, to everyone's amazement, emerged as that young lady's most persistent suitor.

The day finally arrived. Phaedra felt not a trace of nervousness. Her ivory satin wedding gown and French lace veil were her mother's, and the large sapphire she wore on her finger had been given her by Reggie.

When she walked up the aisle of St. George's on her father's arm, she was poised and self-confident. Her wedding vows, repeated in a firm, clear voice, should have been audible in the farthest corners of the church. All doubts gone, she looked forward to complete happiness as Mrs. Reginald Farwell.

Reggie, on the other had, was obviously distraught. He voice never rose above a whisper. His hand shook as he placed the golden band on her finger. At the intimate wedding breakfast for family and close friends that was held at the Duchess' town house, his demeanor did not improve. She overheard several of his friends teasing him as she descended the staircase in her traveling gown to where he awaited her.

She was tempted to pity him. Only tempted, for she still remembered how he had fooled her into believing him silly and affected. Since it was impossible for her to extract revenge from the man she loved beyond belief, she was content to see him suffer a bit at the hands of his friends. After standing silently and listening for a few minutes, she descended until she stood two steps from the bottom.

All the young ladies who had become her friends during the Season gathered 'round. Phaedra held her bouquet high, and looked at their hopeful faces. Some had already become betrothed, some were considered very close to capturing husbands, but a few were still hopeful. She chose, and threw the bouquet directly into Miss Graham's waiting arms.

Finally she was alone in a coach with Reggie, bound for Oakhurst. Since travel on the continent was still restricted by Napoleon's ravaging hordes, they had decided to postpone their honeymoon until they could go to Italy. "Even if I am a grandmother when we may finally go," Phaedra had laughed.

Reggie had promised that they would travel well into the night, if necessary, so they could spend their wedding night in their own home. Phaedra had concurred. "I hope I do not have to return to London for at least a year," Phaedra confided to her silent husband as the streets of Town gave way to open country. All she wanted was peace and quiet.

And Reggie.

He did not respond.

"Reggie, are you ill? You have hardly spoken a single word to me today."

"I am overwhelmed, love. You are finally my wife. I cannot take it all in."

She moved to the opposite seat and looked closely into his face. What she saw reassured her at the same time as it thrilled her. "I should be happy to prove my new state to you, my husband. Only this coach is, perhaps, a bit too public." She held out her hands to him as he returned her smile. "Or could we pull the shades?"

"Wanton!" he exclaimed, taking her into his arms. His kisses reassured her that he was quite well indeed. She had to remind him again that the coach was not as private a place as they could wish to prevent his consummating their marriage then and there.

EPILOGUE

SNOW LAY THICKLY AROUND CASTLE WILDERLAKE. WIND HOWLED ABOUT ITS stone walls. Inside, some rooms were cozy, for the renovation of that great draughty pile had been underway for more than half a year. Greens festooned the mantles of the public rooms and kissing boughs hung in every doorway. The party gathered in the main salon was merry, for it was the first time some of them had seen one another since Spring.

Phaedra and Chloe stood at a drawing room window, watching their husbands and brothers wade through the snow on their way to find a Yule log. "Do you know, Chloe, I have not seen a sign of the willful girl who sometime made our lives chaotic," Phaedra told her.

"Oh, she is still about, I am ashamed to say. Poor Herne! Sometimes I know he must regret his chivalrous gesture. But I keep her firmly under wraps most of the time, and doing so becomes easier every day."

"What did he do, beat you until you became more docile?"

"No, he just... Well, he is Herne. So gentle, yet so unyielding. Best of all, he never lets me forget that he loves me and finds me the most beautiful woman in the world. I am not sure he did love me when we married. I know I did not love him, for I had not the faintest idea what love could be...should be. But I know now, and am so glad that all came out as it has. How could I ever have considered marriage to poor Everingham?"

"I confess I wondered why you chose him to save you from your wicked family."

"Because he was the only one of my suitors lacking in sense, of course.

Herne would have refused, even if I had thought to ask him to elope with me. He would probably have told Papa, in fact. And Mr. Martin was too gentle, too yielding. What has become of him, by the way?"

"He is to marry Sarah Graham in the spring. They became acquainted through the auspices of Lady Mary, whom he pursued all summer, until she convinced him she had no intention to wed for a long while yet. They seem to suit one another very well."

"Is his fortune large enough to please that odious mother of hers?"

"It is merely respectable, but Sarah can be most amazingly stubborn when she wishes. She insisted she would have him and no other. Her mother was forced to give in gracefully."

They stood in silence or a while, watching the snowflakes slowly drift down. When the men appeared, dragging an enormous log behind them, Phaedra said, "Do you regret your sudden marriage? I remember you had such dreams of a grand wedding."

"Like yours? I do and I do not. Oh, I was envious of your wedding, and disappointed that we could not travel to London for it. But there is so much to do here, to make this into a comfortable and elegant home. It is such fun to see how I can contrive to do so with a minimum expenditure. I am becoming quite the housewife, you know." Chloe threw her sister a complacent glance. "Though I should tell Mama first, I will be a mother in June. Herne is delighted."

Phaedra cried her surprise and hugged her sister. "How wonderful. And I was planning to surprise you, having sworn everyone to secrecy. Our children will be the same age."

Laughing and crying, all at once, the sisters embraced one another. "I knew I could depend on you," Phaedra complained, although the tears she shed were happy ones. "Mama will want to be with you and I will have to settle for Cousin Louisa. For shame, Chloe. Could you never let me be first in anything?"

Chloe smiled. "Herne's mother is here and will care well for me. This time, sister, your needs will come first. And about time, I think."

"I love you, Chloe." Phaedra hugged her sister tighter than before.

"And I love you, Phaedra."

The door opened, bringing in a breath of winter air and the men who held their hearts.

THE END

ABOUT THE AUTHOR

On her way to a career as a writer, Judith B. Glad made a lot of detours—into motherhood, short-order cooking, accounting, management, graduate school, botanical consulting. Eventually she decided she had to write those books that had been growing in her head for years—romances all. She believes every story should have a happy ending, even if it requires two or three hankies to get there.

After growing up in Idaho—the locale of several of her books—Judith now lives in Portland, Oregon, where flowers bloom in her yard every month of the year and snow usually stays on the mountains where it belongs. It's a great place to write, because the rainy season lasts for eight months—a perfect excuse to stay indoors and tell stories. Judith has four children, all grown, three granddaughters and a grandson.

Visit Judith's webpage at www.judithbglad.com to learn more about her other books. While you're there, take some side trips to view early 20th century picture postcards, read about 5,000 ways to earn a living, or see what a *Mentzelia* really is.

Judith B. Glad's

WESTERN HISTORICAL

"Behind the Ranges" Series

The Queen of Cherry Vale

Ice Princess

The Duchess of Ophir Creek

Noble Savage

Knight in a Black Hat

The Lost Baroness

The Imperial Engineer

Undercover Cavaliere

Squire's Quest

Lord of Misrule (a Christmas novella)

And her other books:

REGENCY ROMANCE

The Anonymous Amanuensis

A Sisterly Regard

The Portrait (novella)

A Pitiful Remnant (novella)

CONTEMPORARY ROMANCE

Solomon's Decision

Never the Twain

Twice Victorious

A Safe and Welcome Nest

PARANORMAL ROMANCE

Improbable Solution

MAINSTREAM ROMANCE

A Strange Little Band

www.ingramcontent.com/pod-product-compliance
Lightning Source LLC
Chambersburg PA
CBHW071502170626
46811CB00007B/2681

* 9 7 8 1 6 0 1 7 4 9 0 5 5 *